THE INFECTS

THE INFECTS

Sean Beaudoin

CANDLEWICK PRESS

Copyright © 2012 by Sean Beaudoin

First edition 2012

Library of Congress Cataloging-in-Publication Data is available.

Library of Congress Catalog Card Number pending

ISBN 978-0-7636-5947-9

12 13 14 15 16 17 BVG 10 9 8 7 6 5 4 3 2 1

Printed in Berryville, VA, U.S.A.

This book was typeset in Minion.

Candlewick Press
99 Dover Street
Somerville, Massachusetts 02144

visit us at www.candlewick.com

For my father, who took me to see
a matinee of Dawn of the Dead *when*
I was way, way, way *too young*

Don't Fear the Reaper

THE NEIGHBORHOOD WAS TRASHED, FUNERAL pyres in the distance burning against a raw pink sky. Half the street was in rubble, from Thompkins all the way to Main. The high school was gone. The Video Mart had collapsed into firing positions for the few remaining snipers. Dead soldiers lay under timbers, under scrap metal, under their commanding officers. Other soldiers had gotten up again, looking for something to hurt.

Something to eat.

Nick Sole crouched behind a wall, totally strapped. Steel pipe, survival knife, bone-handled revolver.

Problem was, the revolver only had two bullets left.

And a Swarm had just turned down the street.

Moving slow, but not slow enough.

Nick rechecked his supplies.

Food? Not much.

Medicine? Gone.

Synthetic adrenaline?

He'd shot himself in the thigh with a hypo right after the last plane crash. A USWAY Air 767. Just fell out of the sky, broke in two pieces, took out half a strip mall and everything from the parking lot to the river.

Lost a lot of good people on that plane.

Or maybe they were all Swarm, so screw 'em.

Hard to know where you stood these days.

Unless you were standing on neck.

Either way, he and Amanda needed to move. They'd just done a recon of the Boxxmart by the interstate. Other people'd had the same idea. The guns were already looted, down to peashooter target pistols that wouldn't drop a Girl Scout, let alone a hungry Lurker. The propane was gone. The first-aid kits were gone. Even the flat-screen TVs were gone. What were they going to plug it into, a Lurker's ass? The only food left was a bag of Blowritos (nutritive value: zero) and a few sticks of beef jerky — not counting the walking beef jerky Amanda had spent her last hollow-points on.

"You ready?" she asked, tying a strip of dirty cloth around an open leg wound. She had a slash across her face, the shaft of an arrow embedded in her shoulder, and dried blood caked in her hair.

No complaints.

No crying.

Totally ready for action.

Amanda, his little sister, looking more thirty-nine than nine years old in the diesel-heavy light.

"I had a hundred more like her, we might actually hold this city," said the lieutenant in charge of their neighborhood — right before he'd been dragged, screaming, into a sewer. Nick, on the other hand, was appreciated mostly for his ability to carry crates of ammo and open canned food quickly.

"They're getting closer?" Amanda said in her raspy little whisper. "We can't stay here?"

The Swarm was definitely louder, beginning to feed off itself. The first ones had made it over the Prius Barricade, a makeshift wall some long-ago jarheads had built and then died on.

"I know."

Amanda pushed her thick glasses back up her nose, one lens cracked in three places. She spoke with a slight lisp, voice barely audible above the groans and explosions. "I love you? Nick?"

"Me too, A-dog."

"Okay? Enough sap? I take frontal? You flank?"

Amanda clambered up onto the jagged brick, shouldered a rocket launcher, and stuck her tongue out in concentration.

Nick went around the side, through a crack in the fence, and ran hard for the Quickie Slurp across the street. As usual — busy thinking about Petal when he should have been pure commando—he didn't see the Lurker coming. It reached from the cab of a totaled Hummer and grabbed Nick's wrist. Luckily it was still strapped in. Safety first! Nick went with a few front kicks, made the thing eat serious boot, then wedged its head in the door before slamming it shut.

Good old Detroit steel.

There was a spurt, and then there was a *fwooom.*

Amanda's RPG, as always, was right on the mark. It exploded in the main Swarm, concussion to plume. Lurker parts rained down like a late summer squall. Amanda did a front flip off the berm, then stepped nimbly between the remains of a National Guard unit, picking up gear and ammo as she went. In her thrift-store dress and long black hair, she looked like tiny Demi Moore playing tiny Judy Garland, just two ruby shoes and a killer tornado away from waking up in Oz.

"What are you waiting for? Run?"

Nick backed toward the Quickie Slurp, scanned the lot, and opened the door.

A welcome bell rang.

Just as something leaped over the register.

A Lurker chick.

All in leather.

Tight and low-cut, sleeved with tats, from hula girls to thrash bands and back. Seriously a Victoria's Gossip model, blond hair waving in the wind. Except she was also wearing the kind of two-toned blood mask you could only get from burying your face deeply into another person, a demarcation line just below the eyes, the spot where teeth could reach no farther.

"Hi," Nick said, raising his pistol.

The Lurker chick howled, teeth claggy with flesh, and lurched forward.

Totally skipping the foreplay.

Nick managed to get off a shot, which missed, embedding itself in a package of olive loaf even the looters wouldn't touch.

The gun slid across the floor.

He would have screamed, but there was no time.

She sank her teeth into his shoulder.

Then cheek.

Then neck.

His health rating plummeted.

Nick Sole, Totally Fuct.

Amanda was already more than six hundred thousand points ahead, and with yet another Maximum Outwit plus Severe Gouging, there was no chance at all he could catch her, even if he cleared the entire next level by himself. Through a red-tinged screen, Nick watched his sister sprint across the street, eat a glazed ham, collect a string of gold coins, and then pocket double-bonus energy points for finding a gassed-up chain saw.

She pulled the ripcord and held it over her head, the motor howling with bad intent.

Nick dropped the extra controller. Amanda paused her Palmbot. The screen blinked: *S.W.A.R.M. II: What Lurks at Midnight.* CONTINUE? Y/N.

"Sorry? Nick? You lose?"

"I know," he said, smiling at his sister instead of her avatar. "Again."

"What a surprise?"

Nick ran three fingers through his close-cropped hair, tightened his red Chuck Taylors, and then crawled out from under the kitchen table. The clock above the sink said seven thirty. It was dark already. He had a little less than an hour to make his shift.

"Done saving the world?" the Dude asked, spooning Salisbury steak from the metal tray in front of him.

"Hardly."

"You see Miss Sparkle under there?"

Miss Sparkle was the cat. Gender never determined, despite the name. It'd slunk off into the night, without so much as a final meow.

"I don't think so."

"She'll be back," the Dude said, talking mostly to his watch. "Everything comes home eventually."

Nick poured Amanda a bowl of cereal and slid it under the table with his foot. Then he made himself a sandwich, white on white, hold the meat, hold the condiments.

Mostly because there wasn't any meat. Or condiments.

Or anything else in the fridge, except pickle water and crusty foil.

The Dude's philosophy on groceries was pretty much The Dude Has Other Concerns. Which mostly meant lubing up with a tube of SPF 2 after breakfast and crashing on the rubber lawn chair in the driveway. Even in the winter, the Dude was deeply tanned, prominently veined, sporting a pink polo shirt and a headful of silver dadlocks. Suits and ties and wing tips sat moldering in boxes in the front room, where they'd been since the day he retired.

"What's for dessert?"

"Jell-O."

The Dude frowned, addressing his spoon: "Again?"

Nick jiggled a double portion into a large white Tupperware, slipped a paper towel into his father's collar, and then checked his phone.

There were three blinking messages.

All of them to Petal.

All of them unsent.

> 6:14 P.M.: *Hey Pet-l, u wanna hng out 2night?*
> 6:55 P.M.: *Wht r u up 2 l8tr?*
> 7:12 P.M.: *I wuz thinkng aftr wrk we cld talk.*

Nick Sole, texturbating.

Pathetic.

Not that he was ever very smooth, but at least he knew

enough to slouch around the hallway all enigmatic, nodding and yawning, like, "Oh, hey, what's up?"

You liked a girl, she liked you.

Or not.

Get a number, get a name, get shot down.

Whatever.

But Petal Gazes was a whole other universe, a different orbit, a brighter sun. She was a tenth straight espresso, pure feedback, wet-toe-in-socket beautiful.

At least to him.

Which went directly against Nick's long-standing policy: Never Want Anything.

Treeless Christmas? Eggless Easter? Toastless morning?

It's hard to be disappointed when you don't give a crap.

But now he really, *really* wanted something.

Petal Gazes.

Staring across a crowded lunchroom.

Holding hands on the way to French class.

Skipping class and Frenching in the janitor's closet instead.

So why couldn't he pull the trigger on a text?

The Dude's favorite show ended. There were commercials for cars, cars, cars, beer, and cars. Then a newsbreak, special report. A camera panned along desolate farmland, showing close-ups of a row of cows. They stared off into the middle distance, expressions grotesquely frozen. A voice-over began, saying they'd all been torn to pieces.

"Detectives are tight lipped, as you might imagine. There is some suggestion that this incident has the look of an accident, though they're not ruling out the possibility of a frat prank gone very wrong. Back to you, Troy."

"Not cool," the Dude said, reaching into his yellow fanny pack for a Cherokee Spirit. "I dig cows."

"You dig steak," Nick said.

The Dude spun the stove dial and leaned over to light his smoke. An errant dadlock hung in the flame and began to smolder. "And your point is?"

Nick snapped the burner off. The room smelled like scorched hair.

"Um, yuk?" Amanda said from under the table.

"My point is, I'm late for work."

The Dude crossed his tan legs and blew out a concentric plume. "Say hello to Captain Fuld."

Nick found his rubber boots by the sink and rubber apron by the stairs, stuffing them into the black Hefty bag that served as his duffel. It was the Dude who had gotten Nick the job in the first place. Called in a favor with his old boss, the same one who'd "retired" him to begin with. But by now, Management Dude was now so far in the rearview that he and his Jamaican-flag board shorts were officially insulated from the irony.

Or the need to go postal.

Which would at least have earned him some respect.

"I'll do that," Nick said, and then poked his head under

the table, where Amanda sat cross-legged, her dark, straight hair parted severely in the center. "Later, gator."

She didn't look up from her Palmbot, racing a stock car with a gun turret though the streets of Paris.

"After a while, chocodile," Nick said, trying again.

The Arc de Triomphe took rocket fire, collapsed, crushed unwary tourists. Amanda lowered a pinkie into her cereal bowl and then slowly licked off the milk.

"See ya, wouldn't want to be ya."

No response.

"He who smelt it dealt it."

Nothing.

"Betta check yo'self before you wreck yo'self."

Bingo.

Amanda finally looked up, answering in Amandaranto, the raspy whisper she preferred to enunciation.

"Nick? You're going? Where? Nick? Don't?"

"I got the night shift, A-dog."

"But? Nick? Why?"

It was a good question. The answer mostly being that the Dude insisted on rent. Said it was a Total Character Builder. But also that they flat needed the cash, since Amanda dry-swallowed five hundred bucks worth of Asperger's meds a month.

Weird thing was, Amanda didn't have Asperger's.

But she did have something, the doctors at the clinic sure of it. They just weren't insured of it. Until the expensive tests were covered, they decided if it wasn't the Ass Burger, Asperger's was close enough.

The Dude blamed the government.

The Dude blamed the Illuminati.

The Dude blamed excessive fluoride.

Nick didn't blame anyone, put stock in earbuds, and rode the tinnitus train.

Tune the kitchen out; tune Metallica in.

Distortion, unlike Zoloft, actually worked.

Amanda, for her part, pretty much just hunkered beneath furniture, hugged her knees, and mainlined multiplayer action.

And Mom?

Well, Mom's picture watched from the mantel, framed in gold, a look on her face like, "Now you kids get why I split?"

Yeah, Nick got it.

Had gotten it a long time ago.

"You know why," he finally answered.

Amanda nodded, then leaned over and stuck something in his hand. It was a folded piece of construction paper. Inside was a quarter. A shiny new one, the kind with one of the fifty states on the back. Delaware. Underneath, it said *Happy Brithday*.

Nick laughed. "You so spelled that wrong on purpose."

Amanda ignored him, pressed buttons, chest-bursted an alien.

"For starters, *brithday* has two *y*'s at the end."

Amanda ignored him, pressed buttons, tased an anti-union protester.

"Here's an interesting fact: Delaware has the second-smallest square footage of any state."

Amanda ignored him, pressed buttons, grand-thefted an auto.

"Okay, don't wait up."

As Nick straightened from under the table, the Dude raised his arm for a high five. Nick wanted to let it hang, was going to let it hang, *needed* to let it hang.

And then couldn't.

He gripped his father's palm.

"Awesome," the Dude said, lighting another smoke.

The porch door slammed.

Nick trudged to his Celica.

Key, ignition, combustion.

The radio squalled — some news station, pretty much the same routine, except this wasn't cows: "More carnage . . . grievous internal injuries . . . absolutely no motive . . . Dog bites and rabies speculated . . . Police are rounding up local bikers for questioning."

Bikers?

He popped in a tape.

Yeah, a tape. Total old school.

The pounding metal hooves of the first Muttonchopper album thrashed out of stock tweeters — pure fuzz.

Loud. Rude. Righteous.

NICK SOLE, A MAN WITH A PLAN:

1. Jab Dolby Bass Boost™ button.
2. Listen to car whine.
3. Fail to give a shit about blinking engine light.
4. Put it in first gear.
5. Fail to buckle up.
6. Redline, pop clutch.
7. Spray gravel onto (unmowed) lawn.
8. Fail to signal.
9. Hit street at forty, easy.
10. Fail to give way to oncoming LeBaron, causing (a) squeal, (b) horn, (c) finger.
11. Gas, gas, gas.
12. Fail to yield to pedestrian(s).
13. Right on red, despite sign that reads NO RIGHT ON RED.
14. Radio even louder.
15. Press quarter so hard into palm it leaves imprint.
16. Achieve cruising speed, wind in hair.
17. Fail to fail.
18. Entrance ramp, merge, fast lane.
19. Go, baby.
20. Just go.

2

Lying on the Killing Floor

HUGE HALOGENS BURNED ORANGE, AN OVAL of sallow light from poles that spanned the enormous lot. In the middle was a structure, essentially a corrugated metal barn, rusted, pitted, oily. Its waffled sheet metal grinned and flexed in the wind. Bolted to an enormous concrete post was a sign with the company name, Rebozzo AviraCulture, dwarfed by a much larger sign that said NO TRESPASSING.

Fancy name, Nick thought, for a chicken factory.

For a hot-wing abattoir.

For a paycheck slaughterhouse.

At the end of the service road was a guardhouse manned by Officer Danny Sorrel, three hundred pounds of stress and sweat, a dude who'd graduated two years before Nick. The guys on the chicken line all called him Rent-A-Knob. Danny

Sorrel's job was twofold: (1) check IDs, (2) raise the gate. But Danny took his duties seriously. He thought terrorists were everywhere, hunkered in backseats, folded into trunks, lurking in the rye — all busy hating us for our freedom. Also our poultry.

"Purpose?" Sorrel snapped as soon as Nick rolled down the window.

"To make my shift on time."

"Date of birth?"

"Hard to see how that's relevant."

"ID number?"

"Same as it was last night, Danny. There a problem?"

Danny Sorrel narrowed his eyes and dropped the hard-ass act for a second. He pointed to his police scanner. "You listen to the news today, Sole? There's major weirdness going on. Blood in the streets, man. I mean, dang, it makes me glad we're behind a fence, you know?"

Nick remembered the news cutaway he'd heard on the radio. "What, you mean that biker routine?"

Danny Sorrel leaned in closer. "It's not bikers. Get your head in the game, Sole. Don't buy what's being sold by the lamestream press. Cops don't ever sound the way they sound tonight. Scared. Cashing in pensions and moving north. It's ominous and shit."

The line of idling pickup trucks behind Nick began to lay on their horns, first one and then the rest joining in, like dogs in a cul-de-sac. Danny Sorrel handed back Nick his

ID. "Happy birthday," he said, and then raised the gate. Nick looked over, surprised, about to say, "Hey, thanks," when Sorrel waved him through with a big fat middle finger.

The main gate was surrounded by smokers getting in a last puff as the day shift punched out — a circle of grumbling men, pale and dazed, with thermoses and metal lunch boxes, callused hands cupping balls, deeply bored. At the far end was a row of huge chrome tankers where the dipping sauce was stored, the pride of Rebozzo AviraCulture: "You'll Come for the Meat, but You'll Stay for the Sauce."

Nick had worked at Rebozzo's for three years and was pretty sure he had never come for the meat.

"Mr. Sole!"

Jett Ballou, wearing a trench coat, sweats, and fingerless gloves, walked over and held out his knuckles.

Nick bumped them. "Mr. Ballou."

Next to Jett was a girl who was often next to Jett.

Petal Gazes.

A shock to the system, every single time.

If only because Nick couldn't understand why she worked at Rebozzo's instead of behind a nice clean counter blending smoothies or selling perfume or folding tank tops.

Nick Sole, Mall Human Resources.

"Hey," he said, looking at his feet.

"Hey," Petal answered. She was thin, with a shock of white hair that hung over half her face. The other side of her head was shaved, highlighting eyes so large they made her look half anime. She wore a black hoodie with BAUHAUS written on the front in duct tape, American flag cowboy boots, and a Carhartt jacket three sizes too big. In other words: exactly, down to the inch, down to the atom, in every possible way, the girl Nick had been dreaming of since he'd first discovered himself in the bathtub at age eleven.

Half punk, half shy, smart as hell.

Weird, but not trying to be.

Lips offset in a kiss-me pout.

Like she'd just stepped out of a graphic novel about sexy apocalypses.

"I dig your earring," Nick said.

It was a gold hoop with a long white feather hanging from it.

Petal blushed. "Actually, it's kind of a joke. You know, working here? A *feather*?"

Shit.

"Yeah, I get it. Totally."

"Obviously," Ballou said.

Petal turned away, unhooked the earring, and slipped it into her pocket. Jett stretched and yawned, pretending to soak in the night air. The shift horn went off. Rolling gates slammed shut around the parking lot. A belch of smoke wafted from one of the exhaust vents. The line of workers seemed to sag in unison.

"It smells," Petal said, wrinkling her nose.

"Worse than usual?" Nick asked, stepping downwind.

Reeking like beaks at school was a given, no matter how much he scrubbed, all through class hoping no sudden movement would punch a hole in his fog of Irish Spring.

But shift funk was something else entirely.

"It's me," Ballou said, raising one arm. "Max Body Spray. Ocean Cinnamon. Just bought it."

"Gross," Petal said.

"Seriously," Nick said.

"Shaddup," said a guy in a hard hat behind them as the line began to move. "The three of you."

"Sorry," Nick said.

"Sorry," Petal said.

"Eat me," Ballou said.

People began to push forward. Nick untangled his earbuds as they laid their stuff on the X-ray belt. In a second Petal was going to walk away. He needed a good line. Something easy and smooth, a joke or part of a lyric. But he had nothing. His mind was a shiny Scrabble tile, a total reflective blank, like the Dude grinning at the wall after a major wake-and-bake.

Moron.

"Nick?" Petal said, snapping her fingers.

They stopped in front of the men's locker room.

"Yeah?"

"I have something for you."

"What?"

She reached up and slid her arms around his shoulders. Pulling him into a full-on hug.

White hair against his cheek.

Tiptoe, sigh, thigh against thigh.

Workers streamed around them, making comments, whistling, slapping Nick's back.

It was the third-best thing he'd ever felt, transported to some place where paychecks didn't even exist, the smell of scrubbed vanilla and musty jacket and shocking pink.

"Happy birthday," she whispered, then let go and hurried toward the packing department as the final siren went off.

Nick changed in record time, with a massive shit eater of a grin stapled to his face.

"Ready to toil, son?" Ballou asked, now all in white, sneakers to shower cap.

Nick was ready for anything, feeling ridiculously suave in his antibacterial slippers and hairnet, sporting the same Guns N' Roses T-shirt for God knows how many shifts, Axl smelling even worse than he probably did in person.

"You know it, kid," he said as they headed out onto the killing floor.

Red Hand, Blue Room

WIN FULD, PLANT MANAGER, STOOD BY NICK'S
station with his arms crossed, wearing a baby-blue V-neck
and khakis belted just below the armpits. The Dude once
said, "Captain Fuld looks like something you'd poke with a
stick after it washed up on the beach." He was soft and pale,
with thick glasses, random white hairs zagging off his scalp,
and a bow tie covered with his own initials, WF.

Also, he had no lips.

"A talk in my office, Mr. Sole?"

"Later," Ballou said, peeling away.

"Yessir."

Nick followed Win Fuld down a dark hallway, past break
rooms and utility closets and secretaries' cubicles, positive he
was fired.

POSSIBLE CRIMES:

1. Snicker-theft
2. Existential bird guilt
3. Sublimated Jayna lust
4. Dogging it on the beak crimper
5. Being a Sole

Nick was no slacker on shift but did (1) occasionally hook candy bars out of the office vending machine with a clothes hanger, (2) cringe midshift at the remote possibility of bird purgatory, and (3) find himself lingering too long in the stairwell after lunch, hoping to get a glimpse of Jayna Layne, the most pneumatic cougar in processing, as she shimmied each milfy curve back into her rubber apron. Not to mention (4) beaks being self-explanatory and (5) the legacy of the Dude.

But were those canning offenses?

Win Fuld just stared.

Nick wished he had the cojones to stare back. To go deep badass, put his feet up on the desk and say, "Pull the plug, Fuld, you ancient turd. Payroll knows where to send my check—the same place as my father's severance!" But the Nick who could pull that action off was a galaxy away from the one sweating a pink slip on a sticky office chair. That Nick had zero leather running through his veins. Zero gats tucked in his belt. There was no silk do-rag or rumbling Ducati in his future, no sixteen-year-old French model to run away to Cuba and smoke Marlboro Reds petulantly with.

There was just reality.

Rent. Amanda's meds. Anything and everything that needed tending under the shaggy banner of Dudedom.

Real life was about gripping ankle and saying thank you. Attitude was for beautiful hackers and downtown Crips and overly sampled rock stars.

"Sir, it will never happen again."

"What will never happen again?"

"Nothing."

Win Fuld smiled. His teeth were the color of yolk.

"Nick, you may have heard that we've been experimenting with a new product for our connoisseur division."

Nick had heard. And had immediately forgotten, because he so didn't give a shit. New products came down the line all the time. They replaced old products. Change the name, change the package, batter was batter, dip was dip.

"Yes, sir."

"The Rebozzo Fryer has completed testing stages and is now ready to go to market."

"The Rebozzo Fryer?"

"The future of gourmet-quality chicken, Nick. A new generation of bird. A product of impeccable quality and taste."

"Chicken has a future?"

"And so we need a new head butcher to work in the Blue Room."

"I understand," Nick said, although he totally, completely didn't. The Blue Room had been under construction all year, hidden behind huge drapes that hung from the rafters. There were DANGER — NO ENTRANCE signs plastered over all the doors. Guys on the line were taking bets that it was going to be a new lounge for the managers (10–1). Or a managers' racquetball club (7–1). Or a managers' group shower (3–2). Either way, no one had been allowed in. Yet.

"And we want that butcher to be you."

"Me?"

"Yes."

"Um, like, *me* me, or —?"

"Are you interested, Mr. Sole, or not?"

Nick wanted to run outside and do a lap around the parking lot. *He wasn't getting fired!* He wanted to knock on the guard booth and kiss Danny Sorrel's fat belly. *A promotion!* Mostly, he wanted to lie down on the office carpet and weep with relief. *It smells down here!*

But something kept him from shouting out an answer.

Like the fact that Win Fuld could have lobbed a dart between shifts and hit at least forty guys with more experience. With better leadership skills. Who would never consider spelling skills *skillz*. Dudes who needed to shave more than twice a week, had late Camry payments and a stocked wet bar in their rec rooms.

Honestly? Even Jett Ballou was a better choice.

"You have a question?"

"Yessir. Why aren't we allowed to talk about the Blue Room?"

Win Fuld smiled, pure halibut, and then gestured toward the door. "Nicky boy, that's exactly the kind of question makes me think I chose the wrong person. It's funny, though. I was sure you'd be interested in pay slot nine."

"What slot what?"

"Your new compensation rate. Or, rather, what would have been your new compensation rate."

Nick pictured the Dude flipping channels as he scratched between his dreads, pretending not to be amazed. "Fuld gave you a *raise*?"

Nick pictured Amanda, delirious over a stack of brand-new Palmbot discs. "Nick? Thank you? Really?"

Nick pictured Nick, newly titled and with a pocket bulge of cash, bending Jayna Layne over an apron bucket in the laundry room.

"Just out of curiosity, sir, what would that rate be?"

Win Fuld pretended to consult a chart. "Pay slot nine, associate poultry conversion facilitator, stipulates a raise of five and change. Which will nudge you from six to just over eleven dollars per hour."

"Consider me nudged, sir."

"So you're taking the job?"

"I'm taking the job."

Win Fuld clapped his hands, slipped Nick a hundred-dollar bill and a cigar, and then led him across the cutting floor. The nightie crew stared, Ballou making faces next to Petal, who was pretending not to look up from under her bandana. The Blue Room had four locks and six bolts and a thumbprint sensor. The door slid aside with a suctiony sound, like Captain Kirk hitting the release that opens a portal back to dinosaur times. Inside was large and pristine, more like a laboratory than an assembly line. The lights were low, except over the butcher station, which was set up for one. A rack of gleaming deboning knives, never used, waited. The reticulating saw, joint snippers, and Dynablade were all top-of-the-line. All stainless steel. All brand new.

"And this whole room is just for one person?"

Win Fuld did a little jazz-hands thing —"Ta-da!"— before hitting the auto-load button. Rebozzo Fryers began to fill the belt like he'd fired a starter's pistol. "Aren't they beautiful?"

The birds came rolling through the chute, untouched.

They were not beautiful.

They were chickens.

"Knives only?" Nick asked.

Usually machines did most of the breaking down.

"Our tech teams haven't calibrated the gears to handle the Mach IIIs yet, so we're going old school for now."

Fo' shizzle, Win?

The new chickens did seem much larger and plumper than the usual batch. No disease spots or rough patches or weepy yellow whatever-it-was caked all over their backs. They were strong and healthy. Even muscular. Like they'd been hitting the iron, benching two-twenty, doing circuit training and cardio.

"Enough sightseeing. Are you ready, son?"

"Born ready, sir."

"Just like your father, eh? Ambition running hot in the blood?"

"I guess."

Win Fuld put his hands where his hips should have been. "How's he doing, anyway?"

An image of the Dude arguing with the microwave rose in Nick's frontal lobe.

"Fantastic."

"Good man. Top-notch researcher."

"I'll tell him you said so."

Win Fuld winked. A tiny drop of something brown, like chocolate syrup, dribbled out of his ear. He wiped it with one finger and then spread it on his pants.

"Please do. And with that, I shall leave you to it."

The door closed with a hermetic swoosh, and then Nick was alone.

He slipped on his apron and selected a knife, the one he'd briefly considered sinking into Win Fuld's kidney.

And then put in a full week.

Four ten-hour shifts.

Being conversion facilitator meant that he now had lunch alone, in a totally empty cafeteria. He also had break alone, in a totally empty break room. He made coffee for ten — since that's the only way the machine worked — and poured coffee for eight down the pristine drain. It was like being in deep orbit. But at the end of shifts, he still went out the gate like anyone else, the other nighties razzing him all the way across the lot. They called him Win's Boy and Fuld Candy and Soul for Hire. Jett Ballou wasn't making any jokes, but he wasn't talking to Nick anymore, either.

Even Jayna Layne looked pissed, which meant that Nick was now in zero danger of being cougared to death in the laundry room.

But there were too many fryers to worry about anything else.

The belt spun, inexorably.

Birds came and came and never stopped coming. One, three, nine, a hundred, a million, a million and one. Every night Nick lay exhausted in his room, pale and worn, too tired to even shower.

Or cash in on Petal's hug.

Paralyzed with options while ghost-fryers cruised behind his lids.

   1. Text Petal; ask her out
   2. Don't text Petal; don't ask her out
   3. List balls (sold as pair only) on eBay

Amanda lay on the floor under his bed, holding her nose while playing *Unmanned Freedom,* guiding a Predator drone as it rained missiles on xTremists cowering in rugged tribal areas. She already had over a million Coalition Points, six Bribed Mullahs, and a full BeardTrimmer upgrade.

"Nick? Yuk? You smell bad?"

He wiggled his gamy toes. "I know, Boo."

"No? You really? Don't?"

"Just play your game, okay, Martha Stewart?"

"You'll never find a? Girlfriend? Like that?"

"What makes you think I want a girlfriend?"

Amanda laughed, then got a perfect score on the Walled Compound bonus round.

Fine.

On Saturday Nick went to the mall and bought new sneakers, new pants, a Mortis Trigger tour shirt, and some cologne: Ready, Steady, Go! for men.

Sunday came and sped by. Nap, play *Resident Medieval: Gunning for Monks* on the Palmbot, nap, nod at the Dude, consider homework, nap, consider calling Petal, white sandwich, white sandwich, white sandwich. Midnight.

And then Monday rolled around again.

Punch in, punch out.

Straight to the Blue Room and straight back.

Chicken heads, chicken legs.

Gut bucket, feather pile, beak stack.

Tiny little hillocks of claws.

Scary.

which is it? black or red?

Especially after Petal, wearing a black skirt and matching lipstick, cornered him at school.

She never wore red skirts. She never wore lipstick.

Nick's head went blank again, smooth, empty. A flat white glacier of nothingness. Not even a woolly mammoth buried in the permafrost.

"Hi," she said quietly.

It was a brilliant tactic. Short. Friendly but noncommittal. Giving up no information while still requiring a response.

"Hi," he answered.

Less brilliant. Somewhat uncreative. Verging on plagiarism.

Petal didn't seem to notice, eyes practically twice their normal abnormal size, hair pulled away from her face with cheap barrettes, wearing a black T-shirt that had MISSION OF BURMA written on it in duct tape.

Her black skirt had rips in it (there was skin underneath there).

Her black tights had rips in them (there were thighs underneath there).

Her black boots were scuffed and ancient (Feet? He was good with feet).

"Um, Nick?" she said, snapping her fingers. "Anyone home?"

"Yeah. Of course. Where else would I be?"

"You seem kind of out of it."

"Oh, no. I'm in. Way in."

Students milled around them, heading to class, oblivious.

Petal crossed her arms and looked down at her cowboy boots. "You know Sherm Crothers? Who works in frozen foods?"

"Who?"

"The fat guy in the hard hat who always tells us to shaddup?"

"Oh. Yeah. So?"

"Last night he had to be dragged off the main floor."

Nick leaned closer and lowered his voice.

"Wait, why?"

"No one knows, but we all saw him attack Duff for, like, nothing."

Duff was an ancient janitor who had been at Rebozzo's since before the Romans invented aqueducts. He'd probably ridden out the Flood in his mop bucket.

"No way."

"Yeah, and Mr. Crothers was going crazy. Guys were hitting him with tools, trying to hold him down, and he didn't even seem to feel it."

"Wow."

Petal reached out and took Nick's hand.

Hers were small and cool.

His were big and damp.

"I'm scared," she said.

The bell rang.

They were now both totally late for class.

Her: AP chem.

Him: history. Or wait. Maybe biology. Either invertebrates or the British Invasion.

As if it mattered.

He couldn't think at all, suddenly full to the eyebrows with heavy, useless oil.

"Petal? Do you want to go out? Or whatever?"

"Out where?"

He couldn't tell if she was joking.

"Um? Outside? For a cigarette?"

"You don't smoke," she said, letting go of his hand. "Neither do I."

The bell rang again.

He could smell skin.

His own.

Coated with nervous sweat and Rebozzo paste.

"Yeah, no, of course. I was just —"

"Just what?"

"Nothing."

Was it possible for one person to be any more of a stone-cold idiot?

Nick found out when Petal turned and walked away.

Catching the Javelin

REAL SLEEP WAS IMPOSSIBLE.

Reel sleep was inevitable.

He lay there, on a sheetless mattress, waiting for it to come.

Beyond exhausted.

Begging to fall into a dark, soundless box.

For at least a couple of hours.

But his mind refused.

Because as soon as Nick closed his eyes, he was headlong into seriously badass dreams, Technicolor mayhem with a speed-metal sound track.

In the deep hours, running.

And being chased.

Running and being caught.

Caught and being bitten.

Bitten and then eaten.

Molars, throat, stomach.

Nick nuggets.

Nick breaded.

Nick curled up in a bath of golden fry oil.

The chickens were getting to him. The no sleep was getting to him. The nosebleeds were getting to him. The getting to him was getting to him.

He felt sick as a dog, sick and tired, sick of it all.

But calling in was out.

At least for the Blue Room's head butcher.

Who'd already spent Win Fuld's hundred-dollar bill on Mutilhate downloads. And then given the cigar to Amanda, who'd walked around with it clenched in her teeth all day like a riverboat gambler, whispering, "Aces and eights? Nick? The dead man's hand? Aces, Nick? Eights?"

So he chewed a dozen aspirin and swallowed half a grapefruit instead, forcing himself to get dressed and into the Celica.

Time to man up.

Cowboy up.

Suck it up, marine.

Get low.

Get mean.

Unclench the heart.

Unpucker the asshole.

Unsheathe the knife.

And put a serious blade to them yardbirds.

It was only an hour into his shift, but it felt like five. Like a hundred and five. A lone rat watched from the bleacher seats as Rebozzo Fryers cruised by on the belt. One after another. Never slowing. Never stopping. A procession of soldiers marching off to sacrifice themselves in honey-mustard salvos.

Chop, slit, chop.

Every other bird, Nick leaned over to check his reflection in the greasy chrome of the assembly machine.

Snip, gut, snip.

His eyes were yellow slits, skin doughy and practically gray.

Cut, slice, cut.

He jabbed at the next chicken.

Which slipped out of his hand as if it had suddenly taken flight.

And then watched in slow motion as a ninety-weight, pure cold-forged, heavy industrial deboning knife went right through the center of his palm.

Hey. Wow. Ouch.

Vlad the Impaler.

He stared at the geyser of blood as if it were a cheesy special effect, a fountain of red dye and Karo Syrup.

Except this was real.

And very, very wet.

Nick gripped the rubber handle, giddy with pain. It was so ridiculous, he almost wanted to laugh. Instead, he took a deep breath and began to slide the blade back out. It didn't want to come. He had to wiggle the hilt, every slow inch an Old Testament curse. When the tip finally came free, it let loose a sigh, a sound of regret and relief.

Pop.

Then blood began to flow in earnest. It gurgled between the tear of sterile rubber and residue of poultry chum, down his arm, and onto the backs of the Rebozzo Fryers he'd already finished. The little birds didn't seem to mind, posed and on the flex, heading toward the packaging machine a slick and shiny red.

Like postmodern art.

Pollock spatter.

Or a really bad horror movie.

Poultrygeist.

The Fowling.

Nick flung the knife, which clanged across the pristine floor, leaving delicate smears of red. It was hard to think, already down a pint of O negative, platelets jumping ship with abandon.

He was supposed to hit the emergency stop. That's what it said in all the safety protocols. But then the alarm would go off. Half the line would come running. They'd see his hand, send him home, whisper with disbelief. It would be a story told around the gate, an instant legend, shift after shift after shift.

Screw that.

When Nick was little, the Dude sometimes called him Pussy One. Mom would laugh and say, "Oh, leave him alone," but the Dude kept at it, mostly since Nick *was* sort of a pussy, crying while Amanda never did, whining when Amanda never did, demanding attention in a way that Amanda would never deign to.

No way he could crawl home now and tell the Dude why.

"Yeah, um, Pussy One hurt his finger."

Or crawl across the cutting floor and tell Win Fuld why.

"Yeah, um, Pussy One's not up to the job after all."

Nick tore fabric from his lab coat and wrapped it around the wound, then slid a new glove over it.

The old one fell, wet and red, on top of a chicken breast.

Unclean.

Unhygienic.

Nick taint.

But he let it go, because more fryers were booming down the line, sliding through his blood. And he could hear the first delivery truck already backing up to the dock.

Beep beep beep.

At least one tainted load was going to get packaged and make it out of the facility.

Maybe more.

He needed time to catch up.

Nick reached down and flipped the first in a row of huge steel latches that anchored his workstation, the massive springs pinging and expanding, then redirected the assembly belt with his thigh. There was a groan, resistance, the tearing of virgin metal. He pushed again, harder, and the conduit finally separated.

A lone Rebozzo Fryer rolled up between the two belts. It hung on for a second, as if trying to decide.

And then fell wetly to the cement floor.

Splat.

A few more, heartened by the first, went over the edge. Each landed with an oddly human sound.

Splat. Splat.

As long as they weren't making it through the chute whole.

Splat. Splat. Splat.

They actually looked pretty comfy down on the cement, sort of like a yoga class stretching.

Splat. Splat. Splat. Splat.

Except Petal was in packaging.

Splat. Splat. Splat. Splat. Splat.

When the fryers stopped coming through, she'd have to report it.

Splat. Splat. Splat. Splat. Splat. Splat.

Or cover for him.

Splat. Splat. Splat. Splat. Splat. Splat. Splat.

Which would be a big mistake.

Splat. Splat. Splat. Splat. Splat. Splat. Splat. Splat.

He had to warn her somehow.

Splat. Splat. Splat. Splat. Splat. Splat. Splat. Splat. Splat.

Send a message.

Splat. Splat. Splat. Splat. Splat. Splat. Splat. Splat. Splat. Splat.

Like maybe a smoke signal. Or a papyrus scroll.

Splat. Splat. Splat. Splat. Splat. Splat. Splat. Splat. Splat. Splat. Splat.

But first he needed to close his eyes and rest. Just for a second. After that, Pussy One would get his shit together and totally figure out what to do.

CASE NUMBER ___ 07-8834-100025

INCIDENT DATE ___ 09-28-2010

INCIDENT TIME ___ 03:27-04:13 hours

COPIES TO ___ Juvenile court

ARRESTING OFFICER ___ Det. Stefano Malk

SUSPECT(s) ___ Nick Sole

Age ___ 17   Race ___ Caucasian

Height ___ 6'01"   Hair ___ Black

Weight ___ 173   Eyes ___ Black

Distinguishing Characteristics:

Dark complected; almond-shaped eyes; tall,
quiet, distracted. Appears to think no
style is style. Wears skinny but not nut-
hugging jeans. Said he'd once thought
about and then decided against an earring.
Appears weary, exhausted, claims to
"feel every last minute of seventeen."
Covered in (own) blood. Surprisingly calm,
emotionless. Asked repeatedly about a
"Petal," which this officer concluded might
be street slang for some type of narcotic.
Full drug test/tox screen at holding
facility recommended.

Narrative:

On the above date and time, I was assigned
to Car #3 along with Officer Dugluff. We
were dispatched to Rebozzo's AviraCulture,
a facility for ███████████ poultry.
We were summoned by the plant manager,
one Mr. Fuld█ The ████████ showed us to
laboratory-like ███████████ butchering
████ in which the ████ █████
working. The suspect is a ████████
employee ████████████. On the floo
were an ████████ number of raw █████
Some of the machinery had been tampered
with, allegedly by the suspect █████
████ chickens to ███████████ floor. The
suspect refused to confirm or deny that
the destruction of the █████ was either
and accident or ███████ sabotage
or ██████████████ confirmed
████████ value of the ██████ well
over fifty thousand █████ █████
qualified as felony destruction of
███████████████ was given every
chance while receiving medical attention
for what appeared to be a self-inflicted
████████████████ behavior and/or
intent. ████████ seemed dazed, refused █

speak. Plant ███████████ insisted ███████
was a longtime discipline problem, even
going so far as to ████████ his ██████████
insists suspect not supposed to be in room
at time. Due to lack ████████ evidence, at
████ point, we arrested ████████.

- -
DO NOT WRITE BELOW THIS LINE
* INWARD TREK HANDLER NOTES: *
- -

Sentenced   Inward Trek boot camp, 3 months

Camp Nickname   Nero

5

Hell on Wheels

THE INWARD TREK VAN WAS HOT, PACKED, and rowdy.

It roared down the highway, black and sleek.

On the side was a logo, a fist with a pine tree growing out of it.

On the hood was a warning: DO NOT APPROACH VAN.

In the front row, against the mesh window, sat Nero Sole.

He still had soul, but was Nick no longer.

As part of the Inward Trek privacy agreement, every client had been assigned a mandatory "Trek Handle" by the counselors at intake, like it or lump it. At first Nick lumped Nero, thinking he sounded like a boy-band dancer, then decided he didn't give a shit. In the end a name was just another dog collar — an easier way for people to get your attention before telling you what to do.

Nick was the past. Nick was prologue. Nick was some kid who couldn't handle the stick and got sent down to the minors.

The great thing about being a convict was that you got to write your own story.

Act cool; you're cool. Act tough; you're tough.

At least until someone called you on it.

Nero was only what Nero proved himself to be.

Preferably Steve McQueen, but with a better haircut.

The highway zoomed by regardless.

Counselor Jack Oh sat at the wheel. Counselor Bruce Leroy rode shotgun.

Behind them were nine clients on lockdown, names sewn over the hearts of their orange jumpsuits:

1. **Nero:** A Nick by any other name would smell just as sweet. *Rumored Crime:* Silent on the matter.
2. **Tripper:** Squat and manic, a capsule of human Adderall, shaved head, baby face, sleeved in tats, missing his two front teeth. *Rumored Crime:* Repeated steel toe to loser rib.
3. **War Pig:** All pecs and lats and kinky red hair. Shotgun-freckled bulk. Doesn't say much; doesn't have to. *Rumored Crime:* Strictly smash and grab, laptops and old-lady purses.

4. **Yeltsin:** Knife games and card tricks. Purple lips and black teeth. Chechen exchange student. Stubble and a cigarette. *Rumored Crime:* Ukrainian mafia.

5. and 6. **Idle and Billy:** Identical twins. Fake tans, knobby chins, peroxide bangs gelled straight up. Tennis and cashmere gone wrong. Seven grand in chrome braces between them. *Rumored Crime:* It's not a rumor.

7. **Mr. Bator:** Wet eyes, skinny frame, honker so big it looks glued on. *Rumored Crime:* Who cares?

8. **Heavy D:** Guess a weight, pick a chin. So much D he requires his own row. Writes code faster than breathing. Rocks sweatbands, round glasses, and a yellow perm. *Rumored Crime:* Hacked into World Bank computers, tried to sell files to Pakistan.

9. **Estrada:** Slicked back and black; face cruel and implacable; either Mexican or the mailman was; dead eyed like an Aztec carving. *Rumored Crime:* Offed a rival as part of gang initiation.

After two days' orientation in base camp just north of San Francisco, they'd been rousted from their cots in the dark—"Hands off your dicks, gentlemen. It's *go* time!"—and allotted ten minutes to piss, brush, cram half a power bar, and zip into orange jumpsuits before splitting at dawn.

The van made steady progress up the I-5 corridor before beginning the slow curl through the remote Sierra Nevada foothills. Soon Nero (Nick) and the rest of the clients (convicts) and counselors (hacks) would be unloading (taking a final civilized shit) before the fifty-mile endurance hike (forced march) that kicked off (nothing compared to what's coming) the program (punishment).

Scrub pine and asphalt sped by at eighty per. The mile markers blurred and paled in the sun. Nero, hypnotized, considered leaning back and kicking out the window. Not because he figured it would lead to a *Great Escape*–style escape. Or even that his sneaker had half a chance of breaking the reinforced glass. It just seemed like the contact would feel good.

Yeah, and it's been a while since anything's felt good, hasn't it?

Also, it might distract him from the voice.

Huh? What voice?

The one that started two weeks ago.

Has it really been that long?

The one that never stopped, never took a breath, deep and raspy and stupid, banging around inside Nero's head like a wasp.

Hey, that's not nice.

And, worst of all, the voice sounded almost exactly like the Rock.

Who?

Former pro wrestler? B-movie action turd? Couldn't act his way out of a bag of steroids?

I still wrestle, okay? Acting is just a good way to meet the ladies. And I never took steroids. At all. Not even a little. So, yeah, pretty much none.

Nero rubbed his palm. It was red and sore and raw. The stitches, sixty-two to close what the deboning knife had only begun to open, itched.

Bet that really hurt.

"Yeah, it really did."

Maybe you should stick to spoons from now on, huh?

"Hilarious."

Listen, kid, here's what you do. Stand up and punch the biggest guy in the van. Then they'll treat you with respect.

"I don't want their respect."

Well, you gotta make a move soon or you'll end up being someone's wife.

"What does that even mean?"

It means you're talking to yourself, genius.

Nero looked around. Some of the other clients were staring, shaking their heads. He hunched down and pushed a thumbnail between his stitches, releasing a jolt of pain that flashed pure black and then bright yellow, blotting everything else out.

Better the hurt than the voice, better the pain than the insane.

Even if it was only temporary.

Nero Sole, Product of His Crazy Father's Crazy Loins.

The noise in the van reached a frenzy.

"Will you all just shut it the hell up a second?" Counselor Jack Oh yelled, yanking the wheel as he gunned around another Prius.

None of the clients paid attention.

Jack Oh rattled the mesh separator. "Hey! Delinquents!"

None of the clients paid attention.

"Relax," Bruce Leroy said, his Afro slung low over thick glasses. A map was open across the dash. "Just keep an eye peeled for the next exit."

The next exit meant a rest stop. A rest stop meant food. Food meant people. People meant something to make fun of. Something to make fun of meant being distracted from hunger. Hunger meant food. Food meant a rest stop. A rest stop meant the next exit.

"About time!" Tripper yelled, knocking his head against the window in threes. "It's lunchtime, baby!"

The other clients cheered, picking up the beat.

"Lunch, lunch, lunch!"

"Now, now, now!"

"Eat, eat, eat!"

Nero did not stomp. Or chant. Power bars and juice boxes were getting old, but antagonizing the counselors never seemed to result in anything but antagonized counselors.

That's right, Nicky: be a good boy. Good boys always come out on top.

Not in this case. This case being *Rebozzo AviraCulture v. One Astonishingly Stupid Teenager*, a judicial proceeding in which Nick went all in and got called holding seven-deuce, standing there with a bloody hand while half that day's production rumbled across the floor like a screen pass to the fullback. The morning shift called the foreman. Who called the shop steward. Who called Win Fuld. Who called the cops. Nick was fired on the spot. Then stuffed into the back of a cruiser: "Watch your head. You have the right to remain a moron. Anything you say can and will be laughed at."

Charges were brought. The Dude just shook his head. Nick's court-appointed suit yawned his way through preliminary motions while playing *World of Orkcraft* on his iPhone.

Jayna Layne testified (hot, sweaty).

Jett Ballou testified (bored, angry).

Win Fuld testified (hairless, lipless).

Amanda sat in the back row of the courtroom, whispering: "Rebozzo Fryer, Nick? Liar? Rebozzo Fryer is a liar?"

Nick was called to the stand. His mind immediately went blank, as if the chicken knife had reached into him and pulled something important back out with it. Molecules of inaction coursed through his bloodstream, the entire proceeding like a fever dream. A high that wasn't high. The bitter and grainy taste of a pure and deep low. Saddled with enough junk Dude code to permanently crash the servers.

Meanwhile, the prosecutor railed away. Gross negligence. Property crime. Unnecessary bleeding. Vandalism. Willful ignorance. Destruction of fifty thousand dollars worth of poultry. Possible collusion with animal-rights activists. Next step: eco-terrorism. Judge Smails pronounced the sentence: pay full reparations by five o'clock today or do three months in juvie camp.

"Pay?" the Dude said. "Today?"

"Juvie?" Amanda said. "Camp?"

"Inward Trek provides rugged problem solving," the judge explained. "Clients learn the value of restorative exhaustion while scaling up the rock of justice and down the face of teamwork."

The Dude lit a Cherokee Spirit. The bailiff tossed him from the courtroom.

One minute Nick's biggest problem was Axl postponing *Chinese Democracy;* the next it was a scene from *Shawshank,* ankle chained in a van with a pack of deviants and fist fuckers, roaring down the highway, half wishing the thing would blow a radial, roll over, and explode.

Except that would mean he'd left Amanda behind for good.

Could he live with that?

Could he die with that?

Oh, stop being so dramatic. You'll be out in ninety days.

Actually, eighty-eight. But who's counting?

Order Me Something from the Dollar Menu

"YO, NERO!" IDLE SAID, POKING HIS SPIKY blond hair into the aisle. "What you dreamin' about, son?"

"Yeah," Billy hissed through his braces. "Whoever she is, I wanna break off a piece of that action too."

Nero slid his thumbnail from the gash that bisected his palm, blood already dry and almost purple.

He'd passed out.

And wanted immediately to pass out again.

"What," Idle said, "you too cool to answer me?"

Nero eyed the peroxide brothers, perched on their seat like a doubles pair up forty–love in the final set.

They're cat torturers, you know.

It was true. There'd been an article in the paper, whole

neighborhoods missing various Fluffys and Tabbys and Mr. Pickles, people blaming a rabid coyote until they'd found the battle arena the brothers had built in a thicket under the bridge. Headline: "Deranged Prep Twins Build Kitty Octagon, Stage Feline Mayhem!" Followed by "Peroxide Lecters Plead Guilty in Exchange for Reduced Sentence!"

Nero turned back to the window. Behind him, Estrada's reflection was a dare: go ahead and fuck with me. He was the only other client not chanting.

"Lunch, lunch, lunch!"

"Now, now, now!"

"Eat, eat, eat!"

Jack Oh gunned around a slow-moving station wagon full of girls with big hair. On the wagon's door it said *Shasta County Anorex Recovery Team* in delicate cursive. The clients went absolutely crazy.

"Food, food, food!"

"Meat, meat, meat!"

"Tits, tits, tits!"

War Pig stood in the back seat and howled, exhaling a rush of metallic-smelling air. Yeltsin raised up and gripped the front of his jumpsuit. "For quality ladies such as these, I not only pay drinks tab; I let them have the mouth time with my junk."

The seats vibrated with laughter, rocked with the beat.

"To be honest, I'm not actually that hungry," Mr. Bator whispered. Everyone else had refused to sit next to him since he'd been spotted the first night in the camp showers, yanking frank.

The kid had a soapy grip! The kid had two fingers' worth! Bible says it's a sin to abuse your loaf! Leviticus twenty-six!

Jack Oh gave a talk about respecting your body. Bruce Leroy did a karate demo that suggested Boner Indifference could be achieved through flexibility and personal discipline.

"Hunger's just a state of mind," Nero said, thinking it sounded cool and then feeling stupid because it wasn't true at all.

Mr. Bator smiled and nodded, looking back out the window as the van careened across three lanes, clients instinctively leaning into the curve.

"Slow it the eff down," Bruce Leroy said.

"Sorry, I don't speak Ebonics," Jack Oh said, speeding up.

The exit sign loomed: Shasta County Nature Reserve.

"Turn here."

Jack Oh flipped his ponytail over his shoulder and grinned. "Here?"

"Yeah, here."

"You mean *here*? Right *here*?"

"Just turn, man."

Jack Oh floored it into the curve. Tires smoked, marking asphalt. The van went all g-force, weightless. Everyone grabbed something, trying to ease pressure off cuffed ankles.

"Whoa, Danica!" Tripper yelled.

"It is called a brake?" Yeltsin said. "The pedal which is next to the gas?"

They hit a dip, caught air, frame leaving sparks, nearly wiping out a pair of Subarus. There was a chorus of horns. An orchestra of brakes. Cursing and fist shaking. Jack Oh flipped the bird, cleared the ramp, and rolled up to a gas pump.

Silence.

The engine ticked and steamed.

Clients rubbed shoulders and necks.

Nero pried fingers from his thigh one by one.

"Sorry," Mr. Bator whispered, letting go.

I had a beak like that, I'd be sorry too.

"Don't worry about it."

You're just encouraging him. There's no kindness amongst wolves, dog!

"I'm not worried," Mr. Bator said, smiling without guile, his nose leaving a shadow that dipped across one frail shoulder, a glint in his eyes that almost reminded Nero of Amanda.

Happier Meal, Tastier Prize

"HOUSTON, WE HAVE TOUCHDOWN," JACK OH
said, and slapped the sun visor. A can of Skoal dropped into
his lap. He dipped, wiped his finger on the seat, and then
looked over at Bruce Leroy.

"What?"

"Nothing," Bruce Leroy said, refolding the map. Across
the parking lot, Fresh Bukket loomed. A giant neon chicken,
oppressively yellow, spun on a pole. It wore boxing gloves,
doing the rope-a-dope, the bob and weave. People carried containers and cartons and wrappers, Chixx Nuggets
and Best o' Breasts and MayoBake Tenders. In the dirt were
ketchup drips and orphaned fries and half-eaten slices of
Gram Spicer's Hobo Pie.

"Pie," Mr. Bator said wistfully. "I miss it, and I don't even like it."

"Exactly," Nero said.

"Let's go," Tripper yelled, straining against his cuff like a tube of pink roll-on. "We need to order up before the food's all gone!"

"Be more chill," Yeltsin said.

"Dude needs his meds," Idle said. "Pronto."

"Counselor Bruce? Tripper's freaking again," Heavy D said, but Bruce Leroy had gone outside to talk to the driver of one of the cars they'd cut off, the man waving his arms, irate. Jack Oh racked the brake and got up instead, leaning against the mesh separator. He wore tight jeans and blue cowboy boots. An immaculate ponytail hung between his shoulder blades.

"Are we having a client difficulty back here? Anything I can help solve?"

The van, for the first time, was quiet. Eyes were averted, the sound of pumped gas amniotic beneath them.

"No, sir."

"Is no problem."

"It's all good."

Jack Oh's eyes twinkled. "Excellent. Then let's all just sit here quietly until —"

Tripper stood. Everyone moaned. Heavy D tried to grab his shoulder, but Tripper wriggled away.

"Fuck, yeah, there's a problem," he said.

Jack Oh fingered the tooled knife-holder on his belt. "And what kind of problem would that be?"

"What do you think, mangina? We're starving."

The clients burst into laughter despite themselves.

"That's enough."

Tripper looked around, riding the wave. "Shit's the opposite of enough. It's called fuel, son. Goes in your mouth, comes out your rim? It's eatin' time, Busta Rhymes."

Jack Oh snapped open the mesh door. It hit the far wall with a molar-jarring clang. The laughter stopped. Clients leaned away from the aisle. Jack Oh clacked over and bent down in front of Tripper, their faces inches away.

"You got a complaint now, skinhead?"

Tripper looked around at the other clients, none of whom would meet his eyes. War Pig exhaled harshly. Nero just stared at his feet.

That's it, hero. Keep eyeballing those size thirteens.

Tripper lowered his head. "I guess not."

"You guess not, what?"

"I guess not, sir — Counselor sir."

Jack Oh nodded, slowly walking back to the gate. "Gentlemen, I believe we have all just learned our first lesson of the day."

When the door was almost closed, Tripper raised his fist to his mouth and fake-coughed, "Jack Off."

"No," Yeltsin said.

"Stop," Idle said.

Tripper coughed again, louder this time: "Chick gotta dick."

Jack Oh spun on one heel, lifted Tripper by the collar, and banged his head against the window.

Some of the boys moaned.

You gonna just sit there and watch?

Tripper turned red, his air cut off, pulling at Jack Oh's forearms. Mr. Bator rocked back and forth, whispering to himself.

This time it's him; next time it's you.

No one moved, holding on as the van swayed with Tripper's kicking legs. His eyes began to roll back, neck bent oddly. The compartment was hot and airless. It smelled like burnt matches and piss.

Do something!

Nero finally stood. He cleared his throat and tried to sound casual. "Actually, it's totally against the rules to touch a client. I read it in the pamphlet."

They all looked over in amazement, even Jack Oh, who let Tripper go.

"Dude, you can *talk*?" War Pig said.

"Two days and not a word. Suddenly it's the Gettysburg Address," Heavy D said.

"All this time I have thought you were the mute," Yeltsin said. "Or at least the unitard."

Nero shrugged and sat back down, his legs trembling.

Mr. Bator leaned over and whispered, "Misdirection. Nice trick."

Bruce Leroy opened the door, took Jack Oh by the elbow, and pulled the gate closed. "Why don't you go check the oil, Counselor Oh? I think these boys have had enough mentoring for one morning."

Jack Oh fished for his Skoal.

Twist, dip, spit.

He squinted, going for Poncho Clint.

Outside, children laughed.

Cars full of normals whooshed off the exit ramp.

Respect was everything. Standing was everything. Being dissed was everything. Everything was everything.

War Pig coughed, "Loser."

Heavy D coughed, "Douche."

Idle coughed, "Copped a feel."

Billy coughed, "Suck it, hippie."

There was a repeated slapping of five and slapping of Nero's back as the driver's-side door slammed hard enough to rattle pavement.

8

GlenLeroy Glen Nero

COUNSELOR BRUCE LEROY, WEARING A WHITE
headband with a Japanese sun rising in the center, took
Jack Oh's place. His real name was Marcellus Lee, but after he'd
stripped down to the waist at orientation, cut like a welter-
weight, and got all *Enter the Dragon* with a karate demo, the
boys dubbed him Bruce Leroy.

"Everyone feeling all right now?"

There was assorted grumbling.

"The trauma over? The drama squashed?"

There were assorted nods. Bruce Leroy pushed his thick
glasses back up his nose.

"Okay, then. Now I know back at camp we said we'd bud-
get up for some fast food before hitting the trail."

The boys cheered.

"Gimme protein," War Pig said, kissing his freckled biceps. "These guns don't run on salad."

"True enough, Warrior Pig. But that was contingent. Con-tin-jent. Meaning based upon if y'all ramped down your inner hyenas. Do any of you suppose you comported yourselves well — that's com-port-ted, meaning acted in a reasonable manner — during this trip?"

Idle and Billy raised their hands. Heavy D raised his hand. Mr. Bator started to, looked around, and then put it back down.

"C'mon, now, people."

Dead silence.

Bruce Leroy crossed his arms. "Can we seize this opportunity to act like men, or must we continue to lie like dogs?"

Yeltsin sneered.

Tripper barked.

"I vote men," War Pig said.

"Men," Nero agreed.

"Good. Excellent. So okay, let's reload. Did anyone in this van even halfway act like his momma raised him to today?"

They all shook their heads no.

"TripHop?"

"No."

"Boris Y.?"

"Yes, perhaps not so much."

Bruce Leroy put his hands together in the Oriental style and bowed. "Thank y'all for embracing your truth."

"You're welcome," Mr. Bator said.

Tripper fake-coughed, "Whatta douche."

"Now, while the ever-professional Counselor Jack Oh finishes gassing this caravan, I am going to walk on over to Fresh Bukket. If y'all can find a way to tap some inner mellow from now until trailhead, you can eat up on such food as I lug back. Do we have a deal?"

Heads nodded. Spines straightened. Elbows rested on laps.

Heavy D raised his hand.

"Heavy Duty, in the corner. Question?"

"Yes, sir. What're we ordering exactly?"

Bruce Leroy scratched his sideburns. "Oh, I figure a pair of sixty-piece buckets should do it. Plus assorted sides and sauces. Cool?"

Murmurs of assent gave the van a parliamentary feel.

"You look unconvinced, Young D."

Heavy D blushed. His wrists, each ringed by an enormous yellow sweatband, rested across the shelf of his stomach.

"It's just that . . ."

"Yes?"

"Personally, I prefer dark meat."

The van exploded with laughter. Idle and Billy punched each other's arms.

"Wide Load prefer dark meat!"

"Kid an equal-opportunity gobbler!"

Bruce Leroy chuckled. "Me too, Big D. Nothing wrong with being hungry for what you're hungry for. Can I get an amen?"

"Amen!"

"Amen!"

"Amen!"

Jack Oh yanked open the door. "What in hell's so funny in here?"

Sorry, Ponytail. Not everything's about you.

"What isn't funny on this fine morning?" Bruce Leroy said, stepping down and heading across the lot. "You feeling me, Counselor?"

Sun beat through the windshield as the clients dreamed of various things to pour gravy on. Families walked by the van talking and laughing but averted their eyes when they saw the mesh windows. Dads puffed their chests while moms gripped their kids' necks and steered them away as if being a delinquent might be catching.

They're right. Knucklehead is a disease.

One mom in particular seemed on the verge of a meltdown. Eyes unfocused, she dropped four Critter Fritters in the dirt and stumbled against the pump. Her husband tried to help, but she growled and snapped at him like a dog, showing her teeth.

Whoa, hard-core PMS. Glad I'm not hitched to that wagon.

The husband got her strapped in, barely, kids bawling as their Family Truckster tore out of the lot.

Estrada leaned forward and tapped Nero on the shoulder. A blue tear was tattooed just below his left eye.

Watch that kid. He's got a face like a mustard stain.

Nero gulped. "What?"

Estrada pointed with his chin. "Incoming."

Ten seconds later, another Econoline eased into the station and parked on the far side of the pump.

Close enough to touch.

Or at least to want to.

It was the second batch of IT clients.

In all-pink jumpsuits.

The girls' group.

On the side of their van, beneath INWARD TREK, was the company motto, *We're All in This Together.*

"I so want to be *all in* that," Estrada whispered. "Together. Separate. Whatever."

The other van began to rock with commotion as various lips, bangs, and ponytails were framed in the windows, as bra straps and bare shoulders dipped beneath pink uniforms.

From sheer boredom to pajama party in the span of ten seconds.

The girls were tall, short, hot, not. At least two of them made Jayna Layne look like a walking meat loaf.

"That one's almost worth getting arraigned for," Estrada whispered. Nero followed his eyes to a stately blonde sitting alone in the back, even though the others were packed three to a seat. Her name tag said SWANN. She seemed to be the only one wearing wrist cuffs.

Across the aisle, two girls sang into a hairbrush mic.

Another danced one-footed, her cuff bouncing to the beat. Then a cornrowed girl with the name tag RAEKWON grabbed the mic and pretended to deep-throat it.

"Oooooooh!" the other girls yelled at once, pushing and shoving.

Normally, fantastic.

But Nero had other concerns.

For instance, the hard-looking girl with dark purple hair. Who was totally giving him the eyeball.

"Sorta cute," Estrada whispered. "I guess."

Cheech is right. To guess.

Nero leaned against the glass and was just able read the girl's name tag: JOANJET. Her hair was rubber-banded into a severe topknot, like a purple fountain you wouldn't want to toss coins into.

That's one wish that's not coming true.

She had a thin face that was so pale it seemed covered in powder. There was a tattoo under her chin. It flared across her neck in both directions, a pair of unfurled wings.

You're staring. Girls totally love that.

"I take the blonde; you take purple," Estrada said. "We go on a double date."

"I don't think so."

"You scared?"

"Yes."

Joanjet leaned over and whispered something to the girl on the seat next to her.

Not a chance.

Whose face was suddenly pressed against the window.

Impossible.

A girl with white hair tucked behind her ears; it was cut shorter now and pulled into a tight bob. She wore no makeup, hadn't styled her jumpsuit by ripping off the sleeves or putting the collar up like the other girls.

Doesn't follow the crowd. Marches to a different drummer. Nice.

Yeah, she was nice.

Just like she was in the hallway at school or shooting the shit while waiting for the chicken gates to open.

Because that girl was Petal Gazes.

What, you know her?

Not even pretending to be surprised, Petal glanced at Nero, and then handed something to Joanjet.

"It's a pencil," Estrada said, too loudly. It woke up the other boys, who finally noticed the van.

"Holy shit. Girls!"

"Move now, please. Is very important that I see."

They stretched as far as their ankle cuffs would allow, War Pig clearing space with his elbows.

"Oh, man, it's like *Chained Heat*."

"I so, so need to get laid."

"Whatever, Fisty. You so, so are still the virgin."

They could all see a piece of paper in Joanjet's lap.

"Yo, Nero, it's a love note!"

"Way to pimp, pimp."

"Is it her phone number?" Heavy D asked.

"Yes, it is, you muncher of ass," Yeltsin said. "She is giving Nero her phone number. For the cell phone she does not have. So he can call her back. On the cell phone he does not have."

"Quiet," War Pig said. "Here it comes."

Joanjet reached over and pressed the paper against the window with her middle finger.

They all squinted, trying to make it out.

It wasn't a love note.

It wasn't a phone number.

It was a drawing.

A pretty good one, actually, of Nero's face. The dark hair and eyes and aquiline nose that had prompted his nickname to begin with, all nicely rendered. His deadpan expression. The thin stubble on his chin and upper lip.

Then, underneath the drawing, it said, in big block letters: EAT ME.

"You got dogged, dog!" Tripper said.

"Sorry, man," War Pig said. "Brutal."

Idle and Billy laughed, kicking the seat as Bruce Leroy came back across the lot, holding Fresh Bukket bags. Petal leaned around Joanjet and pressed her face against the window.

Her lips parted, about to say something.

Just as the van finished gassing up and moved away from the pump with a chirp.

Which gave Nero an excellent view of the restrooms and the highway ramp.

Unbelievable.

Nero Sole was a convict.

Petal Gazes was a convict.

Because of him.

And he couldn't be entirely sure, but she seemed to be mouthing the words *I'm sorry.*

9

Tchaikovsky's Black Heart

BRUCE LEROY AND JACK OH STOOD OUTSIDE the boys' van with the other two counselors: Exene, a tall brunette, and Velma, a smaller blonde with thick glasses.

The Fresh Bukket bags steamed at their feet.

Nero tore weather stripping away from his window and pressed his ear against the glass. He was barely able to make out the conversation. Mr. Bator asked if everyone could please be quiet. They all kept talking. Estrada told Tripper to shut the fuck up, and he did. So did everyone else.

"We can't handle her anymore," Velma was saying. "She has either majorly pissed off or made an outright enemy of every girl in there."

"What's her name?" Bruce Leroy asked.

"Portia Rebozzo. Trek Handle Swann."

"Oh, shit."

"Exactly. We keep her, there's going to be a real problem."

"It's not so much Swann as the rest," Exene said, a beer pooch showing through her tight shirt. "No way we even make it to the trail before some of them jump her."

"Big deal," Jack Oh said, shaking his hair free. He pulled it tight and then twisted a new band around it. "Let them go at it for a bit. Sounds like she deserves a taste."

"Yeah, normally that's fine. But —"

"But what?"

"But that girl is Bobo Rebozzo's daughter."

Bam!

"Who?" Jack Oh asked.

"You really are new, aren't you?" Velma said.

"Bobo Rebozzo owns practically everything in the valley," Exene explained. "This station. Fresh Bukket. Not to mention, um, Inward Trek?"

"What are they saying?" War Pig whispered.

"They're trying to trade us a girl," Nero said.

There was cheering and a repeated slapping of five.

"Be quiet," Estrada hissed.

The boys fell silent again.

"You have to take her," Exene was saying. "That princess goes home with even a mark on her, we're all screwed. Asshats at base camp overbooked us hard. We got fourteen in a van outfitted for ten. You guys only have nine total."

"But why did this Rebozzo send his kid to us?" Jack Oh

asked as a random dad bumped into him. The guy's eyes were unfocused. His gums looked too red. Jack Oh shoved him away. The guy growled, dropping half a Baster Pastry, and just kept walking.

Velma spun the leather bracelet on her wrist. "Rich girls. You know how it is. Teach her a lesson. Live among the lower castes."

Exene nodded. "Talk to her for ten minutes and you'll be surprised he didn't send her to Devil's Island."

"Feels wrong," Bruce Leroy said, eyeing the growler dad, who was now standing in the middle of the lot, staring at the sun. "Especially now. There's something funky in the air."

"C'mon, you don't have a hard case in the bunch," Velma said. "I saw their sheets. That's one of the softest crews we've ever taken up here."

"What did she just say?" War Pig demanded, rolling his thick neck.

"What a bunch of scary badasses we are," Nero said, wondering if Velma had read his file first: *Keep subject fifty yards away from poultry at all times.*

Bruce Leroy looked over and considered his clients through the window: Nero rubbing his temples, eyes shut. Heavy D probing his nose, three knuckles deep. Tripper idly pinching half-moons into his cheek.

"Yeah, it's hardly *The Dirty Dozen,* but adding a girl . . ."

"Pretty please?" Exene said. "Sugar on top? Sugar on the sides? Sugar rubbed all around where it feels good?"

Velma rolled her eyes.

Jack Oh gulped.

A man chased a woman past the pumps. She ran, laughing. Or maybe crying.

"Okay. Fine. But it's inopportune. That's in-opp-or-tune, meaning y'all owe us a big one."

"A really big one," Jack Oh said, pulling his jeans even tighter.

"Gross," Velma said.

Exene blew them both kisses. Jack Oh caught his and put it in his front pocket. Velma climbed onto the top of the van and lowered a backpack and some gear. There was a big commotion in front of Fresh Bukket, pushing and shoving. Someone's arm bled. A teenager in a fry cook's outfit stood there and moaned. The manager came out and waved the whole group away from the restaurant and threatened to call the cops.

"This everything?" Bruce Leroy asked.

Velma got in and revved the engine. "That's it."

"Wait, what about the paperwork?"

"Suckers!" Exene called as the girls' van pulled away, horn beeping *shave and a haircut*. Swann was left standing in a cloud of exhaust. She was tall and model-thin, with a high forehead and straight blond hair that fell to the center of her back. Her smirk was a dare. Her eyes were a smirk. She held the pink jumpsuit cinched tightly around her waist like a halter top, so they could see her belly button, which was nestled along a plane of tight, flat stomach.

Somehow she'd cut the jumper in half and made separates.

"How'd you do that?" Jack Oh asked.

"Couture is a state of mind."

Bruce Leroy cleared his throat. "I realize this . . . situation is less than ideal, but if everyone stays cool, we'll get through it okay."

"No, we won't," Swann said, pulling a lollipop from her sock. "This has disaster written all over it."

"Candy is contraband," Jack Oh said. "Not allowed."

Swann smiled, stuck the lollipop in her mouth, and swirled it around. The dull orb became bright red. She pointed it at him. "You guys are on crack, agreeing to take me. And not the good kind."

Bruce Leroy picked up Swann's bag and put it in the hold, then adjusted her ankle cuff.

"I know who your father is," he said in a low voice.

"So do I," she answered in a lower one.

"That means you know the drill, right?"

"That means I am the drill."

Jack Oh took her elbow and walked her to the door. "You sit up front. No fraternizing with the boys."

"I don't fraternize with boys. Show me a man around here, we'll talk."

"This is such a bad idea," Jack Oh said, thumbing his inseam.

"Yeah, well, Ponytail, I'm not so happy about it either," Swann said, and then climbed on board.

10

Talking Smack, Smacking Back

IT WAS ANOTHER HOUR WINDING THROUGH the approaches. The van's engine loudly girded against the ascent. As they rose almost straight up, the sun began to fade, snow now visible along the craggy peaks. Sweat turned to frost, the air thin and crisp. Swann had been given the front seat, forcing Idle and Billy to sit in the aisle, chained to the gate. Ten minutes after Jack Oh's warning about appropriate behavior around a female client, Swann planted her boot in Billy's sac when he pretended to touch her leg by accident.

"Oh, sorry," she said, braiding her hair into pigtails. "Did that hurt?"

Billy moaned, curled up, air whistling through his braces.

"Try rubbing it clockwise."

Billy moaned some more.

"Kick me too," Idle said, spreading his legs. "Please?"

"Shut up," War Pig said. "Have some respect."

"My hero," Swann said, pretending to gag.

"She's mean," Mr. Bator whispered.

"It's a curse to be pretty," Nero said, sucking in his cheeks. Mr. Bator just stared, considering the merit in it.

Tough crowd.

They came around a corner and almost drove into the scene of an accident. Two cars on the side of the gravel road had somehow managed to crash head-on; a cooler full of ice and food was strewn in the dirt. The drivers both seemed dazed, drooling, unconcerned with their injuries. In the long grass, one man was chasing another, his arms outstretched.

"Aren't we going to stop?" Swann asked.

"People need to solve their own problems," Jack Oh said.

"I didn't mean to *help*," Swann said. "I just thought there might be something good in that cooler."

Heavy D burst out laughing, a falsetto cackle. His yellow perm shook with mirth.

Yeltsin leaned forward into Swann's seat. "Hello. I am named Yeltsin. And my junk, he is named Trotsky."

Swann yawned. "Trotsky was murdered in Mexico City. In fact, they cut off his head."

Everyone inhaled as one.

Yeltsin began to perspire under his glasses. "That I did not know."

"Karma's a bitch. Also, namewise on your penis? I fig-ure maybe you should switch to Ted. Or Ken. Something . . . shorter."

Billy giggled, still rubbing himself.

Yeltsin cleared his throat and raised his voice: "Of less import is disputed historical precedent. This Trotsky, *my* Trotsky, has laid contentedly between the ass cheeks of many fine American females such as yourself."

"No kidding?"

"Yes. And, further, this is service I am prepared to offer you. Of course, free of charge."

The van was silent.

Full seconds ticked away without comment. The engine thrummed through the floorboards.

"Okay," Swann finally said.

"Okay?"

"But you're going to have to show me first."

Yeltsin shifted position, his grin evaporating. "What, here? Now?"

"Yes, here. Yes, now."

"You heard her," War Pig said.

"Yeah, produce the goods, big talker," Tripper said.

Yeltsin faked a laugh and looked at the other boys as the van went around a tight curve. Tires spun, grappling for pur-chase. Everyone hung on, except Swann, who seemed to have preternatural balance. She half stood, as far as the ankle cuff would let her, like the captain in the prow of a ship.

Tripper knelt in front of her and unzipped his jumpsuit. "I want to ink your name right here." He pointed to a blank stretch of skin just above his nipple, between Godzilla playing bass, a cup of coffee, the Germs circle, a lawn mower, the Black Flag flag, a crate of grenades, the Flipper fish, a jar of varnish, some H. R. Giger eggs, a quote from *Atlas Shrugged,* dead Elvis, robot Elvis, Han shooting Greedo, various caliber bullets, and naked Tawnii Täme.

"Why, I'd be honored," Swann said in a southern accent, touching the end of his nose with her lollipop.

The van skidded to a halt at a fork in the road. A big wooden sign had a map carved into it, showing the two main trails up the side of the mountain.

"Exene and the girls got Overlook Pass this time," Bruce Leroy said, pointing to the right. "That way is us."

"That way's you, maybe," Jack Oh said, turning the wheel. The van rumbled up the final mile of dirt road and parked under the sentinel of an enormous dead oak. The trees around it were black and bare of leaves. Some were rotted, beetles clicking and snapping as their heads poked though the bark. Others leaned listlessly as if they'd smoked their last cigarettes with too many hours left before the bar opened again. Buried half in a stand of pines was an abandoned SUV. Jack Oh turned off the lights and locked the doors while Bruce Leroy uncuffed the client's legs in pairs.

Everyone was issued a backpack and hiking boots while the Fresh Bukket bags were stowed.

"You will march in single file," Jack Oh said, hands on narrow hips and lip distended with chaw. His squint was flat and hard. "No one leaves the trail. No one sprints ahead; no one lags behind. And no one talks to the girl."

"The woman," Swann said.

"No one talks to her. As far as food, when we get to base camp, you will each get the same meal. Anyone who bitches about this arrangement or drags ass or talks to her isn't getting squat to eat. Am I clear?"

"It'll be cold by then," Heavy D said.

"I will bet all is cold now," Yeltsin said.

"Listen up," Bruce Leroy said, going for a smile and not really getting it. He looked worried, repeatedly glancing over his shoulder. "This hike has power. I've seen the miles be trans-form-a-tive, meaning they can turn bad into good. It won't be easy, but nothing worth having ever is."

"What about an orgasm?" Swann asked.

Bruce Leroy pushed his glasses up his nose. "In this world there's two ways to handle your business: the right way and the shortcut. Ask a hundred men in the penitentiary; ninety-nine of them thought they saw a quicker route. So, gentlemen, which path are y'all gonna take today?"

"The short one," Idle said.

"The even shorter one than that," Billy said.

"Can we, perhaps, complete this hike online?" Yeltsin asked.

Estrada shouldered his gear and stood next to Nero. His

eyes looked angry, but his voice was calm and low. "Can you believe it?"

"What?"

"The girl."

All Nero could think of was Petal driving away in the other van.

"Who, Swann?"

Estrada laughed. "No, Jenny from the block. Yeah, man, Swann. One minute it's a rolling sausage fest, and then suddenly we toting around the hottest *chula* I seen in forever."

You keep him talking; I'll go look up chula *in the dictionary.*

Bruce Leroy opened the equipment shell on the roof and handed each pair of boys a tent. Then he gave them sleeping bags, cookware, hiking boots, freeze-dried MREs (meals ready to eat), full water bottles, iodine tablets, orange survival jackets, orange hats, and orange mittens. INWARD TREK was stenciled with black paint on every item.

"Who wears orange?" War Pig said, yanking the pompom off his hat. "We look like a handful of dicks."

"All clients got to gear up," Bruce Leroy said, eyeing the horizon. The clouds were thin, the sun a distant point of gray. "Gonna be cold tonight."

Swann went first, playing an imaginary flute. Estrada sniffed the air deeply as she passed. Nero and Bruce Leroy went second, following Swann past a sign that said FABRIZIO T. REBOZZO MEMORIAL TRAIL, into the first stand of pines. Jack Oh took up the rear.

"Jack Oh's taking it up the rear," Tripper said.

"C'mon, y'all," Bruce Leroy said, clapping his hands. "Time to man up."

"Actually, I believe it is time to man down."

"I'm only seventeen. I won't be a man for another five months."

They humped along the trail until it came to a series of natural stone steps. With all the gear, it was a full-on ascent.

"Is this where we line up for the funicular?"

"What's a funicular?"

"Like a gondola."

"What's a gondola?"

"Like a douche bucket on a string."

"Oh. Why we wanna line up for that?"

Mr. Bator wiped his nose on his sleeve. "Can't we just, like, camp here?"

When no one answered, he peeked up the trail and added, "Because I have a really bad feeling about this."

11

All Along
the Watchtower

THEY SPENT THE AFTERNOON CROSSING
creeks, stepping over mossy rocks, and taking short breaks
between inclines. The woods were unusually dark. The trees
seemed too close, as if they hadn't had the sense to give
each other space. A thick layer of dead leaves gave off a rotting stench, muffled voices and breath and feet. Nothing
seemed to move in the scrub. No happy birds, no angry
birds. No birds at all. Just an insectoid buzz that seemed to
come from everywhere at once, tiny things digging in against
the cold.

Or something even worse.

"Where's all the animals, yo?"

"Yeah, where's Shrek?"

Yeltsin picked a piece of food from between his teeth and then wiped it on Mr. Bator's neck. "Shrek is not an animal, shitdips."

"Then what is he?"

"Um, I believe is called a cartoon?"

Swann kept a steady pace, always twenty yards in front of the group, a pair of braids flitting between mealy redwoods.

"I'm tired," said Mr. Bator.

"Me too," said Heavy D.

"Can't do the climb, don't do the crime," said Jack Oh.

Eventually, Heavy D and Mr. Bator began to lag behind. Bruce Leroy alternated between towing them by their chest straps and pointing out the Latin names for different trees and flowers.

"Great. Tree names in Chinese."

"That's not Chinese, dick."

"How you know what Chinese dick is?"

"I don't."

"Bet you know what it tastes like, though."

Swann laughed. It echoed off the trees as she disappeared around the next bend. Sun backlit the mountain, light spearing through the branches like it'd been Photoshopped. The air hardened, condensed. A predusk gloom drew the clients out of focus, shadows skeletal, a religious procession on the way to a shrine that didn't exist.

"Hold up," Bruce Leroy said, reaching between a pair of

shrubs. He rooted around and yanked on something until it finally came free.

It was a fleece.

A woman's, brand new.

Torn.

Bruce Leroy folded the jacket and stuck it in his pack, but not before Nero noticed it was spattered.

Brownish red.

"Um, Counselor?"

"Not now," Bruce Leroy said, and then took Jack Oh aside.

"Counselor," Nero insisted, "the jacket? I mean, did you see the —?"

"I said not *now,* son."

Everyone lurched forward, moaning. They spread out almost immediately, Swann in the lead as usual. Tripper fell behind, nylon chuffing between his short legs. Estrada stopped to help Mr. Bator. Both counselors argued with Idle and Billy, who locked arms and refused to move.

Petal, find out what supermodel knows about Petal!

Nero doubled his pace trying to catch up.

Swann held branches as if to help but then let go so they snapped in his face before speeding ahead again, a pink triangle disappearing like a deer's tail. After a mile, Nero had a welt on his forehead and two scratches across his cheeks. He threw down his hat and gave up, sweating into the hard pack.

And then Swann was there.

Smelling crisp, like an apple that had just been halved.

They stood side by side at the top of a rise.

Far below, Jack Oh was disentangling Idle and Billy, who'd fallen into a patch of poison oak. On purpose.

"So, uh, what are you in for?" Nero asked.

She yawned. "The fascinating small talk."

Good one. Next time, put her in a figure-four headlock. That's what I used against Hulk Hogan to win the belt.

Swann unzipped her jacket, flashing perfect clavicles and the astonishingly lickable dewy spot at the base of her neck.

"Listen, can I ask you a question?"

"Yes, I have a boyfriend."

"No. I wanted to ask about—"

"Look, you think just because we're standing here for five minutes I'm going to see what a sensitive, misunderstood guy you are and suddenly confide, like, 'Oh, my mom's a rich drunk and my stepdad does coke and I cut my thighs at night with a paring knife while reading dipshit vampire books,' right before we lean in for the most special kiss of your mopey virgin life?"

Crickets cricketed.

Beetles scurried.

Larvae hatched.

The voice in your head remained silently awed.

"That is seriously high-quality," Nero finally said.

"High-quality what?"

"Cynicism. Think you can you front me a dime?"

Swann laughed, chewing her fingernail.

Below them, Bruce Leroy was trying to push Heavy D through the next crevasse. None of the boys helped, except Yeltsin, who kept saying, "You must toss stick of butter up trail as enticement, then he gets himself loose."

"Look, it's a bad habit. I know. But it's hard to break."

"What is?"

Swann fluffed her bangs. "Operating in eff-off mode all the time. It drains the batteries."

"Yeah, I can see that."

"Boning the limo driver."

"Huh?"

"What I'm in here for. You asked."

"Seriously?"

"My father caught us in the carport, practicing with the clutch. I was finally getting the hang of reverse. Three days later, bam, pink jumpsuit."

Nero wiped his nose with an orange mitten. "That's really kind of perfect, actually."

"Yeah."

Petal. Remember her? The reason you ran this steeple-chase? Or are you just going to stand here flirting all afternoon?

"Hey, can I ask you another question?"

"Yes, I still have a boyfriend."

"No, I —"

Bruce Leroy finally pried Heavy D loose. The rest of the clients trudged up the ridge. Swann stepped away and started accessorizing the waistband of her pack with tiny pinecones.

"You want to watch it with Miss Purple, by the way. She's not what you think."

"I don't think anything about her."

Swann frowned. "Will you knock off the innocent routine? Eat me? I saw the whole thing in the van. Everyone did."

Nero shook his head. "No, she was . . . that was . . . I was actually trying to —"

"You've got lousy taste, Fiddler."

"Who's Fiddler?"

"Nero, stupid. Like, what he did while Rome burned?"

You got any clue what she's talking about? I must have failed that class.

"You two! Separate!" Jack Oh yelled, coming around the corner. He took Swann by the arm and pushed her ahead, taking any information about Petal with him.

12

Campsite

AN HOUR LATER, THEY CAME TO A SMALL clearing. A fire pit had already been dug; it was lined with stones and surrounded by worn logs. Branches furled at odd angles. Everything looked exhausted and leached of color. Half-burned garbage was strewn about, wrappers impaled in the dense scrub.

"Congratulations, gentlemen. This is it," Bruce Leroy announced.

Idle and Billy threw down their packs and immediately lay in the dirt.

Nero spread out his tarp.

"Want to share?" Estrada asked, holding a tent. His eyes were flat, fixed. He looked mean, hair slicked down against his scalp, random whiskers and high cheekbones.

That convict will cut your back as soon as breathe on you.

"Okay," Nero said.

Estrada helped assemble the poles. Taking turns holding the sides, they staked each one firmly with rocks.

You guys are buddies now, huh? Hey, that's great. Next stop: marriage equality.

Swann set up her own tent, quick and tight, on the far side of Jack Oh's. War Pig set up lopsided poles, then tried to fix them by jamming them in even harder. Yeltsin and Tripper got theirs upright but argued about who got to sleep near the flap.

"You are to sleep in the back, skinjob."

"Screw that," Tripper said, tapping his head three times. "I need fresh air. I'm not sleeping deep while you cut gravy all night."

"And you are going to squeeze out the lavender? I do not think so. I am sleeping in front."

Tripper tried to kick Yeltsin in the balls, missed, and fell on his back. Jack Oh made Tripper share with Heavy D instead. That put Yeltsin in with Mr. Bator.

"No! I do not share with the Showerbator!"

"No way I'm sharing with Augustus Gloop!"

"We have an extra tent," Bruce Leroy said, helping Heavy D set it up. "You can't fault a man for his size."

"Yes, you can," Tripper said.

"You do realize you're a midget, correct?" Heavy D asked.

Tripper tried to kick Heavy D in the balls, missed, and fell on his back.

Estrada and Nero sat on a rock, watching.

"This routine's better than *Jackass*."

Nero chuckled, unable to shake the suspicion that Estrada wanted something.

He does. Be sure of it.

Or shake the feeling that he was being a tool for doubting that Estrada might just be friendly. Or shake the guilt from talking to him without admitting, "By the way, I'm also having a conversation with someone in my head."

Hey, forget the tent. Maybe you two should share a sleeping bag.

"Can the Rock shut it with the rampant homophobia, already?"

"You're mumbling, son," Estrada said.

Nero blew into his hands. "I said, it's freaking cold. Not like this in Mexico, I bet."

"Wouldn't know, *ese*. I never been to Mexico. Born right there in San Fran."

"Oh. Sorry. I just thought —"

Racist.

"Bet you thought I killed a gang member too, huh? Like, in an initiation rite?"

Nero started to deny it, then didn't bother. "Pretty much, yeah."

Estrada pretended to wipe his blue tear away. "You one of them dudes believes what every convict tells you?"

"No."

"Then why you holding out on me?"

"You mean about what I did to get sent here?"

Bawk bawk ba-gawk. Tell him about the Chickocaust. Tell him about Poultry Bed Death.

"No disrespect, homes, but I don't really give two shits."

"Then what?"

"What you and *chula* blondie were talking about, kid! I saw you together. Would have paid serious Benjamins to be up on that rise instead of your pale ass. No offense."

"Who you calling pale, *ese*? I was born in Tijuana."

Estrada laughed, holding out his hand for a bump. "You all right, Fiddler. Gimme some bones."

They cracked knuckles. Not too soft, not too hard, with just the right clang. It was supposed to hurt a little.

Bruce Leroy walked to the edge of the clearing.

"Lend me your ears, gentlemen. But mostly your arms."

"Huh?"

"C'mon, there's laboring to be done."

They followed him into the scrub to help gather wood. Most of it was rotting or full of worms and had to be thrown back. Nero found a few usable pieces and snapped them under his boot.

"Counselor Bruce?"

"Yeah?"

"What was up with that fleece?"

Bruce Leroy snapped a huge branch over his knee, but it didn't break. It just bent, and then brown sap oozed out. He flung it away in disgust.

"What fleece?"

"The one you found. On the trail. That was . . . stained?"

Bruce Leroy loaded a few logs into Estrada's arms.

"What you think, young bucks? We got enough wood yet?"

He turned and walked back to the clearing. They dumped the kindling, and then Jack Oh built a fire. The other boys immediately gathered around, warming respective hands and feet and asses as the sun went down.

"So can we eat now?" Heavy D asked. "Puh-lease?"

"You sure can," Jack Oh said, sliding the pack with the Fresh Bukket behind his tent. "But whiners don't get rewards. And you all whined the entire way up. That was the rules, and the rules have been broke. So break out your MREs."

"No way. We earned that shit, Ponytail."

"I want my Chixx Nuggets, man. Like right now."

Bruce Leroy stepped forward, making calming motions. "You sure that's the way you want to handle this, Counselor?"

Jack Oh fake-coughed, "Convicts learn a lesson."

Tripper spun around. "But you promised."

Jack Oh coughed again: "Comes around goes around."

"Okay, okay," Bruce Leroy said. "That's enough of that. Listen here, y'all, we'll com-pro-mise, meaning disparate parties coming together."

"You come together." Yeltsin said. "No doubt is not the first time of your Brokeback mingling."

"How about in the morning—"

"Fuck a morning," War Pig said, kicking over the water jug. He hurled his pack out into the darkness, threw his orange hat into the fire, and then rammed into his already leaning tent.

"Oh, well," Swann said. "I prefer the South Beach diet, but I guess this will work too." She gave Jack Oh the finger and then zipped her tent shut.

The other boys slowly followed, grumbling under their breath, "pony dick, starving dick, food dick, cowboy dick, rip-off dick, kill-him dick, nuggets dick, promise dick, jerk-it dick, mayobake dick, dickhead dick."

Within an hour, most of them fell asleep listening to the sounds of Styrofoam creaking, wax paper being unwrapped, and cold gravy being poured as the smell of fry grease settled on the forest floor.

"Six more days," Estrada whispered in their tent as he tore open a pot-roast-and-gravy MRE.

Nero looked at his pork chops 'n' applesauce before throwing it to the side.

"It can't be *that* bad."

"I don't eat meat."

Estrada peered over a spoonful of brackish goop. "You have got to be shitting me."

"Nope."

"Why not, man? Meat tastes *sooo* good."

Nero shrugged. "Childhood trauma, I guess."

"What-hood what?"

"It's not, like, political. I don't think I'm saving the world or whatever."

"Then why get all Gandhi when you could be downing a plate of chorizo?"

"I guess it just freaks me out to eat anything with a face."

Estrada thought about it for a while. "Okay, I can dig that. Good thing, though, huh?"

"Good thing what?"

"Pussy don't have a face."

They both laughed into their sleeping bags, while in the distance, someone began to snore.

In the farther distance, someone cut lavender.

"Hey, I forgot to ask," Nero said. "When we were talking before, how did you know she called me Fiddler?"

"Who called you who?"

"Swann. Fiddler."

"I didn't know."

"What, so that was just a coincidence?"

Estrada sighed. "You're Nero, okay? What else does Nero do but sit on his ass and play violin all day while everything around him burns?"

"Oh."

"It's history, dude. Read up. The Romans? We doomed to repeat them. Or at least resemble them."

Around the clearing, the clients hunkered deep in their bags.

Listening to the crackle of fire and the crackle of wrappers.

As Bruce Leroy and Counselor Jack Oh's low voices rumbled.

It was almost impossible to tell if they were arguing or laughing.

13

No Time for Lattes

NERO OPENED HIS EYES. THE MOON WAS high, skirted by a ring of gloom. Outside the tent was a crinkling noise, like foil being unwrapped. He eased up the flap and peered out, his money on a raccoon.

Or Heavy D.

But it wasn't either.

There was a bare calf, a tight thigh, sheer hotness in pink.

Swann crouched over the garbage pile, jumpsuit top barely covering her panties.

Nero's eyes bulged. Audibly.

She spun around, gnawing a chicken bone.

"What?"

"Nothing."

Oh, that's something, all right.

Swann gathered a pouch of discards into her top. Moonlight reflected off her navel.

"You want some?"

Want some what?

"No."

She held out half a chewed breast. "Come here. Have a bite."

"No."

Her lip curled upward. "You scared to get in trouble?"

Yes.

"No."

"Then what's the problem?"

It's perfectly natural.

"There is no problem."

"There's not?"

"I, uh . . . just can't stand up right now."

"How come?"

Smuggling a crowbar in your jumpsuit?

"My foot's asleep."

Swann laughed. "Want me to rub it?"

"No!"

"No?"

"I also . . . just don't like Fresh Bukket."

"Who doesn't like Fresh Bukket?"

"Me."

"Too bad for you."

Swann bit off another chunk of meat, then stuck the bone entirely in her mouth and sucked off the fat.

Nero wanted to drive a tent stake into his skull.

She tossed the bone into the fire, belched, pulled gristle from between her teeth, flicked it at him, and then slipped into her tent.

You, my friend, are a worthless turd.

Nero rolled over and lay on his back.

And thought.

About varicose veins. And moldy cottage cheese. And waiting in line at the vacuum-repair store.

Which helped a little.

But even so, it took, seriously, almost forever to fall back asleep.

At dawn, light out but just barely, the air smelled like cold MREs and unbrushed teeth. Estrada was snoring quietly, his orange sleeping bag pulled over his face. There was frost on the lip of the tent. It was even colder than the day before.

There was also a smacking noise.

Nero's hand began to throb, all along the gash.

The stitches were red and raw and pulsed.

The smacking got louder.

It had to be Heavy D for sure, already up and into the powdered eggs. Nero pulled on his boots and stepped outside.

The clearing was covered with frost, a fog clinging to the tree line.

It wasn't Heavy D making the noise.

Swann either.

In fact, no one else was up except the counselors, their tents collapsed beneath them.

Bruce Leroy was lying on top of orange nylon. Jack Oh was crouched, leaning over him.

Slip out the back, Jack.

"Huh?"

Make a new plan, Stan.

"What?"

Hop on the bus, Gus.

Nero took a step closer.

"Everything okay?"

Jack Oh's skin was gray and pale, his ponytail unfurled wildly. There was a terrible smell coming off of him.

"Um . . . Counselor?"

Jack Oh looked up and grinned. His knife jutted out of the meat of his shoulder, sunk to the handle. It didn't seem to be bothering him much.

"You need some help?"

Jack Oh didn't answer. His teeth were red and wet, his eyes yellow and pinned. He was stubbornly chewing something, probably a wad of Skoal.

Right?

Nero took a step closer. Didn't want to, but had to.

Had to see.

If it was.

Skoal.

Another step.

Then another.

Nope.

Wasn't tobacco at all.

Matter of fact, Counselor Jack Oh was eating chunks of Counselor Bruce Leroy.

Okay, that's gross.

Nero moaned. And then nearly pissed himself.

Very, very nearly.

Jack Oh stared, no recognition in his eyes, his chin like a paintbrush dipped in red, two of Bruce Leroy's fingernails stuck deep into his cheek.

Nero moved a bit to his left, and Jack Oh growled a warning.

Try tossing him a Milk-Bone.

Nero moved to his right.

This time Jack Oh didn't growl.

Instead, he swiveled and pounced.

Nero dove to the side, and Jack Oh went right over him, collapsing War Pig's tent.

"Hey, get off, assclown."

Jack Oh flailed in the orange nylon, his cowboy boots kicking wildly. The other boys crawled into the clearing. War

Pig saw Nero standing there and jumped up, red hair high-lighted by the rising sun.

"I swear, man, I am seriously about to kick your —"

Nero pointed to Bruce Leroy. Lying on his tent like a crime scene. Missing pieces. Missing parts.

"What the *fuck*?"

"Behind you!"

Jack Oh leaped again. He landed on War Pig's back and pulled him to the ground, teeth bared and snapping. War Pig jammed his forearm into Jack Oh's neck, just managing to push his mouth away. It banged open and shut, razors on springs.

You just gonna watch, Fiddler? Maybe place a few bets this time?

Hands shaking, Nero grabbed a log from the fire pit and charged. Estrada, right behind him, grabbed a tent stake. Idle and Billy had iron skillets. They began to beat Jack Oh as War Pig managed to work himself free.

"Oh, you want some?"

"You want some more?"

"Eat this, bee-yatch."

"Beg for it, Ponytail!"

Idle took three long strides and executed a perfect kick. Jack Oh took it in the temple and rolled into a crouch, growling and spitting. An oval of red smeared his mouth like demented lipstick.

They'd hammered him good. He should have been curled fetal, nursing balls and ribs.

But he wasn't.

"This is so totally insane."

"In the freaking membrane."

The boys came together in a line, backing up slowly, weapons held out in front of them. Jack Oh got on all fours, stalking.

"Now what in the sac do we do?"

"How in the sac do I know?"

Jack Oh feinted. The boys drew back with a yelp. Mr. Bator accidentally stepped on Heavy D's tent, pulling it down. They all looked over at where Heavy D lay, his sleeping bag torn open, like a giant burrito that had been rudely picked at. Dried blood caked his perm and headband. His stomach had been raked apart, tubes and muscle and cartilage visible through a hole in his neck.

The same hole where Swann was feeding.

She was perched on his enormous chest, chewing away, stiff hair jutting at random angles.

She was also completely naked.

"Is not even possible," Yeltsin said.

Blood washed over Swann artfully, like body paint.

"It is just me, or is she still mad hot?"

"You, my friend, are a total degenerate."

"But, yeah, that is centerfold epic."

"Of what? *Skeezer and Cannibal Digest*?"

Swann glared at them, her eyes wide, pupils pinned like a hawk's. She tore a piece of gristle away from D-bone and chewed it intently. Fresh blood spread down her chest, over dried rivulets, and spattered between her legs.

"This is so my best nightmare ever," Idle said.

"I could swear this happened to me once before," Billy said.

"Okay, time to wake up," Mr. Bator said.

Jack Oh howled with rage, loud and plaintive.

Nero felt the sound vibrate through his body, from head to foot.

Ankle to femur.

Nape to coccyx.

Right to the center of his palm.

Inhuman.

Especially when Swann joined in. She threw back her head and then hooked her arms around Heavy D's body.

"*Chica* is marking her kill," Estrada said with a low whistle.

"That is just way *way* too trippy."

"Okay, I go to my safe place now."

Then came a third howl, matching Jack Oh's.

The boys all looked back as Bruce Leroy rolled onto his belly, glasses broken, strips of skin torn away. His headband was bloody, but the rising sun was still intact.

"You okay, dude?" Nero asked.

"His Afro looks fun-ky."

"Bruce, man, help us," Idle said, his voice rising. "It's, like, your job."

Bruce Leroy shook his head as if he was trying to clear it. Black liquid began dribbling from his ears.

"Bruce?"

"Seriously, dude. This is not the time for screwing around."

"Yes, like, now to bust out some of the karate!"

Bruce Leroy growled, then lurched toward them, teeth bared.

"Oh, snap."

"Oh, Jesus."

"Oh, Calcutta."

Time to make a move, G Smoove.

Nero stepped forward and swung his log, catching Jack Oh on the shoulder, just above the knife. There was a cracking of bone. Jack Oh tumbled back into Bruce Leroy, knocking him over. They fell in a snarling pile. Swann clawed at the dirt like a lizard, covering Heavy D with her body, then swiveled her head toward the boys.

And opened her mouth impossibly wide.

Her tongue slowly unfurled.

Dripping wet.

Dripping red.

"Screw this shit," War Pig said. "C'mon!"

The clients turned and ran downhill as a group, but Jack Oh was on all fours, blocking the clearing. Bruce Leroy was preparing a frontal assault. The only choices were to try to bushwack through the scrub, slow and ripe for the picking, or head straight up.

"This way!"

"What about our gear?" Yeltsin said.

"Good idea," War Pig yelled over his shoulder, hurdling the first line of underbrush. "You go back for it."

"What about Tripper?" Nero yelled.

This time no one answered.

Because Tripper wasn't with them.

He was always the hardest one to wake up.

A lousy trait to have.

Especially since now they could hear him screaming.

And screaming.

And screaming.

For a good half mile up the trail.

14

It's a Flashback, Jack

NICK WALKED THE HALF MILE FROM THE BUS stop, threw his books on the sofa, and then poked his head into the living room. Dad was home already. He'd set prototypes out on the dining-room table, poured four fingers of bourbon, and turned the stereo on. Some cool jazz station sqwonked out of the hi-fi as he snapped his fingers and did little dance moves on the rug. Amanda grabbed a steaming prototype, stuffed it into her mouth, and then continued pushing a tiny stroller in perfect ellipses around Dad's mambo-y legs.

It was Nick's twelfth birthday. He figured a present must be waiting in the garage or a closet but wasn't sure if it was the right time to ask. Mom had been making dinner but was now leaning in the kitchen doorway, apron wet, arms crossed, a bemused expression on her face that seemed inclined not to be bemused much longer.

"Ronald, why are you feeding her that?"

Dad took a slug of bourbon. Some of it dribbled down the front of his shirt. He dabbed the spill with his tie.

"Why shouldn't I? Our daughter is only chewing on the future of food. When the future arrives, darling, you don't tell it to come back later. You open the door and let it walk right in."

Nick winced. He knew that *darling* never meant darling. It meant sleeping on the couch. Or slamming the porch door. Or gunning the Continental out of the driveway and just missing the Andersons' mailbox. Nick could feel Mom staring at him, mentally willing him to come stand next to her. Pick a side, prove a point, play a favorite. And he wanted to. Make her feel better. But he wanted to check out the prototypes even more. So he pretended to sneeze and then lifted one from the chafing dish.

It was a chicken nugget, warm, plump, golden, breaded. Shaped like a pristine kidney of deliciousness.

Dad leaned down and smiled. "Bottoms up."

Nick popped it in his mouth.

The nugget exploded with heat. Juice coated his tongue. It crunched and melted at the same time, with a burst of flavor that was both sharp and smoky.

It was totally, completely fantastic.

"See?" Dad said. "The Sole Fryer is the future of gourmet-quality chicken, Lydia. A new generation of bird. Me and

Winnie Fuld are Rebozzo's golden boys now. It's going to sell a million units first year, easy. And do you know what that means?"

"No," Mom said. "I don't."

Dad poured another drink, triple-sipped, and then put it down on the table without a coaster.

"It means we're not going to be living in this dump much longer."

It had been Mom's parents' house. The one she grew up in. Nick knew you never put a drink down without a coaster in Mom's parents' house. He knew you never, ever called Mom's parents' house anything but cozy or charming. Why didn't Dad know that?

Amanda reached for a sample and crammed it into her mouth. Then took another. Nick grabbed one too. Mom strode over and pulled them both away angrily. Amanda just stared at her empty hand, but Nick — much to his surprise, because he was way too old for it — almost started to cry. He *really* wanted that nugget.

Mom held up the greasy samples. Nick was tempted to run over and lick her fingers.

"This is what I put you through school for? This is why you got a chemistry degree?"

Dad flipped back his hair, which was getting long and needed a trim.

"*You* put me through? Did you take the classes? Did you pass the tests?"

"No, I just wrote the checks."

Dad pulled a Fresh Bukket menu from his back pocket and then grabbed the phone. "Forget dinner. We're ordering out."

"*What?*"

"You heard me. We're dialing up a whole mess of the Bukket."

"Yay!" Nick cheered.

"Yay!" Amanda would have cheered, if she cheered. Instead, she hummed in a low voice from under the sofa.

Dad spun his gold card between his fingers like the ace of spades. "We're having a little taste test. See for our own eyes what kind of slop Fresh Bukket is dishing out. And then we're going to compare it to the Sole Fryer. I've got another whole platter in the car."

Mom turned on one heel and slammed the kitchen door.

Dad took another slug of his drink and then ordered one of everything from the menu. "Yes, I'm serious," he kept telling the clerk. Mom swooped through the living room, picked up Amanda, and took her upstairs. Dad grabbed at her dress, missed, and almost fell.

Nick ran over and steadied his father's leg, and then held on, tight, even after the food came.

Chunk o' Leans ———————————— $10.99

Cubed fatback in its own special Estonian gravy, spread over a mound of Larder Fries and Cool Ranch Chicken Strips.

Bread Me, Shred Me ———————————— $7.99

Thinly shredded thigh meat hunkered down in a robin's nest of beer-soaked crumbs, topped with premium Newark dates and fresh Bronx gorgonzola. Don't eat the toothpick!

Neck Hunklets ———————————— $14.99

A chicken lover's fantasy! Tender special-recipe hunklets smothered with our very own Porky Sauce®, then topped with Crispy Neck Cracklins. (One Porky Sauce per customer only, please.)

Frycook's Choice ———————————— $2.99

Troll the bottom of the FryBasket 2000 with Divemaster Stu and surface with a true crunch treat!

Señor Pollo's 9-Spice Fiesta ———————————— $19.99

When the Señor decides it's time to party, who are you to argue? Available in Hot, Hotter, So Caliente, and El Molten.

Mystery Box ———————————— $11.99

Filled to the brim and just waiting to be discovered—there's only one way to solve this chicken riddle, and it's not with your nose!

Best o' Breasts ———————————— $5.49

What could be better? Tender and juicy grade-A breasts cooked to a bulging, tight-sweatery perfection.

Sweet Sweetback's Country-Style Strips ———————————— $7.50

Smothered in lumpy gravy, Van Peeble Paste, and Nu-Okra®.

It's Under the Sour Cream ———————————— $6.99

What is, you ask? Well, stop gabbing, grab a spoon, and send us a postcard when you find out!

Sweet 'n' Sav-O-Ry Chik-n O's ———————— $3.49
Kids love 'em! Shaped like tiny donuts and absolutely swimming in ol'
Gram Bukket's butter-maple glaze.

Larder Fries ———————————— $3.99
Choose curly, straight, home, waffle-cut, or X-tra Lardy.
Now available in a 5-pound Tater Crate ($9.99)
or 12-pound Tuber Cube ($14.50).

Diet Plate ———————————— $12.99
29-piece Chixx Nuggets, lite dip, tomato slice

Dinner on the Go ———————— $24.50
60-piece Chixx Nuggets

Mom's Family Packster ———————— $39.99
88-piece Chixx Nuggets

Hungry Plumber's Night Out ———— $69.50
156-piece Chixx Nuggets arranged in a special platter spread.
(Comes with free* Nu-Butter® Go-Tub.)

CHOOSE YOUR VERY OWN DIPPING SAUCE!
Feel Free to Mix and Match!
(3 tublets for $5.00)

1. **Chipotle, Sweet Corn, and Homecurds**
2. **Blue Cheese/American Cheese Summit**
3. **Loaf 'n' Lickerish**
4. **Sour Bacon Exotique**
5. **Smooth Clammy Chowder**
6. **Salt 'n' Vinegar 'n' More Salt**
7. **Garlic-Cheddar Dunkin' Bukket**

*Technically, promotional Nu-Butter tub is more "freely available" than actually free.

15

The Long March

NERO AND WAR PIG WERE AT THE FRONT, followed by Idle and Billy. Yeltsin was right behind, with Estrada at the rear of the pack. They kept up a steady pace for half an hour, grunting with the exertion of a near sprint, leaping over logs, repeatedly thwacked in the face by branches, ignoring the pain.

Which was nothing compared to the phantom sensation of teeth at their ankles.

When they'd gone at least a mile from camp, the boys huddled on a small rise where they could see down the trail. Mr. Bator was farther back, but not so far that they couldn't hear his sobs. Yeltsin put his hands on his knees and puked an effervescent froth.

It was mostly pink. Everyone stared.

"What?"

"Blondie let you suck her lollipop?"

"Thanks for sharing, douche burger."

Yeltsin shivered. He hadn't had time to put on a jacket. "Who gives such crap about the candy? Um, hello? The counselor Bruce just tried to eat our pancreas."

"Pancreases?"

"Pancrii?"

Estrada looked back down the trail, sweat running from his still-groomed hairline. "Yeah, what in the fuck was that about?"

"It means we paroled, for starters," Idle said.

Billy reached out to slap five. "Camp's over, son."

"Freedom!"

"Anarchy!"

"The freedom to commit serious anarchy!"

"It means we've got to start hoarding water," Mr. Bator said, huffing into the clearing. His nose made an odd whistling sound, like an engine letting off steam. "And canned beans and stuff. And guns."

"Oh, okay," Billy said. "Good idea. I think there's a canned bean and gun store a little farther up the trail."

"I can't believe that . . . thing was Bruce Leroy," Nero said, knowing he had to decide right there, right that second, if he'd gone completely insane.

Nope. You're good. Voice in your head's still here, though.

War Pig nodded. "Not so hard to believe about Jack Oh."

Idle laughed, "No doubt. I smacked that ponytail hard. Left, right, left. Ground and pound. Tapped his shit out!"

"But he got up again," Estrada said. "Didn't he?"

Billy spit on his fingers, moussing his hair. "And what about Blondie's pole dance?"

Everyone inhaled, visions of Swann dancing like sugar plums in their heads. Naked Swann. Blood-soaked Swann. Ravenous Swann.

Did you mention naked Swann?

"Kid, that almost made the whole thing worth it," Billy said.

"Chick was, I swear, totally giving me the eyeball," Idle said.

"She stares at you because you are the walking pork chop. Yes? Just like rest of us."

War Pig held his hands up solemnly. "I believe it's now officially official. Welcome to the Zomb-A-Pocalypse, dudes."

"There's no such thing as zombies," Mr. Bator said.

"I am glad you think so," Yeltsin said. He grabbed Mr. Bator by the collar, spun him around, and pulled off his jacket.

"Hey," Nero said.

"Hey, what? We are in Nintendo World now, no? The game is on, and this meatsac will not last even two levels. He is the zomb-bait. Therefore, is more necessary I keep warm."

Everyone shrugged at the half wisdom of it.

You gonna be a shepherd? Protect the meek? Inherit the sheep? Well, then, make your play.

"Even so, that's not cool," Nero said.

"There *is* no cool in Zomb-A-Pocalypse, there is only survival, or to be an appetizer."

"I wasn't pulling it, by the way," Mr. Bator said. "In the shower? I was just washing."

"Sure you were," Idle said. "Washed so clean your hand almost got pregnant. I say we cut him loose."

Billy nodded. "Time to lighten the load. Get lean and mean. We need soldiers around here, not whiners."

"We've got zero clue what's actually going on," Nero said, "and you guys are already sacrificing people?"

War Pig looked over his shoulder. "Don't need no more clues. This here is pure End of Days. It's the Zombie Rapture. Except no one's going to heaven."

"They're not zombies," Mr. Bator insisted, rubbing his arms to keep warm. "Bruce Leroy must be sick. You should call them infects, because that's what they are. Infected with something."

Like what, a peanut allergy?

"Like what? The ear clap?"

"Who's to say what there's such a thing as?" War Pig asked.

Kid's practically a freckled Nietzsche.

"Argue this, argue that. Is boring," Yeltsin said. "They ate the skinhead! Remember, my shitdip friends? Were many chunks of Heavy D in supermodel's hairline. Whether is virus or meteor or hell is now standing room only does not make difference. Only that we must keep moving."

"So go, already," War Pig said.

Yeltsin rubbed his chin, rubbed his neck, and ran a finger through his stringy black hair. He crouched, then stood, then crouched again.

"Is hard to say, but truth must be admitted — I do not wish to go alone."

"Tough guy needs a boyfriend," Idle said.

"Hardcase mobster needs someone to hold his hand," Billy said.

"Fine, I go." Yeltsin turned and walked into the pines. No one followed. After twenty yards he turned and came back.

"We need an ambulance," Mr. Bator said. "We should get down to the highway and find a doctor."

War Pig shook his head. "Negatory. Only thing Bruce Leroy's going to do with a doctor is snarf him up like a meatball sub."

"Forget the ambulance," Billy said. "Let's just get to the van. Gun the engine, put Z in the rearview."

"You got the keys?" Estrada said.

"No."

"You gonna go ask Counselor Bruce for them?"

"No."

"Then what good does the van do us?"

"You ever heard of hot-wiring?"

"Yeah, on TV. You know how for real?"

Idle looked at Billy. Billy looked at Idle.

"Not so much."

"Besides, what if the highway's swarming?" War Pig said. "The nearest town might be a kill zone."

"We have to find out," Mr. Bator said. "Don't we?"

"What we have to do is make a decision," Nero said. "We can't head down, since they're right below us. But if we keep heading up, we're screwed."

"What is wrong with up?" Yeltsin asked. "I am casting vote for up."

"There's only so much real estate on a mountain," Estrada said. "If they keep chasing us, what happens when we get to the top?"

"Mexicali got a point," Idle said. "We fresh out of parachutes."

"I saw a path a little way back," Nero said. "It's grown over and will be slow going, but maybe we can use it to cut across."

"Cut across for what?"

"The girls."

"What girls?"

Nero cleared his throat. "The other van? Exene and Velma? We gotta warn them."

"Why?"

"Why?"

"Why?"

"Um, because it's the right thing to do?"

Idle laughed. "The right thing."

Billy laughed. "To do."

"It's also the only move that makes sense," Estrada said.

"No," War Pig said. "There's another move. And it's the only thing zombies understand."

"French grammar?"

"Applied economics?"

War Pig reached over and hefted a thick branch. "Battle."

"Fuck, yes!" Idle said, already convinced.

"The dead don't deserve no slack," Billy agreed.

"All we have to do is follow the rules."

"What rules?" Nero asked.

War Pig rolled his eyes. "You know, how you have to aim for the brain stem. How zombie blood can get on your skin, but not in your mouth or eye. How if you get bit, you got one scene to say good-bye to your girlfriend before you turn feral. Whatever. *The rules.*"

"This isn't a movie," Mr. Bator said.

"Mad practically," Idle said, finding a stick. "They're slow. We're fast. They eat neck steak, and we crack skulls."

"Plus tits," Billy said. "And guns that never run out of ammo."

"Exactly. Why make it complicated?"

There was a noise in the woods behind them. Cracking. Cackling. Movement.

"Shhhh," Nero said.

They all crouched, waiting for the noise to come again.

ZOMBRULE #1: *Always assume there's a zombie or six in the bushes when the orchestra begins to ramp up. Because — and this is vital — you can hear the moaning and you can smell the flesh, but the sound track is like GPS — whether's it's speed metal or Doris Day, theme music is the one sound that will never let you down.*

All along the trail, the trees shook violently.

Yeltsin moaned. "The ziggers are here to floss with our intestine, and instead of run, you just keep talking."

"Not cool," War Pig said.

"Yes, okay," Yeltsin said. "I apologize. The ziggers is racist. You are, of course, down with zombie rights."

The trees shook again, louder, closer.

Idle and Billy got in batting stances. War Pig was a lefty who looked to have power to the gap.

"I am ready to rock, son!"

"Come and get a taste, Z!"

Nero put his hand on War Pig's shoulder. "Hey, man, even if you're right about these rules, the first one has got to be: teenagers alone in the scary woods shouldn't ever split up."

"We're fighting," War Pig said, not looking back. He took a few warm-up cuts as the trees closest to them began to sway. "You fags want to run, run."

Some people have a natural gift for dystopia. Others, not so much.

Nero turned and slipped into the woods at an angle he figured would lead back toward Overlook Pass, the trail the girls had taken.

A few seconds later, Yeltsin followed.

So did Estrada.

So did Mr. Bator.

And then they heard an incredible roar.

Followed by yelling.

And the sound of flesh upon flesh.

Upon flesh.

16

Crave the Protein

THE FOREST SEEMED DARKER AND MORE ominous with each step. Mr. Bator whimpered at every noise, Yeltsin telling him to "sac it up" and be quiet before crying out himself at the next. There seemed to be no motion at all, as if they were in a wooded cathedral — no animals, no wind, nothing.

Majorly creepy, huh?

It was nearly impassable. Scrub grew like rolls of wire; the trees were dense and slick. There were bogs of mud and sludge, boulders and jagged shale.

"This sorta blows," Estrada said.

"Was not my idea," Yeltsin said. "Twice I vote for up. Twice no one listens."

Nero pushed through a culvert of nettles and sharp branches, wondering if they should turn back, when he saw something in the thicket to the left.

Blink.

The wind moaned.

Blink. Blond.

The trees moaned.

Blink. Blond. Bloody teeth.

He doubled the pace through waves of brush, ignoring the pain. No one said a word, the crunch of boots over dead scrub counterpoint to Mr. Bator's chattering teeth.

Nearly an hour later, Nero shouldered through a last line of pines and then stuck his head into empty space. It was like leaning out of a packed subway car. He held the branches aside and peered down the trail. There was no movement, no sound. No moaning.

"Well?" Estrada asked.

"We made enough racket to be heard out by the interstate," Nero said. "If Tripper and Heavy D followed, they might have come this way."

"The skinhead perhaps," Yeltsin said. "But Heaviest D? No. That barge, she is stuck in dry dock."

"What does that mean?"

"You did not see the many kilos supermodel chowed?"

Nero closed his eyes, trying not to.

"In very fine movie *Bite Me Once, Shame on Me III,*

handsome Mr. Brad Pitt is chewed upon in exactly such way. Down to the bone. And does not rise again."

"Scientific," Estrada said, and crawled out onto the trail. Yeltsin followed, then Mr. Bator, pale and shivering, hatched with fresh scratches and welts.

"Peroxide twins are for once correct," Yeltsin said, pointing at Mr. Bator's cuts. "Is like sharks. They smell blood in water. He is walking trail of bread crumbs and leads them right to us."

"Will you shut your hole already?" Estrada said. "God, no wonder we won the Cold War."

Nero took off his jacket and held it out.

Mr. Bator shook his head. "I don't want it."

"Wear it for a while, then give it back."

Might as well put on a clasp, wear that kid like a necklace.

Mr. Bator nodded gratefully as he zipped the jacket up to his chin.

"Okay," Nero said. "Here's the plan —"

"Who puts you in charge?" Yeltsin interrupted.

"You want to be in charge?"

"Yes, of course."

"Fine. What should we do now, boss?"

Yeltsin looked around, yawned, and cracked his knuckles. "I do not know."

"Okay," Nero said. "Here's the plan. At a steady jog, we should reach Overlook Pass in a couple hours. When we get there, we tell their counselors what's up and then head down to the other van."

"They're not going to believe us," Mr. Bator said. "I wouldn't believe us."

"You're right. Maybe we tell them there's been a bad accident and Bruce Leroy is hurt."

"Is weak," Yeltsin said. "Forget counselors. Forget story. Instead, we take three best-looking girls and steal van. We will need to repopulate soon. Also —"

There was a loud noise above. They all looked into the trees as a wet chunk of meat plummeted downward.

And slammed onto Yeltsin's face.

Blood spattered in every direction. Mr. Bator screamed. Yeltsin screamed louder, spinning wildly as he pulled at the cutlet that had suctioned onto him. "Help, friends! Help get the zigger off before is too late."

"Calm down, Aryan Nation," Estrada said. "Hold still!"

Nero reached over and lifted the thing by the tail.

"Oh, my *God*," Yeltsin whined, wiping his face on Mr. Bator's back. "Is chunk of Tripper?"

"It's nothing," Estrada said. "Just a dead squirrel."

Yeltsin broke out in a broad grin. "Squirrel attack? Now, fuck that, please! We are officially very screwed when the squirrels have chosen sides."

Nero flung the thing into the scrub. "Let's go."

What, you're not going to tell them the truth?

What truth?

Details are everything.

Details are nothing.

Coward.

The truth was, okay, the squirrel had a lollipop jammed into its mouth.

A giggle echoed through the trees.

Nero turned and took off running.

After a few hundred yards, Estrada caught up. It had begun to snow, the flakes falling heavily as they jogged side by side.

"You smell something burning?" Estrada asked.

The air did seem heavier, rancid.

"Reminds me of Cherokee Spirits."

"What's that?"

"Hippie cigarettes. The kind the Dude . . . the kind my dad smokes."

"Hippies make cigarettes?"

"All the tar and nicotine of the leading brand, but the cancer's organic."

They leaped over a log in unison. Behind them, Yeltsin didn't make it, eating dirt. Mr. Bator helped him up.

"You know what the craziest thing about this shit is?"

Nero checked off a mental list: Petal. Swann. Flesh eating. Lost in the woods. Flying meat. War Pig left behind with a stick. The whole world crumbling. It was a tough call.

"No, what?"

"In the movies, they keep cutting back to NORAD HQ

or whatever, then show a few seconds of New York, a few of Cleveland, and you get a feel for what's going down out there. The army mobilizing, fighter jets, people on container ships, scientists and microscopes, doctors injecting vaccines. But here? Man, we got zero info. It's like being blind."

More like certifiable.

In the distance, there was a giggle. It was impossible to tell from what direction.

"C'mon," Nero said, speeding up.

"Listen, this deal with the van has to work," Estrada huffed. "I got people back in the city to check on."

"Your girlfriend?"

ZOMBRULE #2: *After a fight, avoid turning away from a fallen zombie to hug your girlfriend with relief. Under no circumstances fail to tag that zombie again, or while you have your PTSD face buried in her shampoo-smelling hair, said zombie will stand up offscreen, give the audience time to scream, and then take a big ol' hunk of rib eye out of your back.*

"Yeah, but she wasn't too pleased about the orange jump-suit routine," Estrada said. "Could be she's hooked up with some other dude already. I know some 'friends' been dying to get their chance. On the other hand, maybe San Francisco's zombie central and she's calling my name, busy fighting them off." He cleared his throat. "Either way, I gotta find out."

Nero pictured Amanda in the kitchen, under the table playing *Tourette's vs. Zombettes* while the Dude held off an army of biters with the remote.

"I know how you feel."

"You got a woman too?"

Tell him about Petal. A friend would definitely tell his friend about Petal.

"Not really."

"Slick cat like you?"

"I'm working on it."

"Uh-huh."

"Anyway, as soon as we find the girls' camp, we're heading back to the city."

"You promise?"

"No matter what."

"Good enough for me, man," Estrada said. He held out knuckles, and Nero bumped them. "You haven't steered me wrong yet."

"To be honest, I wish I wasn't steering at all."

"What do you mean?"

"I'd rather be in the backseat. Safe. With the picnic basket and the map."

"Nah, dog," Estrada said. "You a leader. A total natural. I knew it the second I saw you."

17

It's a Flashback, Jack II: Popcorn with Extra Butter

"AT FIRST THIS SEEMED LIKE A TOTAL NATURAL,"
Ely said with a sigh, sitting in the dark next to Nick. "But I
knew we were doomed the second it started."

They'd ridden their bikes down to the multiplex, Nick on
his old Santa Fe ten-speed and Ely riding one of those tiny
tricked-out BMXs that he was constantly doing wheelies and
fakies and deekies or whatever on. All week they'd been talking about seeing *Killsaw Williams IV: The Saw Bites Back*.
It was sophomore year. Nick and Ely weren't really friends
anymore. At one point they'd been scouts together, failed to
make the eighth-grade basketball team together, hung out in
the woods together, had their first beers together. But something had changed over the summer before high school. Ely
decided to start lifting weights, while Nick decided to start

buying his clothes at the thrift store. Ely liked Modest Mouse; Nick liked old Police.

Growing pains. People change. Every piece of lined silver has a silver lining. Friends don't let friends drive with band kids.

Name your cliché.

Bottom line, they barely spoke for two years.

But the week before, Nick had been at his locker when Ely leaned himself against the wall and said, "Know what happens Thursday?"

"No, what happens Thursday?"

"New movies come out."

"So?"

Ely's smile wavered.

"Know what *particular* new movie is out this *particular* Thursday?"

"No clue."

"The new Killsaw Williams."

Now it was Nick's turn to grin. They'd seen the first Killsaw Williams movie in fourth grade. Reggie "Chains" Watts had been a young actor then, relatively unknown. The movie's tagline was: *The city needs a good man, but sometimes a bad man with a blade will have to do!* The movie changed everything. The way they talked, the books they liked, the games they played at recess.

In sixth grade they cut school and thumbed to the Cineplex for a matinee of *Killsaw Williams II: No Succor for*

Suckas. Then in eighth grade, Ely's older sister took them all the way into the city to see a midnight screening of *Killsaw Williams III: Faster Saw, Cut Cut.* The third one pretty much blew, and Chains Watts had gotten so fat that they'd used a body double for the punching and jumping, but it didn't matter since the entire theater cheered wildly every time a chunky and sweating Watts delivered his signature line, "I'm-a gonna cut your back, Sweetcheeks!"

It was as if Nick, Ely, and Killsaw had grown up together.

And now they were old together.

"So are we going to the movies or not?" Ely asked.

"We are totally going to the movies," Nick said, slamming his locker closed.

By the end of the first reel, it was obvious that *IV* was the worst of the Killsaw series, and probably the last one. There was almost no one else in the theater. Chains Watts's Afro had gone gray, he'd ballooned another forty pounds, and all the jokes sounded like they were written by a malfunctioning hard drive. When the credits came up, Ely was bleary eyed and quiet. Popcorn grease smeared his chin. Nick walked into the lobby, ready to fake some story about having to go pick up Amanda's meds at the twenty-four-hour Walgreens.

"Listen," Ely said, shuffling over. "I'd totally love to hang and catch up, but—"

Ely never got a chance to finish because another movie let out. It was called *The Metermaid.* The tagline was *Sometimes even love needs change for a dollar!* The usher opened the door, and a line of red-faced women streamed through.

One of whom was Nick's mother.

Which was weird.

But not as weird as the fact that she was holding hands with some guy who looked like he sold exercise equipment door-to-door.

"Whoa," Ely said.

Nick's mother blanched, trying hard for casual.

"Hi, Ely! Haven't seen you in a while!"

Nick winced. He could practically smell the exclamation points.

"You guys just catch that Killspout movie?" The guy asked, flashing the world's third-fakest smile. "Heard it was way cool."

"Oh, it was," Ely said. "*Way* cool." He patted Nick's back. "Catch you later, man."

"Where's Ely going?" Nick's mom asked, obviously relieved.

"Home. Where his father is," Nick said, and then almost felt bad, watching his mother's face crumble. She was wearing a new dress, blue with little orange shells on it, showing some leg. She was also wearing makeup, something she rarely did at home. In a way it was like seeing her for the first time. Was his mom weird? Desirable? Awful? Or maybe worst of all, just another person who had zero clue what they were doing?

"This is Mr. Gunn. Tedd Gunn Jr. A friend of mine from work."

Tedd Gunn Jr. stuck out his big treadmill-selling paw. Nick stared, trying to summon the balls to not shake it.

Don't shake.

Don't do it.

Do. Not. Shake.

Nick raised his hand and gripped Tedd Gunn's palm, which, of course, was big and rough and warm.

"See you tomorrow, Tedd. Okay? At work?"

"Yeah, okay. Sure. Tomorrow."

Tedd Gunn peeled away in a red sports car as Nick loaded his ten-speed into his mother's wagon. They drove back across town, the radio on low.

"Listen, I just want to —"

"Can we not? I mean, really?"

His mother nodded, gripping the wheel.

"But I want you to understand —"

Nick cleared his throat and began speaking in a cheesy announcer's voice: "Sometimes, even though they love you very much, mommies and daddies come to realize they've developed different . . . priorities."

Nick knew he was being a dick but couldn't stop himself.

"But don't worry — insert child's name — it's not your fault. It's just that —"

Nick's mother slammed on the brakes, almost back-ending a Volkswagen. Nick rubbed his forehead where it'd hit the dash and stared out the window as they accelerated again, watching the cement and broken bottles and orange pylons sweep by.

When they got home, the Dude was convincing the vacuum of something. Amanda stared at her Palmbot, pressing buttons in a frenetic pattern.

"How was it? Nick? The movie? The Saw?"

He crawled under the table with his sister and hooked up a second controller. Upstairs, a door slammed. Nick logged in and was immediately taking musket volleys from a platoon of mutant Quakers. He set up a firing line and then lobbed some grenades.

"You wouldn't believe me if I told you."

"I would? Nick? Believe you?"

Nick led a suicidal bayonet charge, running downhill into the face of heavy fire.

"A-dog, it was totally and completely awesome."

18

Lysol and Quicklime

A HUNDRED YARDS PAST THE POINT WHERE
the two trails intersected was a large clearing with neat fire
pits and gravel walkways and porta potties.

"They have private shitters? Is no way! How come we do
not get the private shitters?"

"Will you *please* be quiet?" Estrada said. "Please?"

Nero motioned them forward, then crept into the clearing and crouched behind a tree. It was silent, still. Pink tents
sat pitched in a row. A fire smoldered. Food hung in a bear
sling from an overhanging branch. A little brook babbled
innocently beneath fringes of ice.

"It's too quiet," Nero said, trying to hide his disappoint-
ment behind chattering teeth. "They must have set out
already."

"But all their stuff's here. Why would they just leave it?"

"Maybe they went for a day hike," Mr. Bator said.

"Perhaps they are in woods together," Yeltsin said. "Getting all lesbo."

Nero and Estrada looked at each other, shrugged, and then walked over.

Those tents sure seem empty. That's the thing about tents, though. You never know what might be hunkered down in there, knitting tendon doilies and sharpening its teeth.

"Don't open it," Mr. Bator whispered. "Please?"

Nero lifted a rock from the fire pit. "One . . . two . . ."

Yeltsin pulled back the first zipper with a rip.

Empty.

Estrada opened the next.

Nothing. Gear. Utensils. Pillows.

They went down the line, all the same.

"Maybe they have a radio," Mr. Bator said.

"Yes, dicknose," Yeltsin said. "Probably a CB, for the calling of truckers late at night. Start a convoy. Hello there, one-niner, keep peeled eye for shamblers in fast lane!"

Nero wrapped a sleeping bag around his shoulders while Yeltsin and Estrada checked out the bear sling. There was good-looking stuff. Crackers. Peanut butter. Hot dogs. They found sticks and began hitting the sling like a piñata.

"Just untie the knot," Nero said.

"My hands are too cold," Estrada answered.

"I am very starving," Yeltsin said. "At this point, as long as there is spicy mustard to accompany, I will eat a dick."

A granola bar fell between the mesh and hit the ground. Yeltsin scooped it up and crammed the entire thing in his mouth.

The rest of them stared.

"Even for you," Mr. Bator said.

"Mmmf . . . yes? what?"

"Nothing."

Yeltsin reached into his mouth and pulled out a chunk with squirrel-blood fingers. "Yuth guyth want thome?"

Estrada began poking the bag again.

Nero found a small daypack filled with socks, a highway map, underwear, Tampax, a lipstick, a wallet. Inside was a driver's license: Exene Doe, age twenty-six, weight 145, eyes blue, hair black, organ donor.

She may end up donating more than just organs.

In the front flap was a ring with two keys. One said APT 3C. The other had FORD TOUGH stamped on the back.

Nero slid the key into his pocket. They'd want to head down immediately once they knew — take the van, refuse to wait.

He had to find Petal first.

Then they could all go together.

Being the big cheese means making tough decisions. Unpopular ones. Deceptive ones. To follow, in the end, is to be lied to. Complicity.

Mr. Bator swayed nervously from foot to foot. "Can we go now. Please?"

"No. We do not leave without this food," Yeltsin said, taking angrier swings.

Nero ducked into the final tent. There was a shirt, a magazine, some loose change. A backpack with cooking gear and underwear. In the side pocket was a tiny notepad. On the front it said GAZES.

A gentleman never, ever reads someone else's diary.

Nero opened it to the middle. Stuck between two pages was a picture, which fell to the ground.

Facedown.

He picked it up and slowly turned it over.

It was cut out of his high-school yearbook.

Nick Sole, Junior. Clubs: none. Activities: none. Academic honors: none. Sports: former varsity track, quit.

Petal had a picture of him.

Carried it around with her.

"What is it?" Mr. Bator asked.

"Nothing."

In the corner of the tent was a balled-up pink puffer jacket with a fur-lined hood. Nero shoved the notepad and picture into the pocket and pulled the jacket on. It was way too small.

"Oh, man, I forgot," Mr. Bator said. "Do you want yours back now? We can totally switch."

"No, it's okay."

"You sure?"

Nero closed his eyes. He was wearing Petal's jacket. His arms stuck out four inches from the sleeves, and it barely covered below his belly button, but when he pressed the nylon to his face and inhaled deeply, he could smell her.

Vanilla sherbet.

"I'm sure."

Also, he didn't want Mr. Bator to see.

See what?

What he'd felt when he'd put his hand in the jacket's inside pocket.

Gold bullion?

Thermite grenades?

A pound of uncut Turkish hashish?

A cell phone.

"Why don't you go do a check of the perimeter?"

Mr. Bator nodded and wandered off.

Nero slid all the way back into the tent, cupped the phone in a sweater, and hurriedly dialed.

It rang six times.

Nine times.

Thirteen times.

Twenty-two times.

And then someone picked up.

"Hello?"

"Amanda!"

"Nick? Is that? You?"

Thank God, thank God, thank God, thank God.

"Yeah, it's me. Listen —"

"Miss you? Nick? Are you? Coming? Home?"

"No, Boo. I'm really far away. Are you okay?"

"Yes? Of course? Why?"

"Is there . . . anything happening outside?"

"Dunno? Can't go? Outside?"

"Why not?"

"Dad says? Not to?"

"Listen to me. Carefully. You need to get in the car, okay? You need to get the Dude and drive to —"

"Can't? Dad says? The highways are? Closed?"

"Why? Amanda, tell me why!"

"Dunno? Nick, I —"

The phone beeped three times. The screen flashed BAT-TERIES LOW, BATTERIES LOWER, BATTERIES CRITICAL, and then died.

Nero resisted the urge to crush it into a ball with his bare hands, then sat up quickly, almost catching a nose in the eye.

Because Mr. Bator was in the tent with him, watching.

Nailed.

"Perimeter's fine."

Nero got on one knee, ready to defend himself. Or abjectly apologize.

Mr. Bator looked back at Estrada and Yeltsin. "Don't worry — I won't tell. I would have done the same thing. Those two would have just fought over it, anyway."

"Maybe. But it was still selfish."

"Yeah, but at least the selfish part bothers you."

Nero nodded. "Thanks."

Outside the tent, the clearing was quiet, peaceful.

ZOMBRULE #3: *When it's quiet and peaceful, it means only one thing: the shark is going to surface and take off the marine biologist's leg, or the capo is going to fork up his last carbonara before getting whacked, or the school bus full of kids is about to head-on a cement mixer, or the hottie with the heartburn is going to pull her hands away as an alien bursts between her double-Ds. Zomblogic dictates a similar outcome. In other words, run!*

"We need to go. Now."

"I definitely have to go," Mr. Bator said, walking toward the porta potty.

No, don't.

"No. Don't."

"Pinch the head of turtle off," Yeltsin said.

Mr. Bator opened the door. Two children in snowsuits sat on the porta potty's bench. A boy and a girl. Probably around six and eight. They were perched on Exene's lap, arms around her neck as if they were posing for a vacation photo.

Except it must have been a crappy vacation, because Exene was dead.

And half-eaten.

Maybe a little more than half.

The girl's face was gray. She had pigtails and wore a pink Annoya the Explorer scarf. The boy wore a blue hat with a pom-pom. Both of their faces were glistening, eyes pinned, demented.

And both of them were smiling.

Before Nero could say anything, the little boy reached out, grabbed Mr. Bator by the neck, and sank his tiny Chiclet teeth deep. Blood pulsed in slow motion, in delicate twin geysers, spraying the picnic area.

Nero grabbed Mr. Bator's free arm, but the girl was stronger. She opened her mouth like Jaws rising under an unsuspecting surfer and clomped down on Mr. Bator's nose. There was a rending noise, the sound of a phone book being torn in half. The girl jerked back.

Nero lost his grip.

The boy pulled Mr. Bator the rest of the way in.

And then the door slammed shut behind him.

19

Rend It Like Beckham

A SERIES OF MOANS ECHOED THROUGH THE woods, sharper than the noises the children were making, which were giddy, brutal, joyous. Mr. Bator's screams ebbed and flowed.

"Sorry, but I'm not opening that door," Estrada said, helping Nero up. "Little dude is done."

"When the porta potty is rockin', is unwise to come a-knockin'," Yeltsin agreed, giving up on the bear sling as the trees at the edge of the clearing began to shake. "And when the forest is a-rockin', is wise to run."

They turned toward the path just as a woman in hiking gear emerged from the scrub, blocking it.

Hooray! Mommy's home!

She must have been pretty once — expensive haircut, subtle makeup, wearing a tight snowsuit.

In one hand she held a water bottle.

In the other she held a foot.

With painted toenails.

Around the ankle were the remains of a pink jumpsuit.

"She got one of the girls."

"Or perhaps all of them."

Mommy let out a hungry gargle and then rushed forward, her nylon pants going *chuff chuff chuff*. Yeltsin squealed, stepped on a log, and fell flat on his back. She grabbed his leg, twenty grand worth of perfect orthodontia snapping open and shut.

"Please, help to get this crazy cougar off of me!"

Nero grabbed a rock and threw it, missing badly. Estrada picked up a rock and grooved a fastball, hitting her flush in the chest. She ignored them both, ready to sink incisor into thigh, when a yell came from below. War Pig tore up the rise, coiled his neck, and leaped. It was like footage from the 1956 World Cup, Pelé in front of the net and ready to redirect a perfect corner. War Pig's cranial bone slammed into the bridge of Mommy's nose, her entire face collapsing inward.

Chick is now officially convex.

War Pig one, Mommy nil.

"Brilliant!" Yeltsin said, getting up. "Is practically move by very fine actor Chuck Norris."

Idle huffed over, picked up a large flat rock, and dropped

it on Mommy's head. It made a sickening pumpkiny sound. Billy stood on top and did a little dance step. First tap, then samba, rounding it off with a little of the old soft shoe.

"What?" he said as they all stared. "Just making sure homegirl don't rise again."

"It's smart policy, yo," Idle said.

ZOMBRULE #4: *Survival is for the ruthless. Everyone else is a hippie poet.*

Billy dipped his finger into the blood pooling behind Mommy's ear and drew an anarchy symbol on his forehead. "Now Z know who they dealing with."

"You sure that's a good idea?" Nero asked.

"Like, anarchy as a concept, or the blood?" War Pig asked.

An HGH existentialist!

"We have thought you guys were doomed," Yeltsin said.

"Or heading back down to the vans."

Idle and Billy shook their heads.

"Not much chance of that, chief."

"Why not?"

"Hate to say it, but we got us a fan base. There a whole bunch of groupies shambling right behind us."

"It's not just counselors down there," War Pig said. "It's hikers, fat chicks in sweat suits, people from the highway. Counter girls, schoolkids, dudes in three-piece pinstripes. After you guys ran off, they rushed us in a pack."

"They came in mad waves," Idle said, covering his mouth and doing a passable beat box. "Not outta Compton, outta the caves."

Billy joined in, spitting flow.

"But check it — it was epic. We dropped a dozen, at least. I was a raging, caging, Z-killing beast."

Idle slapped War Pig on the back.

"And yo! Big boy here? Man got hella skillz with a blunt-force object."

"Dude a Zach thresher," Billy agreed.

War Pig shrugged, embarrassed. Dots of blood on his cheeks mixed with freckles, forming constellations. The Big Dipper. Ursa Minor. Romero. Merging and separating. It was hypnotic.

Romero is not a constellation.

Billy held up the stump of a heavy branch covered in a thin wash of brain. "Seriously, though, yo? I cracked so many skulls, my Q-tip broke."

Idle laughed as two girls in pink jumpsuits came out of the grass at the edge of the clearing.

"Righteous. Some of the ladies made it."

"Hey! Over here!" Estrada said, waving his arms. "Hurry!"

The girls continued forward.

With mechanical, quivering steps.

One of them moaned.

The other gurgled.

"Dang."

"Never mind."

"I am sorry, but I do not wish your phone number after all," Yeltsin said.

It could be her, it could be her, it could be her.

Nero bit his lip and ran halfway down the rise to read their name tags. One said BOBLEGUM. The other said KIM FOWLEY. They were covered in blood and mud and geometric bite marks, evidence of resistance. And failure.

"Okay, can we please now, for sake of fuck, run?" Yeltsin asked.

Nero was about to answer when there was a loud metallic creak.

Ding-dong. Company's here!

The porta potty door slowly opened.

And Mr. Bator staggered out.

"Whoa. The Showerbator forgot his nose," Idle said.

Mr. Bator had a deep hole in the center of his face. Wet ropes of blood and mucus slathered the exposed row of top teeth — his skin ripped free and hanging like a fairway divot.

"Kid gotta new Trek Handle. Check it: Bull's-eye."

"Who needs Botox? Shit's a mad improvement."

Mr. Bator spread his arms, opened his mouth, and roared through strands of flesh. The voice that came out was surprisingly deep and raw. Furious. An echo resounded through the treetops.

"That supposed to scare me?" Idle said.

"I don't even need a stick," Billy said, taking a step forward. "I kill this homo with just my thumb."

Boblegum and Kim Fowley roared back. A second later, there were dozens more roars, coming from deep in the woods.

Yeah, well, that's not so good. Anyone got a machine gun?

"What are they all doing up here?" Estrada asked.

"It's true," War Pig said. "They should be down in the valley, like at Kinko's, chomping assistant managers and shit. Easy pickings. This is way too much work."

A long line of Infects emerged from the bush. First a shambling road crew in bright orange hard hats, chunks of skin torn from their muscular arms. Then a high-school football team still wearing uniforms, a coach with a whistle around his neck leading them along. Behind them were parents, college dorks, people without elbows, with sausage-link viscera, half a troupe of cheerleaders whose teeth were as red as their poms.

"Well, I think it's time to go," War Pig said as a hunter wearing full camo emerged from the woods to their left. His stomach protruded from beneath a red safety vest. He was holding a cooler in one hand and a compound bow in the other.

That could come in handy.

Nero picked up a rock and clocked the hunter in the temple.

Wait, that was sarcasm. I meant run!

The cooler fell, Fresh Bukket wrappers and cans of beer

spilling across the mud. Nero scooped up beers and lofted them toward the others, then pried the bow out of the hunter's hand. As he was trying to free the quiver, a pom-pom girl jumped on his back. Estrada grabbed her by the bra strap and flung her to the ground. A yellowed retainer tumbled from her mouth and got caught in the fibers of her Shasta High varsity sweater.

Rah rah! Yay undead! Go undead! Touchdown!

Nero notched an arrow, steadied himself, pulled back the string, and fired.

Totally missing.

He notched another and fired again.

Missed again.

He fired.

And missed.

Fired.

And missed.

The next one flew true but too high and dug deep into the shoulder of one of the football players.

War Pig, Idle, and Billy clapped mockingly, offered *oles* and *bravos,* then raised their beers in tribute. Nero picked a beer up and cracked it as he ran back over, the horde closing in around them.

"Beer's okay," Billy said. "But it's too bad zombie hunters don't smoke the schwag."

Idle belched. "I'm telling you, this undead shit is way easier if you don't take it too serious."

War Pig killed his beer and crushed the can against his forehead.

Everyone laughed, too hard, almost giddily.

Beneath the laughter was a slick of unease.

Idle's eye twitched.

War Pig looked exhausted, haggard.

Yeltsin, caked in blood, tried to smile, managed a sick grimace.

We got a morale problem here.

They all waited, looking at Nero.

No one was looking at Nick.

"Which way?" Estrada asked.

Don't go down. Go up.

Amanda was down. Amanda needed his help.

The line of Infects cleared the rise, a silhouette of teeth and hands, fingers twitching, ready to sink into fleshy crevices and extract pearls.

"Um, Nero?" Estrada said.

The van was down. Zombies were down. Hell was straight down.

Go up.

They came on, inexorable, like the tide, like a spray of foam edging closer to their toes.

Petal. Amanda. Amanda. Petal.

He had a key. He should use the key.

If they bushwhacked for the van, they just might make it.

But probably not.

Up.

"Dude, make the call," War Pig whispered.

A tall, pale farmer in a leather butcher's apron and overalls shambled out of the brush.

Are you serious? A pig farmer?

Holding a scythe.

Are you serious? They still make scythes?

The blade was rimed with rust. The farmer's mouth, a rude line of snaggly teeth, was rimed with gore.

Now.

Nero was thinking of the foot Mommy had held, the pink toenails.

Did Petal paint her toenails pink?

Did Petal paint her toenails at all?

Now!

Nero finished his beer, belched, turned, and began running.

Upward.

There was never really any choice at all.

The rest of the boys followed.

One by one, without a word.

20

Marlin Perkins Lives

THE TREE COVER INCREASED AS THEY CLIMBED, moving into an area of older growth. The sun was just barely able to poke through, outlining the path in ethereal silver. The group moved as fast as they could, breathing hard, hoping but not entirely certain they were putting distance between themselves and the horde, which could be heard thrashing around farther down the trail.

And why *was* the horde thrashing? Why was there a horde at all? They acted like movie zombies, slow and mindlessly shuffling—except the ones who didn't. Like Mommy seeming to care about her kids. Or the football team all sticking together. Or Mr. Bator almost seeming to laugh.

It all comes back to the elemental question. The ontology of zombiedom. The first great and most enduring mystery: why are they all so goddamned hungry?

At times the path would disappear in the snow and mud, with no clear direction, forcing Nero to reach into black space and feel his way along, like sticking his hand into a dark hole and waiting to be bitten by something rabid.

Or worse.

Watch out for that loose rock.

He stepped over it, palm itching madly. War Pig and Yeltsin were right behind him. Estrada was a few feet back, with Idle and Billy taking up the rear.

"Idle takes it up the rear," Billy said.

"Billy sniffs my rim," Idle replied.

Nero stopped in front of a familiar stand of pines.

Too familiar.

Shit.

"Which way, chief?" War Pig asked.

There were no footprints in the snow, none in the mud. If any of the girls had made it out of the campsite, they hadn't come this way.

"Made it out" is relative. Question is, made it out as what?

The moaning got louder.

Nero slid down a muddy incline. Trail was no longer an accurate term. It was now just the slightest cleft between vegetation, like a rotting green thong pulled tight between the ass cheeks of being lost.

"Nice jacket, by the way," Idle said, tugging at Nero's fur hood.

Billy pointed at the pink zipper and laughed. "Make it work, baby."

Nero had forgotten about the jacket. Cared what it looked like even less. All that mattered was what it smelled like.

At the end of a long incline, there was a fork.

His gut said right. Right felt right.

Go left.

"You sure?" War Pig asked, breathing heavily.

Left again.

"Man, I didn't even see that turn," Billy said, almost sliding off the edge. "You got mad eyes."

They went another two hundred yards, and then Nero stopped. There was an enormous boulder in the way.

"Great."

"Is completely perfect."

"Way to go, Magellan."

There was a sheer drop-off to the north. They could try to climb over the smooth frozen rock or descend for a hundred yards to the south, back toward the Infects, and work around it.

"I say we climb, yo."

"Most definitely."

Work around it.

Nero turned and started down. The van key jabbed him in the thigh.

"Screw that, son."

"They bite in that direction, remember?"

Nero ignored the twins and kept going.

"Kid got a death wish."

"Hella suicidal."

War Pig turned and followed Nero. So did Estrada.

Idle and Billy pouted for a minute and then did as well.

"Hello! Please to wait up!" Yeltsin said.

They took the long sloping curve in a jog, through heavy underbrush, making too much noise.

"Bet every biter for miles can hear us coming."

"Convert that shit to kilometers. Then they're farther away."

The smell of Infects got heavier, a settling mist. Dead rot. Like steaks left on a hot dashboard.

"When is this freaking rock going to end?" Billy whined. "I mean, who makes a rock this big?"

Nero kept going, keeping his left hand against the jagged outcropping. A low, insistent buzz rose, getting steadily louder, like an army of weed whackers advancing in formation.

"They know we're here," War Pig said. "Like, right *here*."

"Maybe we should turn back, huh, Nero?" Estrada said. "Shit, man. I think —"

The children from the porta potty stepped out from between two pines just below the path. They were wet with blood, holding hands, their naked arms gray in the moonlight.

Shamblers hold hands?

The little girl bared her teeth.

The little boy bared his teeth.

ZOMBRULE #5: *The only routine worse than kid zombies is knocked-up zombies. Got a pregnant girlfriend? Guaranteed she's a scene away from being chomped. And then the midwife is all "Push, push" and the boyfriend is all "Don't push, don't push," and suddenly you've got a yowler that wants to bite its own umbilical cord. Forget the rhythm method. Zombception? Zombzygote? Zombbirth? Abstinence is rule one in Plagueville.*

The boulder jutted down another few feet, impossible to see beyond.

"Why don't they rush us?" Estrada whispered.

"Little freaks must be full. That Mr. Bator nose was like an eight-course meal."

"Don't mean they won't bite just for fun."

Rocks began to slide down the trail behind them.

Keep going.

Nero took three quick steps.

The children watched, on their toes, breathing heavily, but didn't move. If they came now, he would have nowhere to go.

One more step.

The boy licked blood off his sister's cheek.

One more step.

The girl shuddered. Then purred.

One more —

Nero almost fell as his hand slipped into a gap in the rock, a shaft cut like a long hallway. It was wet and dank, narrow but large enough for his body. Between two jagged risers led a natural path, extending forty feet. It wound through the rock and back up the hill.

Impossible to find unless you knew it was there.

Exactly. So how about a little love for Uncle Rock?

Nero turned to go back and tell the others.

When something grabbed his wrist.

Hard.

And nearly pulled him off his feet.

He tried to pry the hand away, but it was too strong.

There was no room to move, nowhere to run.

Don't move. Don't run.

The pressure on his wrist increased as he was slowly dragged against a small crevasse, up to the armpit. It wrenched the joint, but he resisted the urge to cry out.

Don't cry out.

Nero set his feet so that he couldn't be pulled any farther and grabbed a heavy rock, but there wasn't enough room to swing it. He had no leverage. And his other arm was going numb.

Disembodied.

He felt pressure points moving down his elbow, incisor points along his wrist.

Then a warmth.

A wetness.

He tensed, waiting for the first bite.

But whatever held him was not biting.

It was licking his palm.

A tongue, soft and pointed, ran along his stitches.

Lapping at the blood.

Moving very slowly along the long vertical cut.

In and out of the tear, along the edges, down the sides.

Softly, clockwise.

Gently, counterclockwise.

It felt good.

Too good.

How can anything feel too good?

Nero arched his back and closed his eyes, could feel himself giving in to it. Wanting to give in to it.

The tongue went deeper.

His entire body pulsed.

He dropped the rock he'd been holding, and it landed on his foot.

Startling him.

Just enough.

To feel the teeth again.

Nibbling along the lips of the gash.

21

Splitting the Uprights

NERO BRACED HIS LEG AGAINST THE ROCK and jerked backward.

There was a giggle.

He pulled again, harder. The momentum threw him back against the shaft's interior face. As he grappled for purchase, something ran past. Something cold.

He knew who it was.

Knew in his (uneaten) bones.

A silhouette suddenly filled the rock opening.

"Swann!"

The silhouette leaped and then disappeared. Nero scrambled the rest of the way down and stuck his head out. War Pig was holding off the children with a pointy stick, jabbing them into the dirt every time they got up and came at him again.

"Did you see that?"

"See what?"

"Never mind. Come on!"

War Pig tossed the stick like a javelin. It nailed the girl in the center of her forehead. They all ran into the gap, Billy the last one through. The little boy reached out and just managed to grab his leg. Billy wailed, trying to shake him off, but the boy hung tight, jaw distended and glistening.

"Yo, can a pimp get some help?"

Idle turned and swung his boot. It was a solid shot, all arch and tip, launching the boy like a football. His little body spiraled end over end, flew back off the ledge, cleared a horizontal branch, and then crashed into the woods far below.

Idle pulled Billy to his feet just as the horde entered the gap.

"Move ass!" War Pig yelled.

They scrambled over the loose shale, pure thrash-metal adrenaline coursing through jangled synapses as they rushed between tall faces of black rock, barely able to see. Hands gripped things that were soft and wet. That grew in the dark. Mold and rot. Guano. The air was thick and fetid, moans and echoes of moans booming over their heads.

Nero finally clambered up the last rise, where the cave mouth yawed and the trail resumed below a small rock ledge.

Just to his left was a perfect circle of fresh snow.

And in the center of that circle was a single footprint.

Could be anyone's. Could be anything. Could be a peg leg who digs spelunking.

It may not have been Petal's, but it wasn't a man's.

Which meant at least one of the girls must have made it this far.

Nero smoothed the print with one hand, a bubble of hope rising in his bones.

"Man, it feels good to be back," War Pig said, holding on to Nero's shoulder. "Above the teeth line."

"It's official. No way I'm ever having kids," Estrada said, sliding onto the ledge.

"Little doinker wanted to drink my milk shake," Billy said.

"Extra-point conversion," Idle said, raising both arms for a field goal. "Knew I should have tried out for the fagball team."

The moaning from below echoed louder, rhythmic, a group exclamation of want, a berserk mazurka funneled between the rocks.

Nero looked down at his palm and shuddered. The wound was fresh and pink and wet, licked clean of dried blood. The stitches were straightened, scabs torn away to the raw skin beneath.

In some circles they call that foreplay.

War Pig tested a boulder, gauging if it could be pushed back into the gap. "We got them hemmed like nine pins. All we got to do is roll a strike."

"That is such genius," Estrada said.

They all worked together, straining, like grunts on Iwo Jima, trying different handholds. The larger rocks had no give at all. They sent down a few smaller ones, which tumbled into the darkness and maybe broke a few toes or shattered the occasional femur.

"With the dynamite, we could wait until last second, take out entire platoon," Yeltsin said.

"You got a few spare sticks on you, Kasparov?" Idle asked.

"No."

"You got any blasting caps?"

"No."

"You got a match?"

"No."

"Right. Other than that? Great idea."

"Enough," War Pig said as the sound of footfalls, mindless and leathery, edged up behind them. "Let's go."

Wait.

Nero crouched and motioned for quiet.

Along the trail, trees began to shake.

"No way."

"So unfair."

"But how did they get ahead of us?"

Pines shook and swayed. There was a low rumbling, like a crowd of angry voices.

"We're screwed."

"Total hors d'oeuvres."

"Oh, well," Estrada said, looking back into the dark chasm. The first empurpled hands, outstretched, were now visible — eyes and teeth reflecting menace in the low light. "Time to die."

The trees parted violently.

And then a horde emerged from the woods.

But it wasn't Infects.

It was animals.

Running in a pack. Deer and raccoon and squirrels. Mice and rats and opossums. A twelve-point buck. A moose. Foxes and ferrets and voles. Skunks and chipmunks and an ocelot. A bear. No, two bears. Breathing hard. More animals came. Dozens. Hundreds. Marmots and skinks and rabbits. Dogs. A ram. Bobcats and weasels and beavers. Woodchucks. Boars. Rats. They tore by in a furry stream, not making a sound, just the padding of their paws and hooves and claws and ragged exhalations.

All of them with flat terror in their eyes.

"Holy Christ, that's weird," War Pig whispered.

"Shamblers eat moose?" Yeltsin asked.

"Maybe they're just freaked out," Idle said.

"It must be the smell," Estrada said. "Rotting lip. Dead sweat. Blue skin. The animals don't get it."

ZOMBRULE #6: *Shamblers do not eat moose. But, my friend, when the day comes that animals run together in terror, having flicked the switch from*

predator to prey and been reduced to abject com-
munal fear, you bipeds should probably take it as a
bad omen. If only because it means Usain Bolt with
a taste for face is closing in on the outside lane.

The last of the animals streamed by — the bedraggled, the slow and the old, the fat and the skinny, the outcasts, the four-legged versions of Mr. Bator and Heavy D. Finally, an ancient raccoon hobbled from the scrub, the very last one. It stopped, looked at the boys, and sighed as if about to offer a pearl of wisdom.

They waited for it, even as Infect hands reached up, just feet away.

The raccoon opened its mouth, pulled back its lips.

And then lay on its side and died.

Pretty good advice, actually.

"What, of old age?" Estrada said. "Now? Are you shitting me?"

Okay, go.

Nero leaped down from the rock and headed up again, the others practically clinging to his back. The path was colder, darker, steeper than before. He shivered, suddenly desperate to be home. Warm and full. In bed. Half studying an algebra text while the comfortable background sonata of Amandaranto hummed beneath him, the reassuring patter of sound effects and three-button combinations. Graphics violence instead of graphic violence. The option to PAUSE.

The luxury of START OVER. Replay the level. Snap off the OFF and make the screen waver; turn the entire horizon into a calming and nonfatal blue.

From within the cave came a high-pitched caw, almost like a bird's.

A large and taloned and angry beast.

They stopped at the next rise and watched as the horde emerged from the cave mouth, like dirty sausage shoved through a dirtier grinder.

Falling onto one another in stacks.

Tangled into a dim, groaning pile.

Getting up. Sniffing the air.

Lurching forward again.

A woman's high moaning could be heard above it all.

"Sounds like *chula* blondie's getting close," Estrada said.

Close? Chick was already as close as it gets without taking your virginity. Or, wait, does that hand job count?

"You really think that's Supermodel?" Idle asked.

Nero pulled down the sleeves of Petal's coat. The seam of one armpit split. He wanted to take the whole thing off and hold it up to his face, breathe her scent in. But he knew it wouldn't smell the same.

The Petal smell would be there, but faint.

Now it was mixed.

With someone else's smell.

Someone who'd held him in the cave.

Tightly.

"I don't care how hot she is, I don't ever wanna see that spinderella again," Billy said.

"Me neither," Nero said, then turned and made like an animal.

Taking off in a flat-out, tail-up, snout-first run.

22

It's a Flashback, Jack III: How I Met Your Monster

MOM WAITED UNTIL THE DUDE HAD LUBED UP and hit the lawn chair in the driveway, then changed back into her sweatpants. She got Nick and Amanda to eat breakfast and brush their teeth, then told them to strap in.

"Mom? No school?" Amanda asked, pushing her glasses up her nose.

"No school today, Amand-O," Mom said, backing the car out too fast.

"Why, Mom? Mom? Huh? Why?"

"We're taking the day off, honey. Just me and my guys."

"Where are we going?" Nick asked.

"The mall."

"Hate the mall? Mom? Hate it?"

"I know, honey, but I need a new dress. And I thought we could go to the game store before we get burgers."

Amanda nodded. *Game store* was the magic password. Mom drove faster than usual, whistling along to the new tune by Tawnii Täme that even people who liked Tawnii Täme hated.

They parked out front, early, the usual bench sitters and speed walkers and bargain rackers clogging the revolving door. At the top of the escalator, Amanda walked into a marble column. And then fell down, rubbing her head.

"Ouch? Nick? Ouch?"

A pack of high-school kids pointed and laughed. The guys wore rap-metal shirts and enormous black boots, the girls' mouths wrapped around smoothie straws. Nick thought about flipping them off, then didn't. For one thing, the guys were bigger than him, with longer hair and dirtier jeans and deceptive punch-you smiles. For another, they listened to rap metal, which was punishment enough.

At the game store, Amanda hit the shelves with purpose. There was no browsing or reading. No comparing or contrasting. She believed in a policy of random volume, within minutes returning with a huge stack of Palmbot titles. Mom picked five and then slid her Visa to the clerk. He had stringy hair and wore a *Pulseman X* hat that was shaped like a clenched fist.

"Pulseman?" Amanda said. "Ten?"

"Heck, yeah," the clerk said.

"Thought it was? Still? Pulseman seven?"

"Heck, no. Where you been? That was last year."

In the corner was a Zombie Corner. It had displaced the vampire displays, which were shoved aside and unperused. There were zombie FPSs, zombie MMOGs, zombie dictionaries, zombie oral histories, zombie shirts, zombie masks, zombie music, zombie Muzak, zombie suntan lotion, zombie noodle soup, and the best-selling and dead-serious *Zombie-Facts Q&A* with renowned necrologist Dr. Henry E. Kyburg.

Mom's Visa was turned down.

Twice.

The people in line behind them began to get impatient.

"Um, don't take this the wrong way," the clerk said, his voice cracking, "but where do you stand on the subject of cash?"

"Seriously?" a woman in line said.

"Maybe you should try Tedd Gunn's card," Nick suggested.

Mom blew a wisp of hair off her forehead.

"Run it one more time. There must be something wrong with your machine."

"Umm? Mom? Umm?"

Amanda was shifting her weight from foot to foot. She hated confrontations. And lines. And stores. And fluorescent lights.

"Any day," someone else said while the clerk fed new paper into the register. A bead of sweat ran from under the bill of his hat. He looked back at a door that said MANAGER on it. The door remained closed. The register tape wouldn't fit into the slot. The Visa was rejected a third time.

"Sorry," the clerk said.

"Need to pee, Nick? Bad?"

"Can you take her to the boys', honey?" Mom asked, the *honey* dripping with arsenic. Nick thought about having to walk past the Headbangers' Ball and their girlfriends again.

"You're kidding me."

Mom tried to smile while upending her purse onto the counter. Tissues, pens, buttons, a small bottle of mouthwash, a checkbook with no checks, a lipstick, matches, an empty box of cigarettes, a Kotex. She slid coins into dollar groupings and lined them up next to a worn stack of bills. The cashier licked his thumb, lost count, started over again.

"Oh, for God's sake."

A tall man tossed his forty-piece *Totally Official S.W.A.R.M. "First Response" Kill-Copter* gas-powered, unidirectional U-Build-It Model Set with twelve-hertz remote, special One-Thumb Aeron Flex Control, and twin .50-caliber "So Undead" machine-gun mounts (with Guaranteed 12x Lurker Stopping Power) onto the counter. It landed with a bang. Some of Mom's dollar bills wafted onto the floor. The man stormed out. A woman followed, pulling her crying child behind her.

"Pee, Nick? Pee? Now?"

Nick took Amanda by the hand and led her the long way around the food court.

Pussy One at your service.

Fortunately, the bathroom was empty. Amanda chose a stall and then turned, dead serious, starting to raise her dress. "I stand and you aim? Huh? Nick?"

"Did you just make a joke there, A-dog?"

Amanda closed the door. After she came back out, Nick washed both their hands at the same time, sudsing up a tall pile of bubbles and then blowing on them as they scattered and clung. A man walked in and gave them a strange look.

"Time to split."

"Was time? A long time? Ago?"

Mom wasn't at the game store. The clerk shrugged and handed them the bag of games, which had been paid for. Inside the bag was a twenty-dollar bill. They passed Fresh Bukket, which was packed, and went to the mostly empty Burger Barn instead. Nick ordered a yogurt and side salad for himself and a Junior Moo Meal for Amanda, since she dug the toy inside — or at least dug pretending not to. For Mom he ordered a Cal-O-Riffic Rib Strip Diet-Plus Plate. Now with 60% less trans fats!

"What are? Trans fats? Nick?"

"It means they replaced the old synthetic lard that they'd replaced the original real lard with, with new real lard."

An hour later, the diet plate was cold. Amanda was already on her second game, having crushed the first, *El Fister's Revenge,* zipping through every level and running up an all-time high score that she immediately uploaded to the company's servers.

"Don't like it anymore? Nick? Boring?"

He riffled through the stack. "Try this."

Amanda ejected *El Fister* with malice. It clattered to the floor.

"You dropped your cartridge," a cute girl said, walking by. Nick smiled, but the girl didn't smile back. The cartridge stayed where it was. Amanda slid *Delicious Warm* into her handheld. It was pretty much just an excuse for Asian girls in pigtails and plaid skirts to do flying kicks. She cruised through a dozen levels before it hit the floor. In went *Akkak Attack Prime*, truck-bots that turned into plane-bots and back again. Floor. Next was *The Adventures of Gary Brain and Eunice*, a riddle game with the famous brother-and-sister detective team. Eject. It was down to *The Evolved 66: Celestial Embryo*. A spaceship on the way to Proxima Centauri was full of sentient babies. The babies were heavily armed. In the hold sat over a million gallons of narco-milk.

There was level after level of raging firefights, forced diaper changes, and booby-trapped snacks.

"This is? Awesome?"

Amanda hunkered down, punching buttons with a precision frenzy. Points doubled and tripled, accumulating faster than the counter could tabulate. The Palmbot started to hum and emit a high-pitched whine. A few junior nerds stopped by to watch.

"Whoa!"

"Are you, like, pro?"

"Badass thumb work!"

"That deaf, dumb, blind girl sure plays a mean pinball."

"What?"

"Nothing."

People came and went. Food was ordered and eaten.

Muzak ingested and then squatted out the entirety of Fleetwood Mac's *Rumours*.

By the time Burger Barn flipped around the *Sorry! There'll be more Yum tomorrow!* sign, there was a pile of game boxes under the table and crushed wrappers spread across the top. Security gates were being pulled shut in front of all the stores. A guard ushered Nick down the escalator and out onto the sidewalk, told Amanda to "Watch your step, sweetie," and then locked the door behind them.

There were only a few cars left in the parking lot, almost all of them tan.

"Who buys? A tan? Car?" Amanda asked.

Nick found a pay phone and called the Dude.

A couple hours later, he swung by and picked them up.

23

Just Knock

A LONG CHANNEL OF WET GRANITE LED TO A slippery carapace they took turns helping each other onto. Estrada was last, gripping War Pig's forearm. From the ledge, it was clear how far they'd risen above the tree line. There was nothing left but a triangle of bare rock, angling straight up. They stood in the cold like cows in the early morning, stamping their feet, not ready to move. Nobody wanted to mention that they were out of mountain, with nowhere else to go.

But down.

Either a ledge or a gullet.

Still, there was a giddy relief in being at the end of the line, no matter what happened when they stepped over it. Or were forced to.

"Wow."

"Is peaceful."

"Almost like shit is mad normal down there."

Below, the valley was laid out in green and white, sparkling under a wedge of moon. It was actually beautiful.

"Wonder if everyone's dead."

"Hopefully only the ones who deserve it."

"And, possibly, some others."

"I would seriously kill someone," War Pig said. "For, like, three almonds."

"Weird there's no gunshots. Aren't people fighting back?"

"Seriously. Why we gotta carry all the weight?"

"I smell smoke."

"Bet they're torching the bodies."

"Yeah, but who's torching who?"

"We are. To them."

"We who? Them who?"

"Dude, like the National Guard. SWAT and shit. Someone gotta be in control, don't they?"

In the fields the bodies burning, as the war machine keeps turning.

"No one has to be in control," War Pig said. "No one's ever in control."

"You guys," Nero called. "Check it out."

The path wound up the rock ledge for a hundred yards, then rose quickly to a peak that jutted above them. There was a gap that opened onto a clearing carved from the mountain like a shallow bowl. In the center, a dark wood Tudor hunting lodge sat forlornly, all spires and gables and mansard. It was grim, a gingerbread house gone wrong. A mirage.

"That's convenient," Idle said.

ZOMBRULE #7: *Convenience is great in a store that sells smokes and Magnums and Big Gulps, but not so hot in a monster plot. In Zomb-World, if it looks too good to be true, it almost certainly is. Next stop: raw fat, red gallons, and patella gnawing.*

"Yeah, huh? But a helicopter with the keys in the ignition would have been even better," Billy said.

"How did you know it was up here?" Estrada asked.

Nero's hand throbbed. "I didn't."

Next to them was a wooden sign buried deep in the granite that said REBOZZO LODGE — CLOSED FOR THE SEASON. Beneath that, someone had spray-painted *Even if it were open, only a fool wood go in.*

"Guy tags all the way up here, but doesn't know how to spell *would*?"

"This is the spray paint?" Yeltsin asked, fingering the letters. "Or blood?"

"Who cares? Check out that pad. It's epic."

The lodge seemed to hunker in an eerie mist.

"If by epic, you mean it looks exactly like every ghost movie ever made rolled into one big Frankenhouse, then yeah."

"I don't like it."

"Me neither."

"Seems like a total trap," Idle said.

"Zombies don't set traps."

"Maybe not, but rednecks do. Inbreds. Bandits. They all out of canned yams already, luring people in for survivor stew."

Billy nodded. "Every Z movie has at least one Texas Chainsaw family eating hitchhiker patties."

"It's called a parable," Estrada explained. "Z are eating people so the script has people eating people too. Even when they don't have to. You're supposed to be all 'What a profound insight into the human condition' and shit."

"Oh," Idle said.

"Oh," Billy said.

"What do you think?" War Pig asked Nero.

The clearing around the lodge was wide open, like a natural amphitheater. Nowhere to hide. Nowhere to run. Nero pictured Leatherface in a *Kiss the Cook* apron, simmering down a hearty mushroom and backpacker stock.

"Seems dicey, but we're fresh out of choices."

"Okay, but how do we get in?"

"Break a window?"

"They're too high up. Must be twelve feet. Looks close from here, but standing below? No way you could reach them."

"You will notice gun notches built beneath each casement?" said Yeltsin. "There is a reason they are so high. I have seen this before. In Chechnya. Is built to hold off attack."

"From who?" Estrada asked.

"Me," Billy said.

"Me," Idle said.

"Only way in is the front," Nero said, pointing to a huge wooden door that looked like the entrance to a castle. It was weather-beaten and ancient, with iron hinges.

"What do you suppose the chances are it's unlocked?" War Pig asked.

Twenty feet below, the horde moaned in unison, their whispers whipping between the rocks like a demented flute.

You got to know when to hold 'em, fold 'em, and walk away. It's pretty obvious when to run.

"Hurry up and start decisioning," Idle said.

"Yeah," Billy said. "It's mad cold."

Nero clambered onto the terrace, which was worn smooth under a thin layer of snow. Dead and withered trees poked through the cracks like sentinels. It was quiet. Peaceful. At least until a figure stepped through hazy gray and onto the carapace with him.

Swann.

White, ethereal, naked.

"Not again."

"Oh. Please, no."

Her skin was beyond pale, except for the wash of red that ran from her chin to her belly button. It looked like she was wearing debutante's gloves, lacquer-red from fingernails to elbows, but hers were made of dried heart blood, deep and glossy.

Other Infects emerged from behind her. The two children, lurching in tandem. The Shasta County Anorex Recovery Team they'd passed on the highway. Cheerleaders. Lumberjacks. Taxi drivers.

Then came Mr. Bator. Velma. Boblegum and Kim Fowley. Tripper, his tattoos obscured by gouges and layers of dried blood.

He was also missing an arm. And a hand. And both ears.

"They ate his freaking ears," Billy said.

Tripper grinned. His tongue flickered between his missing front teeth. And then, over the carapace, as if he'd free-climbed the ice face, pulling himself up with mangled fingers, came Counselor Jack Oh. He scrambled onto the plateau and perched next to Swann's leg, on all fours, like a dog.

"Ponytail knew what he was all along."

"A mutt."

"A leg lifter."

"An asshole sniffer."

Swann reached down and scratched Jack Oh's snarl of gray hair with her bloody nails. He was shirtless, and most of his pants were torn away. The knife, planted to the hilt, still jutted from his shoulder.

> ZOMBRULE #8: *This breaks pretty much all the zombrules. Which means you are teetering on zombarchy. As has been proven in nine out of ten CDC plague simulations, zombarchy is*

26 percent worse than a full-on Zomb-A-Pocalypse. Conclusion? If there's anything tall nearby to jump off of, now would be an excellent time to consider it.

Swann snapped her fingers.

Jack Oh tilted his head, gnashed his teeth, and then charged.

Like a Doberman.

Yeltsin squealed and ran. The other boys followed, making a dash for the lodge. The footing was bad. They cursed and slid and bitched, legs trembling as the door seemed to get farther away with each step, the echo of Jack Oh's peculiar gait closing in.

Hand-hand, foot-foot.

Slap slap, slappity slap.

"How does he move so damn fast?" War Pig grunted.

"Every moaner's supposed to be a slow moaner," Idle said. "It's written in the Z constitution."

"Garlic probably don't work on vampires anymore either," Billy said.

ZOMBRULE #9: *Depends on the director. Zombies move at different speeds. Old-school ones are slow and rotty but dangerous in a pack. Your new breed are young and agile, all amped up on the rage virus, none of that shucking and jiving between a parking-lot-ful of decomposing shufflers. Best bet: try to get cast in something retro.*

Jack Oh came in low, from the left, closest to Yeltsin.

Hand-hand, foot-foot.

Slap slap, slappity slap.

"Help! Friends! Teammates!"

Hand-foot.

Slap, slap.

Yelstin swung around, kicked Estrada's leg, and ran ahead. Estrada fell, carving a groove in the snow with his chin.

Bait.

Okay, that is beyond cold.

Jack Oh tried to stop and bite, but his hands couldn't get a grip. He slid past Estrada like a collie, toenails scrabbling across linoleum, and careened into Yeltsin's legs.

The two of them went down hard.

Yeltsin rolled over, holding his hand out plaintively.

"Help! Again I ask! Please, you guys! Nice doggie!"

Jack Oh bit off three fingers.

They say it tastes just like chicken tastes to other chickens who prefer ham.

Yeltsin screamed and gripped the bouquet of his palm, a trio of gurgling roses. Jack Oh went in for another bite. Nero grabbed a handful of ponytail and yanked it hard to the side while War Pig pulled the knife from Jack Oh's shoulder.

It came out with a sickening *shtunk*, releasing a gout of yellow bile, and then went back in, as War Pig stuck it up to the handle in Jack Oh's eyeball.

Jack Oh collapsed next to Yeltsin, who lay quietly sobbing.

"You need some ointment for your lady parts?" Billy asked, kicking him in the ribs.

"Yeah," Idle said. "I have a whole tube right here. Traitor."

"Don't," Nero said, taking off Petal's jacket and wrapping it around Yeltsin's ruined hand.

"Is so kind. But frankly, why to bother?"

"I'm not sure. You don't really deserve it."

Yeltsin closed his eyes, breathing shallowly. "Is terrible thing, a small time to know you die, but do not die. To see what comes next, this madness."

"Leave the prick to rot," Idle said. "Right, Pablo?"

Estrada said nothing, brushing himself off.

"For my actions, I blame society," Yeltsin said, rolling over. "Also, my mother."

Nero stood as Idle took the knife, sawed off Jack Oh's ponytail, and threw it at Swann's feet.

The other Infects shuffled behind her, closing in from three sides.

Soon it would be four.

The boys ran the last forty yards and slammed into the lodge door as a group.

"What a surprise," Estrada said. "It's locked."

War Pig clanked the huge metal knocker, a bronze ingot

shaped like a snarling wolf's head. Idle and Billy pounded the frozen wood with their hands, digging their fingernails in. Behind them, dozens of Infects fanned out. There was no way back to the rocks, no way around the lodge. The football team, faces gray, a rictus of hunger behind their face masks, howled with victory. The cheerleaders moaned some approximation of a cheer.

Screaming now, Billy clawed at the door.

Idle gripped the knife by the blade and threw it. It hit a cheerleader in the stomach and sank in. She barely glanced down.

War Pig double-timed the knocker: *bam-bam, bam-bam, bam-bam.*

"Open up! Open up!"

Nero just watched. It all seemed so anticlimactic.

This was the end.

And in the end, he'd done nothing but prolong their misery.

Amanda was stuck with the Dude.

Petal was lost.

No one would be left to tell their story.

And what about Uncle Rock?

The football team slavered forward.

Fifteen feet.

Ten.

Yeltsin rose jerkily, sucked his fingers, and began to howl.

The boys gave up on the door and turned to fight.

"This is such bullshit," Idle said.

"Totally," Billy said. "I deserve mad better."

War Pig began to hyperventilate. He bent into a crouch and flexed, arms extended for battle.

"They get you, promise you won't eat me," Estrada whispered to Nero. "Promise you eat someone else."

Six feet.

"Deal," Nero said, bracing against the hinges.

This is gonna hurt.

"Oh, man!" Idle whined.

"Word," Billy said.

Three feet.

The shamblers converged, arms raised, mouths open, in a pack, drooling as one.

And then the doors spread wide.

The boys fell backward in a heap as the doors shut again and the bolt was thrown. Infects slammed against the heavy wood.

Howling with pure rage.

24

Many a Benefactress

NERO HELPED ESTRADA UP. IDLE AND BILLY scrambled away from the door, which buckled inward. The sounds of frustration and hunger from outside were muffled, the highs and lows cut out, resulting in a steady middle of want. Which somehow made it worse.

The boys took turns flinching with each bang. Especially when Swann's voice, higher than the rest, keened with fury.

Like an ax that might cleave through the heavy wood.

But the doors, crossed with steel braces, held.

They were in a large room, dark except for a flickering glow. Nero could just make out the walls, but not the far corners. The ceiling was spanned by massive exposed beams. Torn furniture and broken glass was strewn across the floor, legless chairs and stained rugs rolled up and shoved into corners. There was a single staircase leading to a second-floor balustrade that ran along one wall, rusted armor mounted in the eaves. Huge oil paintings, torn and rotting, hung without frames. They were grotesques, headless viscounts and skeletal maidens. Knights-drowned water nymphs. Ghouls knelt among rapt animals, teeth yellowed and ready.

In the center of the room was an enormous stone fireplace.

In the fireplace was a roaring fire.

And by the roaring fire were five girls.

Half an IT van's worth.

None of them Petal.

Wait, are you sure? Check again.

Joanjet stood in front, purple topknot severe as ever, wiry arms crossed over her chest. Raekwon stood behind her, pink jumpsuit pants hacked off into short-shorts over thermal underpants that clung to her long legs. Her tight cornrows had little shells crimped onto the ends. She held an ancient musket that looked like something Roger Williams conquered Rhode Island with.

The others held fireplace pokers and kitchen knives.

"Right on," Estrada said.

"Seriously," War Pig said.

Idle and Billy slapped five. "We must be a couple of dead martyrs, 'cause here's our seventy-two virgins!"

"Quiet!" Joanjet said.

The boys stopped cheering.

Raekwon raised the musket.

Behind them, Infects continued to pound.

Joanjet gave a half smile. Her jumpsuit top was sleeveless, a strip of pink nylon wrapped around each wrist like sweatbands. "Save that frat routine for someone who gives a shit. If you want to stay in our lodge, you need to learn the rules."

ZOMBRULE #10: *Girls with muskets make the rules.*

"*If* we want?" Estrada said.

"*Your* lodge?" War Pig said.

"We know the rules," Billy said. "We're fast; they're slow. They eat neck steak; we —"

"Not the zombie rules, foolio," Raekwon interrupted. "The Delinquents Are Lucky They're Not Outside rules. The Complain One More Time and You're Plateau Buffet rules. The I Don't Trust You Assholes as Far as I Could Kick a Lemon Pie rules."

"Oh," Idle said.

"Oh," Billy said.

Sad Girl and Lush looked embarrassed, hugging their arms and shivering. Cupcake covered her eyes with a corner of the huge flannel shirt she wore over her shoulders like a cape.

"You're guests," Joanjet said. "Where I'm from, rude guests get sent home early."

"Can you dig it?" Raekwon said.

"Totally," Nero said.

"Absolutely," Estrada said.

"What about you, muscle-head?" Joanjet asked, but War Pig wasn't listening. He was staring at Raekwon.

"Yeah, sure, whatever you say."

"Good."

The two groups eyed each other warily.

"There's only five of you left?" Nero asked, reading the names of the girls from their jumpsuit tags.

Lush was Asian, plump, with a schoolgirl bob and a silver nose ring. Sad Girl was tall and angular, a permanent frown battling the manic sparkle in her eyes. Raekwon, even holding the gun (or maybe especially holding the gun), was sleek and hot. And scowling. Cupcake was farthest away, a pale brunette with short bangs and cat's-eye glasses. She seemed to be in shock — hugging her knees, rocking back and forth and humming to herself.

"Are there only five of *you* left?" Joanjet answered, as the wings tattooed on her neck seemed to flex in the firelight.

"We lost a few good men on the climb up," Idle admitted.

"What good men?" Billy said.

"Okay, so we lost a few men on the climb up."

"Anyway, there's six of us if you count Pacino."

"Who's Pacino?"

Raekwon held up the musket. "My gun."

"You named your gun?"

"Why not?"

"Hell, it's the Zomb-A-Pocalypse," War Pig said. "I had a gun, I'd probably name it too."

Ask them, already.

"Where's Petal?" Nero blurted. His voice, raw and desperate, seemed to echo around the room.

Cupcake began to cry, burnt-firewood mascara leaving black trails down her cheeks.

The other girls looked at one another.

"Where do you think she is?" Raekwon said.

The pounding on the door increased, infect weight making the braces bow inward.

"More importantly," Joanjet said. "Where's Swann?"

Billy shrugged. "She the one out there sounds like a demented bird."

Joanjet slipped into the darkness and then reappeared at the window on the second floor.

"Wait. She's *naked*?"

"It wasn't our idea," War Pig said as Joanjet came back into the light. "She tried to eat us about six times on the way up here."

"I'll bet."

"Skank."

"Zomb-bitch."

"It's not funny," Estrada said. "People are dead. A lot of them."

"I don't think it is, either," Sad Girl said, taking a step closer to Estrada.

There was a long, uncomfortable silence.

"Can you at least put down the guns and knives so we can get closer to the fire?" Nero asked quietly.

"Not yet," Joanjet said. "Are any of you bitten?"

"No," War Pig said. "We would have turned already."

The girls shook their heads.

"Some turn faster than others."

"Either way, we're not taking any chances," Raekwon said. "Strip down for a body check."

"Screw that," Idle said. "You guys strip down for a hottie check."

Raekwon pointed the musket at Billy's chest. The other girls formed a half circle with their knives. Sad Girl looked at Estrada and shrugged.

"That antique even work?" War Pig asked.

Raekwon thumbed the hammer back. "Want to find out?"

"Yeah," he said. "But not about that."

Raekwon blushed, lowering the gun until Joanjet glared at her.

"We did a check ourselves," Lush said. "Okay? First thing when we got in here. It's nothing personal. Just . . . smart."

"It's true, you guys," Sad Girl said.

"You don't want to, the exit's right there," Raekwon said.

Idle and Billy flashed gang sign. East coast, west coast.

Those boys about to bust a move. And then it's gonna get ugly.

"I don't mind," Nero said. He stepped forward, took off

his boots, and unzipped his jumpsuit — wearing only smiley-face boxers. His lucky boxers.

"For real?"

"You leave your Snoopy ones at home?"

Idle laughed and went to slap five with Raekwon. She shoved the barrel in his face.

"Your turn, honey."

The other boys looked at one another.

"Hey, why not?" Estrada said. He unzipped his jumpsuit and took off his shirt.

Sad Girl gasped.

Even by the dim firelight, it was clear that he was covered with scars, from his neck to his knees.

He looked like a keloid yakuza. Or a brown whipping post.

"What are you, a pirate?" Joanjet asked.

"More like a galley slave, yo," Idle said.

Estrada shrugged. He and Nero stood side by side.

Nearly naked.

In front of a burning log.

And five angry girls.

25

It's a Flashback, Jack IV: The Amand-O Reveal

ANGIE JESKEY LOOKED A LITTLE LIKE PETAL. But harder. Less refined. More like a sketch of Petal on a bar napkin. A bad sketch that had gotten wet, some of the marker bleeding toward the edges. Still, when Annabelle Lu came up in the caf and said, "Angie Jeskey likes you," Nick listened. In fact, he doubled up on some balls and called her that night. But Angie wouldn't answer. Her mom picked up and went, "Sorry, Nicholas, Angela is not available," even though he could practically smell her grape gum through the phone. Angie most certainly was available, right there, at the kitchen table, shaking her head *I'm not here.*

It wasn't until he'd given up, actually pretty relieved about it, that she started to text him in class, text him in the hall, text him in gym, inviting herself over to study.

"Okay," Nick said. "I guess."

Angie laughed and the next afternoon was sitting in his room wearing an orange sweater, a turtleneck, and a ponytail. Blond with black roots. She slipped off her shoes. There was a hole in one of her stockings. They looked at her calculus book for about twenty minutes while her toes rubbed his beneath the desk, and then she leaned over. The book fell to the floor. The binding split open. They started making out.

Her lipstick on his lips, her lipstick on his teeth. The lipstick that was on his teeth back on hers.

Tongues swirled clockwise, counterclockwise. Rhombus. Tetrahedron. Ellipse. Push, pull. Her mouth tasted like chips and gum. She'd obviously had a lot of practice, running him through the paces like a quarter horse getting his morning workout.

They shifted neck positions. Banged teeth. Soft kisses, hard kisses, long kisses, short kisses.

But no matter what Nick tried, she didn't taste like Petal.

At least what he was fairly sure Petal tasted like.

Angie put his hand on her leg and then pretended to push it away. She slid his fingers into her waistband and then angrily pulled them back out.

He accepted this paradigm as their clothes began to come off, item by item, sure she would soon rear back, shake her mane, clip him with a hoof, and then gallop off over the hills, never to be seen again.

Which he was half hoping for.

It felt good to be holding someone, but she was the wrong someone. In every way. He wanted to stand up, make some excuse, but couldn't find the strength. He knew if his friends could see him, they would laugh, call him a pussy. "What, you gonna turn that shit down?"

The skirt came off. Nick could see the top of her panties, green with a pink frilly trim. They didn't look new. There were little pills of thread balled at the hem, like an old friend he'd never been introduced to and wasn't sure he ever really wanted to meet.

Angie put one hand on Nick's shoulder and stared into his eyes like an actress in a lawyer show trying to remember her lines.

Nick's pants dropped, gathering around his ankles, for the first time in his life almost naked in front of someone besides the guys on the track team.

Just a pair of boxers between them.

A thin layer of fabric holding back the elemental truth.

They made out standing up. Angie locked on to him like a remora. Nick couldn't breathe. He started to push back, to groan, which she took as encouragement and wrapped even tighter. Her mouth was too warm, tiny bumps of tongue rubbing sourly against the grain. He managed to lever his forearm against her chest, about to shove, when the door swung open, pinning them in a coffin of hallway light.

Amanda.

She stood there behind ridiculously thick glasses, eyes magnified to enormous size, holding the Palmbot against her thin dress.

"Nick? Why in your boxers, Nick?"

Angie screamed. She let go, grabbing a pillow off the floor to cover up with.

"Why the girl scream, Nick? Huh? Nick?"

"God," Angie said. "Can't you put her in her room or something?"

"A-dog, buddy? Think you can go back downstairs?"

"Too loud, Nick? Want to play? Up here?"

The Dude was in the kitchen, arguing with the blender.

"What's he doing?" Angie asked.

"Probably making a smoothie."

"Nope? Homemade? Suntan lotion?" Amanda said.

"I swear, your family is so fricking weird!"

Amanda lay down on the floor next to Nick's bed, in her usual spot. There was a divot practically worn into the floor. She got comfy, popped in a disc, her arm lying over Angie's foot.

Which caused Angie to scream again.

There were footsteps at the bottom of the stairs.

The Dude cursing.

Angie pulled on her sweater and stuffed her bra into her backpack. When the Dude reached the doorway, she pushed past him without a word. A minute later, the front door slammed.

"There a problem here?"

The Dude had smoothie on his chin. He smelled like a barrel of coconut oil.

"No, no problem."

"Smiley faces?" he said. "For real?"

Nick looked down at his boxers. "Well, yeah. You know."

Amanda paused her game, *Jack Drac and the Guzzleblood Six.*

"Different disc, Nick? This one? Boring?"

The Dude went back downstairs, chiding the handrail the entire way. Nick handed Amanda one of her favorites, *Multilevel Smurf Target Practice for Small-Caliber Weaponry,* and then sat on the bed, head in hands.

There were two hours before his next shift.

And then eight hours of chopping up chickens.

Tiny little bodies.

Pluck, gut, quarter.

Bread, pack, freeze.

Plenty of time to come up with something to say to Petal.

Something besides, "Don't take this the wrong way or anything, but I totally couldn't stop thinking about you pretty much the entire time my tongue was clamped inside Angie Jesky's mouth."

26

I'll Show You Mine if You Show Me Mine

THEY STOOD THERE BY FIRELIGHT, NEARLY naked.

Everyone staring at Estrada's scars.

"What happened to you?" Sad Girl finally whispered.

"I got an uncle into discipline."

No one said anything.

"Had an uncle," Estrada clarified, pulling his clothes back on.

"I don't understand," Cupcake said.

"You don't have to," Nero said.

Estrada looked at him and nodded as Joanjet examined the gash on Nero's hand.

"This is fresh."

"It's a cut, not a bite. It has stitches, not teeth marks."

It really should have teeth marks, though, shouldn't it?

Joanjet frowned but let it go.

War Pig stripped down. Raekwon whistled. The other girls all turned to look. He was lean, cut, with abs like a run of moguls. A knot of red hair gathered at the center of his chest and ran in a line down to the elastic band of his underwear. He looked like a guy who wanted to kick sand in your face and then kick you in the face for swallowing his sand.

Joanjet, unimpressed, checked him carefully for bites.

"Okay, you're good."

Idle stepped up next, tan and smooth, no muscle to speak of, rocking Yves Saint Laurent underwear. He grinned, a mouthful of chrome, posed and flexed.

"Okay. Clean."

Relatively, but could probably use a quick taint scrub.

Billy was the same, down to his silk Hilfigers. He walked fierce and thigh-first, hand on hip, then spun and returned like a runway model. Sad Girl and Lush giggled.

"Clean."

The boys put their clothes back on and then knelt by the fire.

"So now what?" Estrada asked as the pounding outside became rhythmic, call-and-response. The noise reverberated through every wall, the lodge surrounded.

"That's what we been talking about since we got here," Raekwon said. "Rest? Run? Fight? Dig a freaking tunnel?"

"I think we should separate," Joanjet said. "Girls on one side of the room. Boys on the other."

How . . . Catholic.

"Wait, what?" Estrada said.

"No," War Pig said. "Why?"

"I don't want to separate," Sad Girl said.

"Me neither," Lush said, her nose ring twinkling in the firelight.

Joanjet looked at Raekwon, who looked at War Pig, who shrugged.

"We're staying together," Nero said. Everyone stared at him. He cleared his throat. "It's just, you know, the more of us the better. No one wandering off alone into the darkness."

"*Thank* you," Raekwon said, flexing her calves. "Splitting up is just a cheap way to kill off the secondary cast, and I am totally part of the first cast."

Everyone laughed.

"But sooner or later there's going to be too many Z for that front door to hold," Nero said. "There's got to be something we can do besides just wait for them to bust in."

"What if the whole country's like this?" War Pig said quietly. "Surrounded. Maybe even the whole world. For an escape plan to work, there has to be somewhere to escape to."

"But won't people come?" Cupcake asked, her bangs pasted to her forehead. "Like, someone in a Jeep? In a uniform? And tell us what to do?"

Billy laughed. "Yeah, right. There ain't gonna be no rescue. No news crew. No one even knows we're here."

"They got pressing business, even if they did," Idle said. "Delinquents are hardly first on the save list."

"But our parents," Cupcake said. "The police."

"Any dudes left down there are going hand to hand, busting skulls just to survive. What kinda crackhead's gonna hike over to see how the ol' abandoned lodge is holding up?"

"They're right," Joanjet said. "We're on our own."

ZOMBRULE #11: *Teenagers. All alone. In an isolated cabin. In the middle of the woods. In the dark. What a fresh and original setup. In any case, immediately find someone to pair off with, a paring knife, a can of pears in heavy syrup, a* Pere Ubu *boxed set, an autographed Luke Perry 8x10 glossy, a headstone map of Père Lachaise, a pair of nunchuks, and a quart of paregoric.*

"Let's go over what we know," Nero said. "How did it break off for you guys?"

Cupcake closed her eyes and covered her ears.

"Well, Eeyore went crazy during the night," Joanjet said. "She attacked Kim Fowley first. I guess she . . . did things to her . . . for a while. Until we woke up. Juicebox went to see, but she never came back. There was . . . you know, screaming.

Something tore my tent down and grabbed Abzug Belagosi by the ankles and just . . . pulled her into the dark. Then I heard Raekwon calling out and followed her voice. We met by the fire and all just sort of took off up the trail."

Nero swallowed, hard. "And Petal was with you?"

The girls all looked at one another.

"No."

So she got separated. Maybe she headed down to the highway.

Raekwon cleared her throat. "Yeah, so we ran. And, you know how they do — the meat freaks followed us."

"Picked us off one at a time," Lush said. "First Hera. Then LadyMac, Buffy, and Macy."

"So we headed up."

"Until we couldn't head anymore."

"And here we are."

Scratch.

"What is that?"

Scratch scratch.

"It sounds like fingernails."

Scratch scratch scratch.

"It is fingernails."

Scratch scratch scratch scratch.

"Tell them to stop!" Cupcake yelled, pulling at her hair.

Scratch scratch scratch scratch scratch.

Joanjet walked over and put her arm around Cupcake.

Scratch scratch scratch scratch scratch scratch.

Then kissed her on the mouth.

Ooh, snap!

Cupcake kissed her back, and they held each other. When Joanjet finally pulled away, she turned, daring someone to say something.

No one did.

Except Idle.

"Shit, Deep Purple, you a dyke?"

Billy laughed. "Total bull dagger."

"Not cool," War Pig said.

Sad Girl stood up, green eyes flashing in anger. "The world's falling apart but you idiots still need to make fun of people comforting each other? I mean, don't you hear those fingernails outside? Doesn't it make you not want to hurt anything? Even with words? Like, ever again?"

Idle and Billy looked at each other, pretending to consider.

Pretending to be swayed.

Pretending to hold headphones to one ear and spin records on a turntable.

Scratch-a scratch. Scratch-a scratch scratch.

"Not really."

"No, we pretty much still want to hurt stuff."

Nero stepped in front of Idle so that Joanjet was looking only at him. So she understood that not a single person left alive cared what the twins thought.

"You guys want to know what we should do?"

"Yes," War Pig said.

"Yes," Lush said.

"Yes."

"Yes."

"Yes."

"Good. Let's break into pairs and see what we can scavenge. Someone should reinforce the door. We need to find food and weapons. Water. Communications. And we need to set up a bathroom, as far away from the fireplace as possible."

There was nodding all around. Sad Girl and Estrada held hands and got to work.

Nero turned toward the twins. "You born-agains want to help, or are you going to sit on your asses until our dinner guests break in?"

"I vote asses," Idle said.

"Help, I need somebody," Billy said. "Anybody."

No one laughed.

There was too much to do.

Especially since the scratching had gotten louder again.

A lot louder.

27

Redrumming
with Scissors

RAEKWON AND WAR PIG PICKED UP EITHER
end of a heavy bureau and used it to reinforce the front door.
Lush dragged antique chairs and elaborately carved frames
back to the hearth to burn. Estrada and Sad Girl took turns
breaking them apart. After a while, Sad Girl unzipped the top
of her jumpsuit and tied the sleeves around her waist, just a
wifebeater underneath. She wasn't wearing a bra.

Estrada stared at his feet.

Idle and Billy found a can of paint thinner and poured
some into a rag, mashing it to their noses. They giggled, glaze
eyed, making fun of each other's huffer's rash.

Joanjet stood next to Nero. "So are you the quarterback of
your football team or head of the student council?"

He smiled. "I'm just another delinquent."

Joanjet raised a plucked eyebrow. With her pink sweatbands and lean frame, she looked like the bass player in an obscure L.A. punk band. "Whatever you say."

They walked the perimeter of the great room, looking for something to salvage. In the far right corner was a bar, empty of booze but filled with broken glassware and dusty stools. Pitted dining tables covered with sheets ran along the near wall with nothing beneath them. In the lower right was a kitchen with an ancient icebox, empty. Nero walked up the stairs and paused in front of a window. Hundreds of Infects surrounded the lodge, four deep, pushing and pounding. Some stood farther back in the clearing, mouths open like children as snowflakes softy settled on them.

Nero turned away, afraid he'd see Petal. Shuffling in circles. Drooling.

"I'm sorry about in the van," Joanjet said. "My note."

"Eat me? Not very original."

She shrugged. "I have anger issues."

Nero watched the twins take turns punching each other on the arm. "Join the club."

"I can't believe you made it all the way up here with those knuckleheads."

Nero looked at Raekwon. "Seems like you had your hands full too."

Joanjet nodded. "The price of leadership is that your raw materials are chosen for you."

They walked back downstairs as War Pig shoved another table against the front door.

"Okay, check it out," he said. "You're an Infect, right? You got a choice of anyone in this room. Who do you eat first?"

"No dangles," Idle said, leering at Lush.

"Exactly," Billy said, also leering at Lush.

"Estrada," Sad Girl said.

Cupcake and Joanjet just held hands.

"I'm on Jenny Craig," Nero said.

Raekwon laughed. "Forget who. What *part* do you eat first?"

War Pig gulped.

Idle and Billy looked at each other.

"Kidney and fava beans."

They went down the rest of the line.

"Ass."

"Ass."

"Ass."

"Ass."

"Calves."

Lush sighed. "Uh, I guess that soft stuff around your fingernails?"

"Hey," Estrada said, walking out of the darkness with an old boom box. "Look what I found under the stairs."

"Nice!" War Pig said, grabbing it away. "Does it work?"

Estrada stared at him. "Not yet."

War Pig looked up, blushed, and then handed it back.

Estrada pried open the back compartment with Sad Girl's knife. He dislodged a rusty screw, and the battery cover popped off.

Six gleaming D cells sat lined up, nose to nose. Except the final one, which was out of alignment.

"I can't believe there's actually batteries in here."

ZOMBRULE #12: *There are never any batteries. There's also never any gas, any flashlights, any shotgun shells, any propane, any directions, any rubbers, any paper, any wireless signal, any fishing line, any socks, any adults, any toothpaste, any zombie-dispatching meat axes, any dimes, any socket sets, any Band-Aids, any forks, or any nose plugs when you really, really need them. Unless, of course, the plot requires one to make some scene plausible, in which case it'll magically appear. In the meantime, plan on not having what you will probably never have.*

Estrada looked up at the ceiling, whispered a novena, and then nudged the last battery back into place.

The radio squalled painfully.

Everyone let out a cheer.

Sad Girl raised the antenna as Estrada licked his fingers, then slowly turned the dial to the right.

There was nothing through the low 90s. Not even static.

"Shit," War Pig whispered. "Can it really be that bad?"

"Maybe there's just no signal up here."

"Even in Antarctica, you can get static."

At 95.1, there was a station that made tiny blip noises. At 98.9 a faint but steady Emergency Broadcast System signal droned. They waited for an announcement, but it never came.

Through to the hundreds. Nothing.

At 104.3 there was a man's voice, deep and scratchy, like he was inside a well. Talking about a small town called Linda Rosa. Where aliens had landed. And were killing citizens.

"No way," Idle said. "Aliens? *That's* what the fuckers are?"

"I knew it," Billy said. "That's what I've been saying all along. Mars mad attacks."

"Where's Linda Rosa?" Sad Girl asked. "Near Oakland?"

"They're not aliens," Nero said. "And that's not a real place."

"Guy on the radio just told you they were."

"It's Orson Welles."

"Like I give a crap what his name is?"

"You should. He's been dead for years, for one thing."

"Wait, aliens *and* ghosts?"

"Who is he?" Estrada asked.

"Used to be a famous actor. It's an old recording. He's reading from *The War of the Worlds*."

"I saw that shit movie," War Pig said. "Five-foot-tall Tommy Cruise muscles up and saves humanity with, like, a gallon of water."

"Exactly," Nero said. "This is the radio play the movie was based on. A long time ago, like in the 1930s. It freaked out half the country, but it was just a hoax."

"So maybe the shamblers are just a hoax," Billy said.

"Yeah, maybe we're being Punk'd," Idle said. "Where's the cameras? Bruce Leroy is probably in the trailer watching the feed and laughing his ass off."

Estrada kept dialing.

Nothing up through 105.3.

And then, at 107.7, music.

Riffs.

Feedback.

The raw, manic voice of Diamond Dave.

The finger-tap mastery of Eddie V.

The chubby, stubbled void of Michael Anthony.

"It's Van Halen!"

"'Running with the Devil'. This song is practically all about us!"

"It means someone's still out there, broadcasting," Nero said.

"And they have good taste."

"Whatever it takes to drown that freaking scratching out," Lush said.

Estrada put the radio on the table. They sat through two songs, "Mob Rules" by Black Sabbath and "Kill 'Em All" by Metallica.

"Dude's got a sense of humor at least."

"Who says it's a dude?"

And then two more.

"I Ran" by Flock of Seagulls and "The Final Countdown" by Europe.

Cupcake curled up on the floor, her head on Joanjet's lap. Estrada and Sad Girl got up without a word and danced, slow, like at the prom, their foreheads resting on each other's shoulders.

As the last synthesizer note droned, there was a squall of feedback, and then a voice came on.

"Shasta County Community Radio . . . had the gate downstairs chained, but they got through somehow. The booth has a soundproof door, nice and heavy, but it's not gonna last. . . . They're right outside, pressed against the glass, and more just keep coming. . . . It's like . . . It's like all teeth and bloody handprints. . . . My station manager, he's . . . he's right there, staring at me. Man, I walk in and first thing he's eating the drive-time guys in the lobby. Franklin and Spazzer from *The Morning Zoo*. Chowed on Spazzer like nobody's business. I'm . . . I'm just an intern. I barely know how half this equipment works. Hey, is anyone listening? Am I just talking to myself? The phone's so totally dead. My cell has, like, no bars. No bars! Can you hear me now, motherfucker? Seriously, I don't want to get eaten! If I had a gun, I'd shoot three of them and then off myself, but I'm too much of a wuss to do it with the stapler. . . . I mean, I know we all have to die sometime. But like this? Oh, man, the glass is cracking! A hand is coming in. Hold on. . . . Okay, I shoved a rolled-up piece of carpet in there. That should hold for a minute. . . . Well, if anyone's listening, I think we got time for one more tune. I'm not going to turn the mic on in here. When they get in, it's gonna get . . . ugly. No one needs to hear that — you know what I'm saying? I don't even want to hear *myself* scream, let alone broadcast it over twenty thousand watts. But, hey, check it out, my name's Alec. Alec Schwartz. You got that out there? If this isn't, like, the end of the world or whatever, could someone please tell my mom what happened? Let her know? Oh, shit, the glass . . . it's crumbling. They're making the hole bigger. . . . One of them's got its head in. God, he's all teeth. Anyway, you be cool, rockers! If there's any of you even left . . . I'll see you . . . I'll see you on the other side. . . ."

A song started. "All Along the Watchtower" by Jimi Hendrix.

Halfway through, the song stopped.

And then the signal went dead.

I regret that I have but one DJ to give for my country.

Cupcake moaned and hid her face.

Estrada snapped it off. "Save the batteries," he whispered. "Try again later."

Lush and Sad Girl hugged.

Raekwon wiped a tear from the corner of her eye.

And then the scratching got louder.

Scratch-a scratch. Scratch-a scratch scratch.

"How can their fingernails not have worn away yet?" Idle whined.

It sounded like they were digging into the walls.

Through the walls.

Through all of their skulls.

And then there was a howl.

That came from inside the lodge.

Cupcake screamed.

The boys jumped up.

The girls grabbed their weapons.

Shadows danced madly in the firelight.

And then the howl came again.

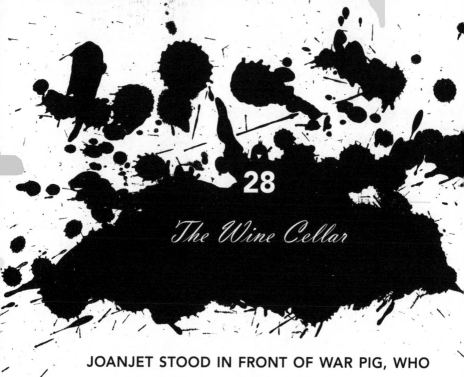

28

The Wine Cellar

JOANJET STOOD IN FRONT OF WAR PIG, WHO was in a crouch, ready to tear something apart. "Before you all lose your minds, don't. There's something we haven't shown you yet."

"What?" Idle said.

"What?" Billy said.

"What?" War Pig said.

"What?" Estrada said.

"What?" Nero said.

Like Grandpa Rock always used to say, you can't trust a woman as far as you could drag a dude in drag.

"It's downstairs," Lush said nervously. "They're —"

"Wait, there's a downstairs?"

"Why the eff didn't you say so?"

Joanjet picked a knife up off the hearth and started cleaning her fingernails, skin was so pale it looked almost ceramic in the firelight. Her tattoo fluttered as she swallowed. "We didn't know if we could trust you yet."

"Doesn't look like you trust us now," Nero said.

Infect moans revved up, overpowering the silence. The howls came again. Joanjet reached for an iron candelabra stashed behind the fireplace, lit it with a twig, and walked through the dark hall. In the corner, near the bar area, was a door none of the boys had noticed, set back behind a tapestry of entwined vipers where the firelight didn't reach.

"Well, are you coming, or do you want to stand around all night with your feelings hurt?"

When they walked over, Joanjet slid the bolt and flung the door open.

The stairway was blue-black and steep.

A fetid smell wafted up into the room.

Like tar and copper.

Shit and blood.

Fear.

There was moaning and scratching.

Hissing and spitting.

Close and personal.

"Please don't make me go down there again," Cupcake said.

"So stay up here."

"Please don't make me stay up here again."

Nero did not want to walk into the dank maw either. Every part of him, every molecule, screamed not to.

"What, then you slam it behind us?" War Pig said. "Lock us in? No, thanks."

The howls rang out in volleys.

"What's down there?" Estrada whispered. "For real."

"You coming?" Joanjet asked. "If not, I'll close the door."

"Close it." Cupcake said. "Forever."

"Oh, God," Lush said, holding her hands over her eyes.

Go and see.

"Last chance."

Do it.

Nero stepped into darkness.

Darker darkness.

It smelled like retch. Like decomposing wretches. The rest followed single file, candlelight bouncing off the cement walls, a quivering halo. Raekwon and Pacino came last. The final stair, broken in half, led to a smallish room filled with cardboard boxes and folded chairs and broken lamps. The floor was earthen and maroon colored.

Charnel house. Abattoir. Coffin. Cage.

In the corner was a pile of bones. Horns and hoofs. Antlers. Femurs. Ulnas. Long dried, yellow-white. Next to that was a pile of skins, never tanned, rotting. Nero gagged. It set off a chain reaction, the others covering their mouths.

Joanjet held the candle up. Heavy chains hung from the ceiling along one wall, sharp hooks dangling at the ends.

"I've got such a bad feeling about this," Idle whined.

"Fuck a feeling," Billy whined. "This is just bad."

Joanjet walked to the center of the room. Rusty water stains led from all four walls to a metal drain. Next to an enormous boiler, two hunters were tied to chairs, still in their camouflage and orange reflective vests, hands bound tightly.

They were going crazy, howling through slavers of drool.

"You took *hostages*?" Idle asked.

Billy giggled nervously. "Wow. That is majorly badass."

A third hunter, lying on the floor dead and half-eaten, was chained by the ankle to a thick iron standpipe.

As Nero stepped into the oval of candlelight, the hunters struggled against their ropes. One was chubby, with a mustache and a greasy forehead. He looked like someone's uncle. Like a guy who ran a hardware store that had a bowl of lollipops by the register. The other was tall and thin, with a once-kind face that could not be entirely obscured by his infected features. It was almost hard to believe that either one truly wanted to do violence. Until you looked in their eyes and saw how badly, mortally, and marrow-deeply they wanted to do violence.

"They were already in the lodge when we got here," Joanjet said as reflections from the candle bounced off the walls, into the corners, retreating, then reaching out again. The hunters' bloody mouths opened and shut in tandem, trying to chew their way from dark to light.

"There's something deeply wrong about this," Nero said. "Even for this."

"Tying them up was easier than dragging them upstairs and throwing them out," Lush said. "These two were so busy eating the third one, they barely noticed us. Until it was too late."

The hunters strained forward as if they wanted to argue the point, get some testimony into evidence. It was unsettling to see them up close. Not running. Not fighting. Just watching.

As they battled their demons.

Or were their demons.

"Freaking Z, man," Idle whined, looking back toward the staircase, which none of them could see any longer.

"How could you just leave them?" Estrada asked.

Joanjet took Cupcake's hand and crossed herself with the candle. "I don't know, it sounds stupid now."

"What?"

"I guess I thought they would come in handy?"

"As sex slaves?"

"Bring in the Gimp, and shit?"

"No, morons, to get an idea of what's going on. What they have."

"Oh, like find a microscope and discover up a cure?"

"Splice some genes with your jelly knife?"

"That was before we figured it out," Cupcake said.

"Figured what out?"

"They're not zombies," Lush said. "The chicken was bad. What they are is food poisoned."

Now is not the time to smugly bring up your vegetarianism. Trust me.

"Why do you say that?" Estrada asked.

Joanjet switched the candle to her other hand. "It's the one thing that connects them all. Fresh Bukket is the last place to buy food for fifty miles. Everyone stops there. Including the IT vans. Our counselors bought some. So did yours." She pointed to the hunters. "And there were wrappers up here with these guys. Plus an empty sixty-piece bucket."

"Sure, that's a coincidence," Nero said. "But almost anything could have set them off."

Raekwon shook her head. "Our counselor Velma was in love with two of the girls. Always letting them skip chores, carry lighter packs. Last night most of us got MREs for bitching the whole way up the trail, but Velma's favorites got to have the Chixx Nuggets. When we woke up, guess which two were already infected?"

"Boblegum and Eeyore," Sad Girl said sadly. "They ate chicken last night; they were eating Exene this morning."

Nero's stomach tightened. "At the campground . . . those kids —"

"What campground?" Cupcake asked. "What kids?"

"They had food," Estrada said. "In a bear sling. There was Fresh Bukket in there. I saw it."

Fresh Bukket chicken is Rebozzo chicken.

Rebozzo chicken was Nick Sole chicken.

Convict chicken.

Four thousand pounds of poison.

"What about Swann?" War Pig asked. "She went to bed hungry, just like the rest of us."

"Swann ate Bruce Leroy's leftovers," Nero said, the entire weight of it dropping on him like a thirteenth-story piano. "I saw her picking through the garbage in the middle of the night."

Nick Sole, Ground Zero.

Outbreak monkey.

Plague Boy.

ZOMBRULE #13: *Chicken doesn't kill people. People kill people.*

"Anyway," Raekwon said. "Now that we done getting all CSI? It don't change much. We're still in here. Still surrounded."

Sad Girl put her arms around Estrada and laid her face against his chest. He stroked her hair as if he'd been doing it for years.

"Don't get too cozy," Joanjet said, biting her lip. "There's one more thing."

"There's always one more thing," Idle said. "You said one more thing last time there was one more thing."

"Fuck a more thing," Billy said, spitting on one of the hunters, who extended and contorted his black tongue, trying to lick it up. "I want out of this hole. Now."

"What is it?" Nero asked, dying to race Billy to the steps, slam the door shut, and nail it closed.

Dying to have spent the last hour almost anywhere else.

Even outside.

Amid the throng of hands and teeth.

Where at least there was fresh air.

And everyone knew exactly what they were.

But he wanted to know what the "one more thing" was even more.

Joanjet held up the candle and then led them around the cast-iron boiler.

Behind it was a single folding chair.

In the folding chair sat a person.

Tied up.

A girl.

"The other thing is her," Joanjet said.

Oh, no, you didn't!

The girl raised her head.

"What the fuck?" Nero said.

It was Petal.

29

Getting Middle-Grade on Your Ass

PETAL WAS TIED TO THE CHAIR, HEAD DOWN.

Nero choked back something that wasn't a sob.

It was relief; it was thanks; it was a debt owed that could never be repaid, a God to be acknowledged, a psalm to be learned — or just an appreciation of sheer luck, a few numbers that had finally come in, dice that had rolled snake eyes for so long finally adding up in his favor.

It had all been worth it. The carnage, the run through the forest, up the mountain, not giving in, knowing that somehow — eventually — he'd see her again.

That she would be safe.

That he'd made the right decision, instead of heading back to the vans.

Petal. Alive.

She looked up at Nero, eyes deeply set, a shock of white hair hanging over one side of her face. She bit at the rag tied around her mouth and made low straining noises.

He leaned forward to release her.

"Don't," Raekwon said, raising the musket.

"Don't what?"

"Step on back, hero."

Nero didn't move.

"Do it," Joanjet said.

"But why?"

"Because she's infected, fool!"

He felt a rush from ankle to toe, from atrium to ventricle, an infusion of pure, uncut guilt, revulsion coursing through every last bend and valve and fatty stoppage.

You idiot!

Petal was slightly gray but seemed normal otherwise. No smell. No noises. Nothing coming out of her ears. Her eyes were clear. Enormous. Still beautiful.

Nero the leader ceased to exist. Nick the chicken schlub was back in force.

Confess!

He opened his mouth but could not bring himself to tell them. That he knew Petal. Not biblically, but mortally and morally. That he was the reason she was here. That he'd followed her all the way up the mountain. That way back in pre-van civilization he'd stuck a knife deep into himself and maybe started it all.

That you love her.

Nero's voice was a raw croak. "So why isn't she acting like them?"

"We don't know why."

"So you just left her down here?"

"To rot? Pretty much, yeah. That's how this works, right?"

Nero was about to answer when there was a loud bang.

Cupcake screamed.

Billy screamed.

Joanjet swung the candle toward the hunters, whose orange faces flashed in and out of the darkness as they hissed and growled and chomped their teeth. The closest one had managed to rock his chair over and was pulling himself toward War Pig.

With his lips.

"Lip power?" Idle said.

"That is so epically messed up," Billy said.

Raekwon stepped forward. "It's time to remove the contagion."

"No," Nero said. "If all they did was eat bad food, it's not their fault."

ZOMBRULE #14: *Be wary of Ztockholm syndrome. The pre-eaten have been known to sympathize, fall in love with, and even sacrifice themselves to their idealized undead tormentors. It's particularly common among sweatpant housewives, redheaded orphans, fans of vampire lore, teenage boys obsessed with Linux, teenage girls with paint-by-numbers horses on their bedroom walls, and those hopelessly trapped in remote hunting lodges.*

War Pig raised his boot and brought it down as hard as he could on the hunter's temple.

Once. Twice. Three times.

Bruised melon. Cracked melon. Fruit salad.

"Gross." Lush said.

"What the hell are you doing?" Joanjet asked.

"Why pretend to be reasonable?" War Pig said. "There's no reason. There's no able."

"The first rule of the Zomb-A-Pocalypse is that taking prisoners is stupid," Billy said.

Actually, that's not the first rule of the Zomb-A-Pocalypse.

"Please stop," Nero said.

Raekwon walked over and crushed the skull of the other hunter with the butt of Pacino. The chair fell apart. He bent back awkwardly and cracked.

Cracked?

Yellow liquid leaked from his nose and mouth as he folded in the wrong direction, like an old sofa. The tip of his spinal column peeked out above his pants, wagged like a dog's tail, and then stopped moving.

"That is so, so far beyond what I can process," Lush said.

Idle and Billy clapped, giving Raekwon an ovation.

"Chick getting all Foxy Brown."

"Cornrow Lara Croft. Except with better legs."

Raekwon turned and scowled, her voice low and steely. "You can't keep Z around like house pets. Leaving Petal down here ready to turn was bullshit. Like dangling James Bond over a shark tank and running away instead of just shooting his dumb ass. Sooner or later she gonna escape, and I'm not getting eaten over that kind of foolishness."

"You mean we should kill her?" Nero said with disbelief.

"Of course not."

"Thank God."

"You can't kill what's dead," Raekwon said, holding up the gun. "I mean to help homegirl more fully transition into what she already is."

"No," Estrada said.

"You can't," Cupcake said.

Nero walked over and stood in front of Petal, his back to her face.

"She gonna bite you, fool!"

"She's not biting anyone."

"You sure about that?"

Yeah, are you?

The candle wavered.

The tiny flame popped and hissed.

Blood and stink and rage welled up from the floor.

There was a long, ugly silence.

"The main thing," Petal finally said, "is that everyone needs to just calm the fuck down."

Bam!

Joanjet swung around, putting Petal in the center of the glow.

"She can talk?" War Pig said.

"Of course I can talk."

Girlfriend's the missing link! Homo zerectus! Found in the zombie caves of Chauvet!

"Then why didn't you say anything before?" Estrada asked.

Petal spit out the rest of the gag, her lips red and tortured and utterly pouty. "Um, I guess because someone shoved this strip of towel in my mouth?"

"Wait, so she's not infected?" Billy said.

"Okay, now I'm officially confused," Idle said.

"She is." Sad Girl said. "I mean, at least we all saw her get bitten."

Lush leaned over and raised Petal's jumpsuit leg. Caked blood surrounded a raw-looking bite mark on her shin, a dozen teeth clearly outlined, practically down to the bone.

J'accuse, mothersucker!

"Okay, she's on a delay," Raekwon said. "Time release. Whatever. She's gonna be Z soon, so let's get this over with."

"I don't want to eat you," Petal said. "I totally promise."

"An undead promise is as good as the meatsac it's bitten on."

"Word."

"But what if she's, like, immune or something?" Nero said.

"Yeah, and what if she gets a sudden rush of Zach and chows your spleen off?"

"Does she look like she's about to attack anyone?"

"I say we put her down," War Pig said. "Right now."

Nick was officially canceled. Nick was gone. Nick never existed.

"No one is hurting her," Nero said. "Period."

You sure he's not right? Like, maybe you should hurt her? Even a little? Just to see?

"It's three against two."

"This isn't up for a vote."

War Pig stepped closer. "No?"

Nero kept his eyes flat and steady. "No."

"Who's the two and who's the three?" Lush said. "There's ten of us."

"And why are the boys suddenly in charge?" Sad Girl asked. "This is our lodge, remember?"

War Pig made a muscle and then kissed his biceps. "These put me in charge."

"God," Cupcake said, "that is such . . . such . . ."

"When did you guys become cops, eh?" Estrada asked. "Digging the power rush? Being storm troopers and shit. Killing."

"They're already dead, moron."

Idle and Billy laughed and stood next to War Pig, who

put his other arm around Raekwon. "And this fine young lady with a musket confirms it. You got a problem with that?"

Nero nodded. "Yeah, I do."

Estrada walked over and stood next to Nero. So did Joanjet, Sad Girl, and Cupcake.

"Taking sides is stupid," Lush said, standing between the two groups. "We have to stick together."

"It's not us against us. It's us against them," Sad Girl said. "Remember? Outside?"

"There's one of them inside, though. See the difference?"

"I'm not one of them," Petal said. "I'm me. I'm still totally me."

"War Pig," Nero whispered.

"What?"

"Don't freaking move."

War Pig squeezed his fists together, flexing from waist to neck. "Why the hell not?"

"Because the third hunter is off the chain. He's right behind you."

"Yeah, right."

Joanjet swung the candle back around. The hunter, with a bloody foot left behind from where he'd bitten through his ankle, leaped. War Pig jerked to the side. The hunter landed on Lush's shoulder and bit deeply. He tore a roll of flesh away, swallowed it, and then dug in again.

Lush's screams rebounded off the walls, echoed, multiplied. Joanjet grabbed the hunter by the jacket and flung him off. The candelabra clattered to the cement. The room went black, except for a tiny flame that sputtered as the candle rolled across the floor. Everything moved in slow yellow strobe, like an eyelid being opened and closed.

Blink.

Cupcake screamed.

Blink.

The hunter got up again.

Blink.

And rushed at Idle.

Blink.

Who landed a spinning kick.

Blink.

The hunter lurched to the side, teeth wide with flesh.

Blink.

Raekwon shoved Pacino deep into his mouth.

Blink.

And pulled the trigger.

Muzzle flash, red aura, singed hair.

You cannot blink long enough.

A bucket of pink and black milk splashed against the far wall.

"Wicked," Idle said.

"Mad bull's-eye," Billy said.

"I guess that thing works after all," War Pig said.

Nero picked up the candle, put Lush's arm around his shoulder, and helped her up the stairs. The rest packed behind him, trying to stay in the envelope of light. He looked back, just able to make out Petal's face in the chair, and mouthed the words *I'm sorry.*

When everyone was at the top of the steps, War Pig kicked the door shut. "It stays down there. Period."

"It?" Estrada said.

"She!" Sad Girl said.

"Chick rubs the lotion on its skin," Idle said. "And then puts it in the basket."

War Pig dragged over an enormous hutch, straining against the ballast, and jammed it at an angle against the knob. "Anyone even thinks about opening this door goes outside. Got it?"

No one answered.

Nero carefully laid Lush on the floor next to the fireplace. She was breathing shallowly, already convulsing.

"No more, no more, no more," Cupcake kept saying. "Please please please *please.*"

"We need, like, antibiotics," Sad Girl said.

"Hold her down," Joanjet said.

"Believe it or not," Idle said, "I've lost girlfriends before."

"Women," Billy said. "They come and they go."

"Mostly go, though, huh?"

"Shoot her," War Pig said.

Raekwon palmed the remaining ammo. "There's only two of these shells left."

Nero leaned over and examined Lush's wound.

It was an ugly tear. Raw. Suppurating.

"Don't touch it, or you go outside with her."

"Wait," Lush said weakly. Her nostrils flared, utterly human. Ripe. Alive. "What if I'm like Petal? What if it doesn't take?"

"It took," War Pig said as a drop of black liquid dribbled from her ear. "Trust me."

"I love . . . you guys. . . ." Lush said, and then groaned, holding her stomach in pain. Sweat poured off her forehead. "I would never . . ."

"What's it going to hurt to wait and see?" Joanjet asked, putting a pillow under Lush's head. "Huh?"

Raekwon shrugged. "Fine. This is your fault. You deal with it."

They circled around, watching as Lush slowly degraded. First, her eyes seemed to lose focus. The light in them failed. The hole around her nose ring festered and began to leak. Her hair lost its luster, skin leached of color. Even her teeth seemed to yellow. An awful smell began emanating from her pores.

"I'm okay . . . I'm okay . . . I'm okay. . . ." she kept saying, quieter and quieter. "Okay . . . okay . . . okay . . ." until her eyes finally closed. "K . . . k . . . k . . ."

"She's peaceful," Sad Girl said. "See?"

"Flesh," Lush whispered, so quietly they could barely hear her.

"What, sweetheart?" Sad Girl asked.

Lush bolted up, froth coming from her mouth. She grabbed Sad Girl's arm and dug her fingers in. Idle hit her on the temple with a piece of firewood while Billy grabbed her shirt and dragged her across the dirt and broken glass. War Pig ran to the second floor and threw open a window. The twins tossed Lush out like a sack of laundry as she groaned and scratched, clawing for them.

Her body slammed into the crowd of Z below. Other Infects in the clearing turned as one, letting out a roar, and rushed toward the new meat.

War Pig slammed the heavy frame shut again and bolted it as Infect hands banged against the timbers in a frantic rhythm.

"You two, always smarter than everyone else," he said, pointing at Nero and Joanjet. "It's not their fault. Let's tie them up. Let's keep them down in the basement like dogs."

Thing is, he's right. Bleeding hearts? Liberals? The collapse of empire is always fueled by good intentions, the rubble presided over by the strict and the cold.

Raekwon blew on her chipped fingernails. "I said all along it was foolishness."

War Pig grabbed the other candle off the mantle. Raekwon, Idle, and Billy followed him back up the creaking steps.

"We should really all stay together," Sad Girl called.

"You stay together," War Pig said.

One of the guest-room doors upstairs slammed.

"Well, that didn't take long," Joanjet said, looking at a watch she wasn't wearing. "You see why I didn't want to show you right away? T minus *Lord of the Flies* in less than an hour."

Cupcake retreated to a dark corner, talking to herself and pulling her hair. Sad Girl began to weep softly as Estrada comforted her.

Nero put his head in his hands, while downstairs Petal Gazes, or what *was* Petal Gazes, sat alone.

In the dark.

In the middle of a room that had been splattered with death.

Again and again and again.

30

Here, Let Me Break It Down

WAR PIG, RAEKWON, IDLE, AND BILLY TOOK the two rooms on the left, numbers 100 and 110. Nero could hear the twins laughing all the way down the hall. There were three rooms on the right: 200, 220, and 237. They picked the first one and all piled in, exhausted, starving, delirious. Lips dry and chapped. Nervous. They stank. Sad Girl went out and gathered snow from the windowsills and carried it back in her cupped palms. As it melted, they took turns lapping at it like dogs.

Nero found a pile of dirty blankets in the closet and handed them around.

"Everyone needs to sleep. We're all going to lose our shit if we don't."

As if on cue, the scratching outside became languorous, adagio. For a few minutes they sat around the candle, listening to each other breathe. No one wanted to talk about Lush. And yet everyone was dying to talk, terrified of closing their eyes and finding out which hunter waited for them in the basement of their imaginations. They all knew they were spending the night down in that butcher's room no matter what. In dream after dream after dream.

> ZOMBRULE #15: *Bedtime is when bad things happen, and dream time is even worse. Drink coffee, pound Red Bulls, snort speed, tell ghost stories, poke each other with sharp sticks, staple open your eyelids, redo that sudoku, teach yourself to cobble, learn Javanese verb conjugations, memorize Deuteronomy, guzzle sixty-two hours' worth of 5-hour ENERGY, and/or stay up till dawn playing strip poker instead. Do. Not. Go. To. Sleep.*

"The first movie? *Night of the Living Dead?* That was good," Estrada finally said, his voice low and without inflection.

No one answered.

Or said anything at all.

For at least five minutes.

The wind howled. The scratching was steady and raw.

Then came another voice, equally low and worn.

"Yeah, old-school. In black-and-white. Totally creepy. My father says it's a metaphor about anti-Communism. Not joining groups. Being an individual."

"*Dawn of the Dead* was better."

"Is that the one that takes place in the mall?"

"Yeah, I remember thinking it was hilarious. Doesn't seem very funny now."

"I know. I can't believe I actually laughed at that. Sitting there, all safe. With Sno-Caps and popcorn."

"It was directed by the same dude. These guys lock down the mall gates and clean up the Z inside. Then they get to shop in every store. Eat all the food, take the clothes, whatever they want."

"And there was a gun store too."

"Bet that came in handy."

"I wish we had a gun store."

"Did they survive?"

"Nah, bikers broke in and ruined everything."

"That's another metaphor. Like, about consumerism. All the Z hang out at Hot Topix and American Apparel because they don't know any better. It's like, even when they were alive, they were still zombies all along."

"Sorta heavy-handed, don't you think? A little preachy? Shopping makes you a moron? Okay, great. Thanks."

"I saw the remake. It had fast zombies."

"Fast zombies?"

"Ran full speed. Not this shambling business. All busting

the ten-second mark and biting your back. I thought that was dumb. Humans didn't stand a chance. Actually, I guess that part was pretty accurate."

"You should have seen *Day of the Dead.* I couldn't eat for a week after."

"Entrails, gristle, entrails. And then, you know, occasionally acting."

"*28 Days Later* was cool."

"Yeah, but it didn't make sense."

"What about Z makes sense?"

"Remember when you could just get up and walk out of a movie when it was over? Into the sunshine?"

Nero's head spun. Thick and feverish. He wasn't listening. But the voices helped him forget.

What he had to do.

As soon as they all fell asleep.

"I used to dig the Resident Evil ones. Milla? She was totally hot."

"Was?"

"Well, Infects must have reached to L.A. by now, right? That means Milla's dead or homegirl really *is* a zombie, shuffling around in thousand-dollar pumps."

"Oh, the irony."

"Nah, I bet she has a huge walled mansion up in the hills. She's probably got a security team and a generator and enough diet smoothies and B12 suppositories to last a lifetime."

It was quiet again.

Joanjet untied her topknot. Purple hair hung limply over her face, like a tarot reader's scarf. Cupcake, who hadn't said anything, lifted her head from Joanjet's thigh and sat up, entering the circle, candlelight reflecting off her glasses.

"It's no secret I'm scared shitless, right?"

No one answered.

"And so I'm lying here asking myself, Okay, fine, but what is it that I'm really scared of? Dying? Not seeing my mother again? Blood? Swann?"

"Bitch," Estrada said.

"All of the above," Sad Girl said.

"I figure it's not so much being bit, you know? It's the being eaten part. The being torn apart part. I don't want to die, but I especially don't want them . . . pawing through me."

Joanjet rubbed Cupcake's back. "I'm with you there."

"Uh-huh," Sad Girl said.

"Me too," Estrada said.

"And then I thought, well, maybe there's another way." Cupcake leaned over conspiratorially. "What if we leave the front door open?"

"Perfect."

"Sheer genius."

"No, listen, we lock ourselves in this room. But first we cut a hole in the door. A small square, the size of a deck of cards. When they come in, we're in control. We decide how it works."

"I still don't get it."

Cupcake smiled. "We stick our hand through the hole one at a time."

She sat back and waited for it to sink in.

"We let them get a quick bite," Estrada finally said. "Just enough."

"Exactly. How bad can that be?"

"Then, after a while, we are them," Joanjet said. "They won't want to get in anymore."

Sad Girl nodded. "I can't believe I'm saying this, but that's actually not that bad an idea."

"We're fuct anyway."

"I mean, it's probably like being bit by a dog," Cupcake said. "It'll hurt, right? But pretty soon the infection kicks in. . . ."

Estrada exhaled, closing his eyes. "Maybe it's like heroin. Spreads through your body, feels nice. Warm."

"No more fighting."

"No more running."

"You're on the team, like getting an Evite."

"All in this room together."

Sad Girl looked at Cupcake gratefully. "God, you're almost a genius."

"That's why I can't let them eat my brain."

Everyone laughed.

Except Nero.

"I can't believe this. Will you listen to yourselves?"

"Whoa, man," Estrada said.

Nero stood up. "So it's not suicide, then, huh? It's just changing addresses?"

"Hey, now —" Sad Girl said.

"No, you 'hey, now.'" Nero let the pure cold anger surge through him, toxins being released, fury like methane rising from the ice pack. "No way I'm just giving up. No way I'm letting myself be bit. What did we fight all this time for? All the way up here?"

"It's a last-ditch thing," Estrada said gently. "Only if we don't have no choice."

"Shhh . . ."

"It's okay, Nero."

"Calm down."

"You calm down," he said, biting his lip and trying not to cry.

"Hunger delirium."

"Posttraumatic shock."

"Totally understandable, really."

Cupcake took Nero by the arm and led him to the corner, where she rubbed his neck and laid him down.

Sad Girl climbed onto the bed, making the springs squeak. The noise sounded like a gunshot in the stillness. Estrada joined her.

Cupcake and Joanjet curled up by the dresser.

Nero rolled over, feeling lost. Wanting to scream.

They did have some success with primal-scream therapy in the seventies. Seems like now's a bad time to start, though.

He wiped his mouth instead.

What was a mouth if not just a bag of teeth?

What were teeth if not made to rend skin?

What was skin but a flimsy pink enclosure people hid behind?

Ten billion of us, Nero thought. Each one just a spill waiting to happen.

"'Night," Sad Girl said, blowing out the candle.

And then it was beyond dark.

31

A Cheap Date

THEY WERE ALREADY SNORING. IT WAS HARD to tell who.

Nero kicked off his shoes.

Don't take off your shoes. You have work to do.

And closed his eyes.

Just for a minute. Only until you're sure they're all asleep.

He rubbed his eyes and wished, more than anything in the world, for a huge glass of milk and some French toast.

> ZOMBRULE #16: *There is no French toast in the Zomb-A-Pocalypse.*

But mostly he wanted a girl lying next to him.

Everyone else in this lodge has one, huh?

If only to be able to get up on one elbow and grin at her, all deadpan, like, "So . . . this has been a pretty weird day, huh?"

Go downstairs. Your zombie shortie is waiting.

"Yeah, she's waiting," Nero whispered. "In that room. In the pitch black. With no way out. And three zombie corpses."

Well, technically it's four.

"Call me paranoid, but the whole deal with her being dead and everything is freaking my shit."

Joanjet snored deeply, spluttered, rolled over.

I did notice you're not really in a hurry to loosen the ropes.

"Truth is, the Rock?"

Yeah?

"I'm scared."

Of what?

"Uh, lessee. Raekwon. And Raekwon's gun. And War Pig. And War Pig's fists. And flesh eating. And the dark. And the sound of those fingernails. And the end of the world. But mostly? I think I'm scared of Petal."

I understand. I get scared a lot myself.

"You do?"

Only every time I climb into the ring.

"But, um . . . wrestling's fake. Zombies are real."

Hey, man, the only thing fake is the take. Now, get down there and rescue your lady.

"In a minute."

You don't have a minute.

"But what if she's turned?"

State's evidence?

"No, what if I go down there and the timer went off and she's not Petal anymore?"

You mean if she still looks like Petal but is a late bloomer and since you last saw her has been incrementally and virally transformed into a human flank-eating machine just waiting for you to naively approach in the dark so she can glom on and do unspeakable things to you while everyone else sleeps?

"Exactly."

Yeah, I can see how that'd be a tough call.

Nero pulled at his stitches. He was surrounded by bad choices and zero options and no hope and creaking wallboards and Infect moans.

Buuh-huuh.

Muuh-huhr.

Errrf-graurg.

The sounds Z made were bad enough alone, but in a group they were especially weird and creepy. They pounded and churned, rhythmic, piston-like. Brainless, greedy, rote. And yet when he really listened, Nero could hear another tone further down, buried gut-deep.

Primal.

Feral.

Dirty.

Buuh-huuh.

Muuh-huhr.

Errrf-graurg.

Was it possible the Infects got busy with each other?

Buuh-huuh.

Muuh-huhr.

Errrf-graurg.

Stuck outside with nothing to chew on, no marrow in sight, just killing time until the End-Time with a little late-night cannibal grope? Infect on Infect love? They were already stripped down to their elemental selves, all drives and needs. If the first purely human (or post-human) impulse was to eat, the second one had to be to screw.

Or maybe to lawyer up and sue.

If nothing else, they didn't have to worry about birth control. No mortifying shamble through the aisles at 7-Eleven working up the courage to ask the clerk for a pack of Trojan ZLs — lubricated, ribbed, and covered in zombicidal foam.

Lord, do you have problems.

Nero pulled the dusty old blanket over his head.

The last of his adrenaline leached away.

Every single muscle and ligament ached.

His breathing slowed, caught in the back of his throat.

Don't fall asleep.

He closed his eyes.

Do. Not. Fall. Asleep.

And fell deeply asleep.

* * *

Nero opened his eyes.

The scratching had gotten louder, more frenzied.

It raked the lodge walls.

It pulsed, in and out.

Buuh-huuh.

Muuh-huhr.

Errrf-graurg.

There was movement.

Above him.

On the ceiling.

A white outline.

Creeping diagonally, from the corner.

Like an insect. A lizard.

But large.

He blinked.

Buuh-huuh.

Muuh-huhr.

Errrf-graurg.

The thing stopped, turned its head 360 degrees, and looked down at Estrada and Sad Girl. A pendulum of spit hung from its mouth, swung, and then lowered onto Sad Girl's leg.

In the shape of an *N*.

And then an *E*.

And then an *R*.

And then an *O*.

Written like maple syrup, darker than her skin.

Burning in.

Nero was about to yell but couldn't.

Scream but couldn't.

Warn them but couldn't.

Sad Girl cried out, tossed and turned, rubbed her leg in her sleep.

The thing moved again, crawling upside down until it was directly over him.

A form, beyond pale.

White neck. Long legs.

All thigh and ass.

Swann.

The moaning sped up.

Double time.

Buuh-huuh. Buuh-huuh.

Muuh-huhr. Muuh-huhr.

Errrf-graurg. Errrf-graurg.

Nero could see her eyes and a glint of teeth in the darkness.

He could see her blond hair, hanging down like stalactites.

He could see her skin, bare, acres of it.

The moans went triple time.

Buuh-huuh. Buuh-huuh. Buuh-huuh.

Muuh-huhr. Muuh-huhr. Muuh-huhr.

Errrf-graurg. Errrf-graurg. Errrf-graurg.

"Nero," she whispered.

"What?"

"Don't move."

"Why?"

Swann let go.

And fell directly on top of him.

Her arms on his arms.

Her legs on his legs.

Buuh-huuh. Buuh-huuh. Buuh-huuh. Buuh-huuh.

Muuh-huhr. Muuh-huhr. Muuh-huhr. Muuh-huhr.

Errrf-graurg. Errrf-graurg. Errrf-graurg. Errrf-graurg.

The others tossed and turned, moving restlessly around them, their sleep shallow and bothered. From deep within a dream, Estrada whispered softly, *"Chula."*

Swann laughed and swept her hair across Nero's chest.

Tickling him.

She let it cover his face, dragged it along his neck.

He pulled back, looking into her eyes.

Her crazy blue eyes.

And then her mouth was on his mouth.

Not biting.

Not tearing.

Not attacking.

Kissing.

Swann pinned Nero's arms and tore off his shirt. Then held each of his wrists flat against the blanket.

She was covered in red, both dried and fresh.

Buuh-huuh.

Which meant that he was covered in red, both fresh and dried.

Muuh-huhr.

She stuck her thumb deep into the gash in his palm.

Errrf-graurg.

And then they were one.

NERO WOKE UP, NOT SURE WHERE HE WAS.
The Infect voices had lapsed into a moaning rumble, followed by the usual scratching.

He sat up on the floor, alone.

His pants were on.

There was no blood.

There was no Swann.

The ceiling was dark, empty.

A surge of embarrassment washed across his chest.

They call that nocturnal remission.

Had the others heard him cry out?

Did they watch him toss and turn?

And even worse, did they know how much he'd enjoyed it?

Nero reached for the candle before remembering that Sad Girl had put it out before they went to sleep.

For those of you who "slept," that is.

He felt his way across the room. The hallway was silent, the darkness almost physical, enveloping, not even a sliver of moonlight through the thick windows.

Nero listened at War Pig and Raekwon's door.

No sound, except for a light snoring. He found the hand-rail and made his way down the steps. The fire was low, mostly embers, emitting an eerie orange glow that barely penetrated the room.

A long way across.

So go, already.

Nero forced himself to walk.

The scratching increased, as if the Infects could sense his movement.

All of them, just a wall away.

Hundreds of rending hands.

A thousand sharp teeth.

What if one had gotten inside?

One is inside.

Nero kept his head down, trying not to step on broken glass. At the three-quarter mark he could almost see the grain of the floorboards.

No way he should be able to see the grain of the floorboards.

Look up.

There was a light on in the dining room.

A light.

On.

In the dining room.

Better go back and get in bed with Sad Girl and Estrada.

Nero tiptoed over and pressed hard against the wall, taking shallow breaths, then forced himself to peer around the edge.

The bar was one long slab of mahogany. Two huge chandeliers hung from the ceiling. They sparkled softly, glittering across the leather stools. Art deco sconces glowed. Rows of liquor bottles refracted amber light, so much that he had to squint.

Behind the bar stood a woman.

Wearing a crisp white dress shirt, black pants, and a leather apron.

She appeared to be waiting for customers.

Don't talk to her. Go see Petal.

Nero walked over, picked a stool, and sat down. In front of him were two small bowls, peanuts and olives.

"What'll it be?"

"Bourbon," he said, because it was the only thing he could think of.

The woman poured. Nero took a sip. The liquor burned, making him even thirstier.

"What's your name, barkeep?"

"Lydia. My husband sometimes calls me Liddy. Or at least he used to."

Nero's head shot up.

His mother grinned, then held out her palms in a sort of jazz-hands pose.

"Ta-da!"

She looked good. New haircut. New nail polish. Happy.

"Mom? What are you doing here?"

"What am I doing here? What are you doing here?"

Nero thought about it, had no good answer, shrugged.

She picked up a martini glass and studied it for dirt. "Have you considered, Nick, the possibility that you're starting to lose your shit?"

"Um . . ."

"You're wearing an orange jumpsuit. Toting around an imperial nickname. Fighting ghouls. Having dirty dreams. And you smell like a compost pile. Sounds to me like someone needs a Ritalin script, pronto."

ZOMBRULE #17: *American teenagers are medicated 40 percent more than teenagers from other industrialized nations. Which means, by extension, that 40 percent of teenager-munching zombies now have vastly lowered serotonin levels, especially after they stumble upon an abandoned bus full of plump sophomore mathletes down by the river. Nevertheless, zombie chalupa, Arizona Iced Tea, and Almond Joy levels remain dangerously elevated.*

"How did you know about my dream?"

"What else do boys dream about?"

Nero looked down at his torn palm, felt the sweat of a fever in his scalp.

And then it all fell into place.

"I'm infected, aren't I?"

His mom shrugged. "Maybe."

"That's why I can see you. The virus is totally eating into my brain."

"Why would it bother? Talk about a light snack."

Nero frowned. "I thought bartenders were supposed to give advice."

His mom leaned over the bar, looking to one side and then the other.

"You know what I'd do if I were you?"

Get divorced. Leave you at the mall with a twenty. That's what she did last time things got tough.

"No. What?"

She pushed an ancient Zippo across the bar with one finger. "Start a big ol' fire."

Nero looked the lighter over. The gold was soft and worn. It had the Rolling Stones' logo on it, huge cartoon lips with a tongue sticking out. Underneath, it said *Altamont '69.*

She nodded. "Warm this place right up. It'd be the perfect encore."

He spun the strike wheel but nothing happened.

"Wait, how is that going to help—?"

"Who are you talking to?" Cupcake asked, standing in the doorway. Nero spun around on the stool.

He was sitting in the dark.

There were no chandeliers. No bartender. No glass, no olives, no bourbon.

"Nobody."

Cupcake stood just at the edge of the glow from the fireplace, hands stuffed into her pockets. She looked exhausted. Like she needed a hug. Or an IV of pureed steak.

"Then why are you sitting there?"

"I couldn't sleep."

"Me neither. I don't ever want to sleep again. But that didn't make me want to hang out at the bar talking to myself."

"No, I just—"

"You're going down there, aren't you? To see Petal."

Nero didn't answer.

"It's okay—I won't tell. She was my friend too."

"Was?"

"I mean, she was nice to me. At camp. When some of the other girls . . . weren't."

Nero got up and felt his way toward the basement door. "Thanks for not saying anything."

"If she's turned, are you still going to untie her?"

"No."

"Maybe you should. Anyway."

"Why?"

Cupcake shivered, hugging herself.

"I dunno. I mean, when it gets to the point that we have to be scared of Petal, there's definitely nothing else left, you know?"

He nodded. "I'm sorry we haven't had a chance to talk until now. I think I've . . . underestimated you."

"Know what I like about you, Nero?"

"No clue."

Me neither.

"I could tell right away, even when we were alone, you weren't going to ask lesbian questions."

"What questions?"

"You know—how does this feel? How does that feel? Is it just a stage I'm going through? The kinds of things boys always ask to make themselves seem open-minded but are actually just pervy and rude."

"Oh."

"It's cool that you have no idea how cool you are."

Cupcake turned and walked back to the stairs. "Goodbye, Nero."

"Hey, don't act like you're never going to see me again."

"We're never going to see any of us again," she said, and then was gone.

33

Den of Iniquity, Ned of Inequity

NERO GROPED HIS WAY ALONG, EXTENDING one hand into the darkness.

Wall.

Wall.

Wall.

Bookcase.

Wall.

Metal ball.

> ZOMBRULE #18: *An unturned doorknob is like a collection of Hungarian folk poems or discount sushi: best left alone.*

As quietly as possible, Nero moved the hutch that War Pig had pinned the door with. Which wasn't very quiet since it was heavy and awkward. He crept down the stairs one at a time until he reached the floor. Except the floor wasn't there. He'd forgotten about the broken bottom step, tripped, and fell flat on his face.

Princess Grace.

He held totally still.

Nothing.

No noise.

No slither. No rasp. No howl.

Nero crawled past where the bodies of the hunters were. At least where he thought they were. With each foot, the smell got worse. It was hot and fetid. Stink blanketed his sinuses, settled in his nose. It bought furniture at IKEA, adopted a puppy, got a job, met other stink, went on a date, and talked about moving in together.

He slid through the wet and dry, the soft and hard. At one point, something tiny skittered around his hands.

Finally, he got to the boiler.

Where there was breathing.

Slow and low. Raspy.

"Petal?"

Chair legs scratched against the floor.

Nero got on all fours, ready to run.

And then a match was struck.

Z can light matches?

"I knew you'd come," she said, wavering into view face serious but calm. Her eyes seemed normal, large, expressive. Her nose was still her nose, small and slightly flared. Her cheeks were still pale and drawn and soft. She smiled, partly obscured by tendrils of white hair, beautiful in the glow of the flame.

And you left her here. By herself. With them. All this time.

"God, I'm so sorry," he said, immediately working at the knots. "I'm such an asshole for not getting you out of here sooner."

"It's okay," she whispered.

"No, it isn't."

"Raekwon had a gun. What were you supposed to do?"

"I don't know. Something besides go upstairs and be afraid."

"You stood up for me."

"I stood in front of you. There's a difference."

Petal lit another match.

"Where did you get those?"

"Lush slipped them to me. While you guys were arguing."

"Why?"

"Because she's my friend."

Nero had forgotten that friends actually existed. That the whole world hadn't turned into teeth and fingernails and betrayal and rot.

And voices in your head.

Hey, now.

"Is Lush okay?" Petal asked.

"No. She's dead."

"*Dead* dead, or . . . ?"

"She's outside. With them."

Petal nodded as Nero freed the final knot.

"Can I ask you a question?"

"No, Jett Ballou and I never hooked up."

"Um . . ."

"What, that's not what you were wondering? Every time we waited for the gates to open at Rebozzo's?"

"It was that obvious, huh?"

"All boys are obvious."

They are?

"Actually, I wanted to know how it feels to —"

"Be a zombie? Like, if it's just a stage I'm going through?"

Nero smiled. "Sorry, I'm just trying to sound open-minded."

Petal reached out and gripped his palm.

His immediate instinct was to yank it away.

Every organ in his body demanded that he yank it away.

Every voice in your head demands that you yank it away.

She could bite. She could drink. She could smell the fresh blood in his palm and be driven insane with hunger.

But he didn't move.

Petal gently kissed his wound and then pressed it against her cheek. She was warm. Not cold. She was soft, flushed.

He could feel a vein pulsing at the base of her jaw, just under her ear.

A cute pulse.

A steady pulse.

"Being Z feels normal," she said. "If I even knew what normal was. Like the flu, I guess. Except there's no pain."

"So, are you like this . . . forever?"

"I don't know."

"But how can you be only partially infected?"

"Maybe I have some kind of resistance. Or whatever bit me had a weak strain. Or we're all already building an immunity. Or I'm just too damaged to even turn Z right."

Nero laughed softly. "If it makes you feel any better, I'm damaged too."

True, you did just get done talking to your mom, who wasn't there. And air-sexing a blond catwalk murderess, who, you know, may or may not have been there.

"You mean the way you're always trying to act so hip and relaxed, leaning against your locker like an indie band drummer?"

"No, because I hear voices in my head."

Petal cleared her throat. "You hear voices?"

"Actually, just one. The Rock."

"The wrestler?"

Um, actor? Um, product spokesman? Also, I write poetry.

"You know him?"

"I guess not as intimately as you do."

"Seriously, Petal? I spent half the night wondering if I was really in an asylum somewhere, high on Sugar Smacks and Thorazine and banging my skull on the rubber floor of a cell."

She pushed his hair behind his ears, shushing him. "Trust me. This is no dream."

"You swear?"

"I swear."

"Because this part especially seems like a fantasy."

"Which part?"

"Us. Finally being this close. All the way up the mountain, I was sure you weren't dead. It was the only thing that made me not quit."

They were quiet for a second.

"Actually, I can hear thoughts too," Petal whispered.

She knows about Jayna Layne! She knows about Swann!

"Whose? Mine?"

"No, silly. Ever since I got bitten. I can hear *them*."

"The Infects? Right outside?"

She nodded. "But it's not really voices. They buzz. All at the same time. Like locusts. They communicate without words."

"Okay, so what are they thinking about?"

"It's hard to explain."

"Then keep it simple. Why are they trying to eat us?"

Petal closed her eyes and concentrated. "Because that's what zombies do in the movies. They're going through the motions. Confused about how else to act. Embarrassed. When everyone's bitten, no one will be left to judge, and then they can all just relax."

"You're shitting me."

Petal lit the final match. "Actually, yeah."

He smiled, absolutely loving how much smarter she was than him.

"What?" she said shyly.

Nero braced her shoulders and pushed the hair out of her face. It was dirty, with a slight gray tint. Her jumpsuit was in tatters. He could see glimpses of bra between the rips. Glimpses of panty. And her name tag.

"How come they never gave you a Trek Handle?"

She frowned. "Exene said I looked too much like a petal to ever call me anything else."

"It's so true," he said, then leaned over and put his mouth against hers. She pulled back at first, but then gave in, holding him tighter. It was the exact moment Nero had been thinking about, creating, replaying in his mind for a year of Rebozzo shifts. All those nights in line, making small talk. Making jokes. Playing it cool. Feeling like a total Nick. Wishing for this.

Their tongues touched, electric.

It was fantastic.

At least until Petal stepped back and kicked him.

"Are you crazy? What did you do that for?"

"To prove something."

"What, how easy it is for you to get infected?"

"No," Nero said. "To prove that I don't think you're infected at all."

"Yeah? Than what am I?"

He took a deep breath.

"I think you're evolving."

ZOMBRULE #19: *Never. Kiss. A. Zombie.*

Petal held his hand.

His throbbing hand.

You sure that's just your hand throbbing?

There was nowhere else to go, and they both knew it.

There was nowhere else to hide, and they both knew it.

He thought of the picture of him she kept in her notebook. He thought of the picture of her he kept in his head.

Nero Sole and Petal Gazes were going to die.

Don't say together! Don't say together!

Together.

ZOMBRULE #20: *Oh, hell, why not? Go ahead and kiss a zombie.*

He reached for her waist.

They kissed again, slowly, in stages.

Eventually she drew back, into the light of the smoldering match end.

There was something in her hand.

Something she'd pulled off of his shoulder.

Four hairs.

Long, blond, catwalk hairs.

"Whose are these?" Petal asked.

And then a shotgun went off upstairs.

Twice.

34

Final Flashback, Jack: I Don't Live for Today

THE DUDE WAS AT THE KITCHEN TABLE, TALK- ing to his checkbook. A trio of uppity checks was insisting there weren't enough of them to cover that month's bills. Pretty soon, he'd start arguing with the pen, an extra-fine point with a snotty attitude. Nick was doing algebra homework. Or at least pretending to. Amanda was lying under the table, reading comics.

It was a year after the Dude had been canned. His prototypes had gone into production with a new name, U Dip Itz, and a full regional marketing campaign. *Self-dipping Bon-E-Less buffalo wings! A delicious and nutritious meal for the whole family in under five easy minutes! Moms love them because they're loaded with calcium! Kids love them because they're loaded with X-treme® flavor!* The secret was that the wings were infused with barbecue sauce before cooking. With the application of heat, the sauce slowly leaked out through trademark micro-perforations. All the early test procedures had come back positive. The wings tasted delicious.

But weeks before the unveiling, there had been a little glitch. When put in certain older convection ovens at too high a heat, the sauce in the U Dip Itz became volatile and failed to leak. Instead, the wings gushed. They swelled and bled. They looked like car wrecks. Like alien chests. Like Chixx stigmata. Children screamed. Fathers called lawyers. Moms in focus groups broke out in tears.

Win Fuld was pissed.

The rollout was canceled.

The stock grant was canceled.

Partner Dude was canceled.

On his last day, the Dude brought home a file cabinet full of notes, a pink slip, a *Hang In There, Baby!* poster, and two dozen cases of prototypes.

Amanda was the only one not buying it.

She had no fear of U Dip Itz.

In fact, she ate every last one down in the garage freezer, gobbling more than a thousand of them over six months.

Two years later, the Dude had a full beard, talked to the Cuisinart, and insisted Nick get a job.

His state check was late again.

Co-pay had rolled over into you-pay.

They needed rent.

Bendover Dude made a call.

On Nick's first day, Win Fuld said, "Another Sole enters our midst, and with excellent timing! We are in dire need of strong young backs!"

Nick wanted to say, "Are you high?"

Instead he said, "Yes, sir."

U Dip Itz got revamped, became Chixx Nuggets. They'd been released to the public that fall and were a huge hit, which spurred a full sponsorship/marketing/merchandising deal with Fresh Bukket, now the tenth-largest fast-food franchise in the country, right behind Hot Doggity Dog, Scallop Scow, and Morty's The Deep & The Fried.

It did not go unnoticed that Chixx Nuggets were the exact same thing as U Dip Itz, but without the perforations.

Who knew you could plagiarize chicken?

Can't Afford a Lawyer Dude gnashed and wept.

Transitioning Off Scotch and Onto Paxil Dude muttered and gesticulated.

Chronically Unemployed Which Is Different from Unemployable Dude didn't come out of his room for a month.

And then even when he finally did, he didn't.

They were all sitting in the kitchen, just another Thursday, when Nick heard the music.

He thought the Dude had turned the TV up.

Except the music was fast, chunky, distorted. It rocked.

And the Dude hadn't moved. The TV was the same, blurry and not making a sound. Nick stuck a finger deep in one ear, dug around, wiped it on his jeans, and flipped the page of his algebra book.

Then another song came on, slow and heavy, a power ballad.

Nick looked behind him. The porch door was closed and locked. He got up. No one was in the living room. Nothing was on.

The music abruptly stopped.

He shrugged, grabbed a spoon, jabbed it into the peanut-butter jar, and twirled it around until there was a small mountain lapping over the edges. He pressed a hole into the center like a volcano, scooped grape Smucker's into it, and made sure to get the right amount of jelly and peanut butter with each bite.

Sudden volume, full blast, an orchestra, a thousand strings, woodwinds, brass.

Nick almost fell over.

He wasn't "hearing" the music.

He was experiencing it.

Direct current.

A hallelujah chorus tore through the reedy soundbox of his head.

It itched a tiny bit as it came, and he could almost "see" the notes, like subtitles floating by in cartoon script.

Nick bent under the table. Amanda was sitting there,

cross-legged, reading a copy of *Burt Hurts Bernie III: The Healing.* Huge '80s headphones, unplugged, sat on her head. There was a tiny smirk on her face, but she didn't look up.

A bass 'n' drums thang started. Boom-chicka-boom.

Amanda nodded in time with the beat.

Nodded. In time. With. The beat.

Nick jerked the headphones from around her neck and put them on.

Silence.

"Ouch? Nick? What are you? Doing?"

He dropped the headphones and closed his eyes and tried to think the music away. He concentrated, bearing down. Sweat ran from his armpits to his belt. He could almost feel a breach forming in the center of his skull.

For a second there was nothing.

Just a tiny little yip.

Sort of like a brain fart.

. . . e . . .

Amanda went back to her comic, turned the page.

And then manic jazz drums percussed around him, cymbals and triplets and snare.

Nick walked to the other side of the table and read the comic over Amanda's shoulder. Burt was in therapy and making progress getting past the effects of Bernie's emotional cruelty. In the background of the drawings, Burt and Bernie had a radio playing. Little cartoon notes blipped out of the speaker.

He heard the notes. Heard the background noise. Heard the static from the radio.

"Amanda?"

She pushed her glasses up her nose.

"Yeah? Nick? What?"

Her eyes were normal, no hint of understanding, of playing a joke.

"Did you hear that?"

Amanda pulled at the hem of her dress impatiently.

"Hear what? Nick?"

The music in his head swirled, Technicolor. It became multi-instrumental, shifted into other tempos, associations, atonal, snatches of pop, a girl from Ipanema. Gregorian, gamelan, alt-rock, alt-country, alt-alt, back in black. His brain flooded. It wasn't just one song or image; it was thousands of them — quotes, ideas, keys, symbols, staffs, time signatures. They filled his cranium, made it ache, eyeballs bulging.

A hot rush of letters rose and fell apart, re-formed, grew again.

And then stopped.

Or at least petered out, remnants of notes dribbling from his ears.

It scared the shit out of him, even as it faded.

A week later, the mind-songs tapered off entirely.

A month later, he couldn't remember if it ever happened or if he'd imagined the whole thing.

Something in Nick had been pressed down, and the coils had warmed up.

But when the spring released, it was gone.

And when he looked under the table again, Amanda was gone too.

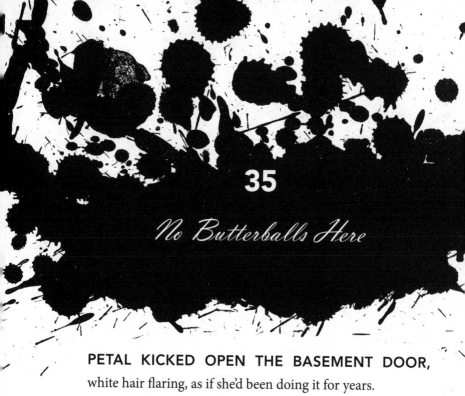

PETAL KICKED OPEN THE BASEMENT DOOR, white hair flaring, as if she'd been doing it for years.

Total badass.

The main room was quiet. They sped across the broken glass and took the stairs two at a time.

Put leather pants and a push-up bra on your woman, she's got a career in straight-to-cable.

"Which one?"

Nero tried the knob to 110 as yelling came from the other side.

It was locked.

Estrada and Sad Girl came out of 227, saw Petal, and kept their distance.

Don't ask, don't tell, don't bite.

"What's going on in there?"

"That musket fired at least once," Nero said.

"Lover's spat?" Sad Girl guessed.

"I hear moaning," Estrada said. "Could be a good thing. Or maybe not."

Nero channeled a huge dose of Killsaw Williams and kicked the door.

Which did nothing but hurt his foot.

"That only works in the movies," Joanjet said, staring at Petal. "How did she get loose?"

"Does it really matter?" Nero asked.

"Not anymore," Estrada said.

There was a long scream from within 110.

Joanjet and Cupcake ran to one of the dressers in the hall-way and tried to push it. Estrada and Nero grabbed either end. It was stuck.

"Move," Petal said, and then gave it a shove.

The dresser slid four feet.

"Whoa," Estrada said.

Petal shoved again. The dresser rammed open the door. In the far wall of the room was a hole just big enough to crawl through, made by a shotgun blast. Infect arms reached in up to the elbow, trying to widen it. Below the hole, pom-pom girls had formed a cheerleader pyramid and were moaning as other Infects climbed their backs.

A ladder. Group approach to problem solving. Intelligence. Not good.

Against the near wall, a naked War Pig wrestled with Counselor Bruce Leroy.

Cold shrinkage + Zombie shrinkage = the kid gets a pass.

Idle and Billy lay on top of each other in the corner where Bruce Leroy had tossed them.

Raekwon was standing on the bed, trying to find a firing angle for Pacino.

"Push him away!" she yelled.

"What do you think I'm doing?" War Pig said. Bruce Leroy's mouth opened and closed like a guillotine, snapping at soft neck, frenzied by the closeness of it. His eyes were blanks, chunks of his arms and chest and face missing, hair soaked and matted.

War Pig swiveled his hips and kneed Bruce Leroy in the balls. No effect. Nero picked up a desk chair and swung it, hitting Bruce Leroy in the face. No effect. Raekwon fired the musket, which punched a hole like a submarine portal in Bruce Leroy's chest. A little girl's hand poked through, groped around, grabbed a hunk of fatty tissue, and then poked back out.

"Shoot him again!"

"That was my last shell!"

Petal grabbed Bruce Leroy's belt, lifted him over her head, and rammed him back through the hole. His body was yanked free and tossed to the ground by other Infects trying to pull themselves in. Some of the arms wore nice watches. Some bracelets. Some Silly Bandz. Some LIVE STRONGS.

Some handcuffs. Some corsages. Some had razor scars. Some just had wiry hair.

The boys beat them back with legs from the broken chair, cracking bone, tearing skin, until they finally fell away.

War Pig turned and looked at Petal. "What is she doing here?"

"Saving your ignorant ass," Nero said.

Raekwon stepped off the bed, put her face against War Pig's chest, and covered him with a blanket.

The room was quiet.

"Why did they just go away?" Cupcake asked.

"That's what they do," Idle said. "Run. Like bitches."

"They scared," Billy said. "That's all."

Swann leaned in through the hole, up to her torso, and screamed, a high-pitched noise that forced them all to cover their ears in pain. She grabbed Idle, bit a ham-size chunk out of his arm, and dragged him back through.

"Patterson! Help!"

Patterson?

Billy grabbed his brother's ankles, barely able to hang on. The Infects swarmed up the cheerleader pyramid and began to chew ravenously, digging into Idle's face and neck and shoulders like an ear of corn. His screams were so manic and shrill they sounded fake.

ZOMBRULE #21: *When a zombie is about to bite, don't scream and wave your hands in the air,*

exposing your vital parts. Do something smart, like
jamming a jar of pickles or a rolled-up newspaper
in its mouth.

Idle's body was jerked completely through. A blood mist hung suspended in the air. The momentum pulled Billy to the edge of the hole. He struggled as a dozen hands grabbed on. Exene, standing on the shoulders of another Infect, took a bite out of the crown of his head, like topping a coconut. Blood pulsed from the opening onto the Infects below, who raised their arms and luxuriated as if taking a hot shower. War Pig tried to grab Billy's leg, but it was too late. Petal and Nero watched him disappear into the swirl of fists and mouths, then be carried away on outstretched hands like a trophy, the bloody mosh pit taking bites as they went.

The cheerleader pyramid collapsed as hungry pom-pom girls gave up their support positions and tried to get a few mouthfuls of their own. Dozens of Infects fell hard into a squirming mass. Nero could swear they were laughing.

Cupcake rocked back and forth, holding her knees to her chest. "I can't do this," she whispered. "Anymore."

"It's okay," Joanjet said, leaning over to comfort her.

Cupcake threw off Joanjet's arm, then got up, ran past Nero, and dove through the hole. She landed face-first in a sea of roiling Infects. They enveloped her. It sounded like a log stuck in the guts of a lawn mower.

"What the hell did she do that for?" War Pig asked,

shaking. His eyes blinked uncontrollably. Nero hustled everyone out of the room. Petal slammed the door and pushed a sofa against it, wedging it tightly against the far wall. It held for a minute, before hands began to reach through the crack and grab at the air.

Joanjet leaned against a tapestry, head in her hands, sobbing. Petal rubbed her back. At first Joanjet let her, but then she looked up, pulled away, and ran down the hall. The door to one of the other rooms slammed.

"Should we go after her?" Sad Girl asked.

"Why?"

There was no argument, no answer. They were all exhausted, spent, starving, numb.

"I guess this is it," Estrada said. "Shouldn't someone say something?"

"Like what?"

"I dunno. Something important. Like about society."

"Society blows."

"Or religion."

"If there was a God, there would be no zombies."

"Unless it's a zombie god."

"Yeah," War Pig said. "Maybe this is all supposed to happen."

"What a bunch of shit," Nero said.

"This isn't supposed to happen," Petal said, looking out the window. "And we're not supposed to give up."

Below, Cupcake was happily spinning around the clearing.

"What's she doing?"

"She's dancing."

It was true. Eyes wild. Flesh in her mouth.

Covered in blood.

Torn to shreds.

Dancing.

"That's bullshit," Raekwon said.

The sofa fell away from the wall. Half an Infect came through, stuck, writhing and moaning.

"We have to go outside," Petal said, starting down the stairs.

"Screw that," War Pig said.

"No, seriously. It's the only way."

"Like we're gonna listen to you?"

"I'm listening," Sad Girl said, taking the steps two at a time.

"Me too," said Estrada, running after her.

More arms reached through the crack and shoved their way into the hall, several middle-aged women in bloody sweat suits, half a lacrosse team. A man in doctor's scrubs and two policemen with chunks of flesh in their teeth. One had a disembodied hand in his leather holster where his gun used to be.

War Pig turned, ready to fight.

Raekwon stepped in front of him.

"Don't."

"Why the hell not?"

Raekwon held up her forearm.

There was a bite in the center of it, blood already black and half-coagulated.

"Oh, no," War Pig said. "Oh, babe."

Raekwon nodded slowly, her breath already ragged. "I swear, I didn't even feel it."

More Infects surged through the gap, knocking each other over, struggling to stand, roaring with hunger.

"C'mon!" Nero said. "Now!"

The first Infect made it to the end of the hall. It grabbed War Pig by the neck. He tossed it through the window and punched the next one in the face. With his other arm he picked Raekwon up like he was going to carry her over the threshold. The blanket fell away.

"Go," he said.

Nero walked down a few more steps. The top of the stairs was now lined with Infects. Raekwon was starting to scream in pain.

"Stay with me," War Pig said as she nibbled at his shoulders like a baby. He didn't stop her. He even shifted her weight to make her more comfortable. And then bulled down the hallway like a fullback, heading toward 237. Infects began to bite him along his sides and thighs.

A few seconds later, Nero heard the other door slam.

Then he turned and ran after Petal.

36

Everything Falls Apart— Limb by Limb by Limb

IN THE BACK PANTRY WAS A HEAVY STEEL service door, welded shut. On top of the ancient icebox was a butter knife, eight screws, and a louvered exhaust duct. Freezing air poured through the hole in the wall. Nero climbed up and stuck his head through the metal housing. Petal, Sad Girl, and Estrada were sitting on the little A-frame roof that formed an alcove above the back steps. Below them, oblivious, were hundreds of Infects, pressed against the exterior of the lodge, pushing and shoving like travelers around a luggage carousel.

"About time," Petal whispered.

"Warrior Pig?" Estrada asked. "No?"

Nero scooped up handfuls of snow and shoved them in his mouth. "No."

The rear of the lodge was a mess. Garbage cans sat empty next to piles of metal and discarded tools. The clearing itself extended all the way to the edge of the cliff. In the distance, random Infects were stumbling around, moaning as if talking to themselves. There were a few football players, a chef, and a man in an expensive suit with the kind of glasses people who aren't architects but want other people to think they're architects wear. He had a chunk the size of a plum bitten out of his temple. You could almost make out the compressed gray maze of brain tucked away like a gift. Otherwise, he could have been waiting for a taxi.

"We're all going to jump at the same time," Petal whispered as the Infects began to moan and sniff the air like dogs. "After that, stay together, and don't look up. Okay? Look only at me."

"But we can't just run for it," Sad Girl said. "We'll never make the edge of the clearing, let alone the path. And even if we do —"

Petal turned and hugged Sad Girl roughly, then rubbed her arms. She slid her lips across Sad Girl's neck, ran her hands up and down her legs.

Whoa. The Rock likey. The Rock likey mucho.

"What are you doing?"

Petal leaned over and did the same thing to Estrada.

"Hey!"

She slid over to Nero and licked him next. His scalp and chin. She ran her wrists up and down his sides and legs, ran her tongue along his arms, kissed his palm, kissed his lips deeply.

"What's going on?" he asked, breathless.

"You don't stink enough. Yet."

"Huh?"

The kitchen behind them was now full of Infects moaning and trying to climb up the icebox. Arms poked through the vent, scratching and gripping the exterior wall.

"Go," Petal said.

Sad Girl and Estrada held hands and jumped, rolling in the snow. Estrada quickly found a rusty hammer. Sad Girl picked up a length of pipe.

Nero took a deep breath, looking down at all the mouths. At all the bloody teeth.

"Trust me," Petal said.

ZOMBRULE #22: *Things to Trust: Your gun. A dead bolt. A wrench. A strong piece of rope. The flammability of a can of diesel. The edibility of a can of tuna. Brass knuckles. A survival knife. Things Not to Trust: Everything and everyone else.*

"I can't."

"Why not?"

"I'm scared."

Petal grabbed Nero with two hands and tossed him off

the roof. He landed with a thud. She followed a second later as the Infects against the lodge began to turn around. Some shuffled; some hobbled on one leg. Others crawled.

All of them roaring with hunger.

"I can't believe you threw me off," Nero whispered, getting up.

"I can't believe I had to, Nick."

Me neither.

"Nick?" Estrada said, raising an eyebrow.

"No clue who she's talking to," Nero said.

"Walk," Petal said as Infects came from all directions. She turned and aimed for the cliff edge. "Calmly. Don't make eye contact."

They moved together, making as small a target as possible, flanked on both sides by slaver and teeth, rotted hands reaching out, swiping the air like groupies trying to get an autograph.

"Why aren't they closing in?" Estrada whispered.

"They're confused by me," Petal whispered back. "My smell. And the smell I put on you."

Wait, she wasn't licking you just for the hell of it?

Infects began to mob them, cutting off the path. Estrada gripped his hammer. Sad Girl held the pipe up, ready to bring it down on the closest forehead.

"Drop those weapons," Petal hissed.

"What? Why?"

"Do it."

The hammer clanged to the ground. The pipe followed, rolling past a pair of sneakers that Nero recognized.

He shut his eyes and kept moving.

Do not look.

Absolutely. Do. Not. Look. Up.

Nero looked up.

And found himself staring into Yeltsin's face.

Yeltsin foamed and spit, 160 pounds of stubble and teeth and the desire for flesh. The right side of his jaw was visible through the skin, two rows of yellowed teeth broken off at the roots, jagged peaks ripping through blood-caked gums.

There was nothing in his eyes.

No recognition.

"Is anything human in there?" Nero whispered. "Yeltsin? Nod if you can hear me."

Yeltsin did not nod. He stepped closer.

"You don't have to bite. You don't have to follow a script. You're not a *zombie*, Yeltsin. You're human. Fight it."

Yeltsin did not appear to be fighting it.

He seemed even hungrier.

The other Infects sniffed and drooled behind him.

"We're not going to make the ledge," Sad Girl whined.

Honestly? You guys are screwed.

Two feet.

It's been fun kicking around in your head, dude.

A foot.

I'm gonna miss this shit.

Six inches.

"Will they eat you?" Nero asked Petal, holding her hand. "I mean, *can* they?"

"I don't know," she said.

Yeltsin ran his destroyed hand up and down Nero's arm. His fingers were gone, a smear of syrupy red fat left behind.

His mouth opened wider, jaw almost locked.

About to bite.

"Wake up, Yeltsin," Nero whispered. "There's still you inside you. I know you can hear —"

There was a ripple through the crowd, a heavy stink that rose and descended at the same time.

Flowers. Manure. Estrus. Beef.

Dirt. Coffee. Rut. Marrow.

Swann.

She reached out, grabbed Yeltsin by the neck, and tore off his head.

The body fell limply to the ground, where the Infects dove and hissed and cursed, fighting over it.

Swann casually put her bloody hand on Nero and stroked his hair.

Like a pet.

Sad Girl moaned. A dark spot ran down the inseam of Estrada's pants and immediately froze.

Maybe it was time to stop fighting, Nero thought. Let

Swann feed, give himself to the horde, give the others a chance to escape.

ZOMBRULE #23: *Self-sacrifice is for chaste vampires, widowed uncles, and grizzled detectives with only one week left until retirement. A wise man sacrifices someone else instead, scoops up their food and water, and runs.*

Petal stepped forward and hissed, long and low. Swann hissed violently in response, her shoulder blades arched, as if she were about to spread wings and take flight.

They got in each other's grills, although Swann was almost a foot taller.

Cat fight! Cat fight! Oh, yeah!

The other Infects went crazy, cooing with hunger and lust. They jabbered and spit, circling in frustration.

Petal closed her eyes and extended her arms by her sides, like a preacher. Who was about to deliver a sermon. On the Infects Mount. Part the flesh sea and demand that Pharaoh let her uncorrupted people go.

Swann wrapped her long fingers around Petal's neck. The pack surged forward, pawing at Estrada and Sad Girl.

But instead of fighting back, Petal began to hum.

An insect noise, deep in her throat.

A clicking.

The sound of mantis wings.

Bow and rosin.

Gut and tension.

Hairy legs being rubbed together.

As it rose in volume, Infects in the back of the pack joined in. All across the clearing, they began to kneel and lend their voices. Petal's soprano whine rose high above the chorus, darting in and out, playing with the tone, using the noise as backbeat, as support. The sound got louder, picking up intensity, falsetto highs and deep lows. It was like listening to a needle on a seismograph.

Like gospel music on Mars.

Even Swann let go of Petal, closed her eyes, and joined in.

The hum picked up depth, vibrato clicks and breathy gasps, the crowd lending a deep bass, spreading through the frozen ground. It got louder, fuller, became a swelling chorus. Bus drivers, Indians, firemen, hunters, counselors, construction workers, and pom-pom girls raised their arms and gave in to the rhythm.

The chorus swelled, a group expression of either pleasure or dissatisfaction, either want or despair. It reached a clucking, buzzing intensity and then broke at the high-water mark, falling away and reverberating toward the cliff's edge.

Infects stopped humming and opened their eyes.

One by one, they began to stand and growl again.

"Keep going," Estrada said.

Petal put her hands on her knees and gulped in air. "I can't. They're not listening anymore, anyway."

Your turn to do something, hero!

Nero looked over to where Estrada had dropped the hammer.

Fighting was pointless.

And then at the cliff's edge.

Running was pointless.

He reached into his pocket and felt something rectangular. Something solid.

The Zippo.

The one his mother had given him in a bar that wasn't real, during a conversation that never happened.

But it sure felt real.

Solid, cold, rectangular.

Rolling Stones, Altamont '69.

Maybe it had just been sitting on the bar, rusting away, left behind by some long-forgotten hunter.

Who cares? Stop overanalyzing and get to it!

Nero popped the top and thumbed the strike wheel.

The flint sparked, lighting on the first try.

Always pay extra for a name brand.

A tall flame, blue and orange, rose two inches, burning purely.

He held it up, like at a concert.

As if a hundred other lighters were all around him, waving in unison as the crowd chanted, begging for an encore.

The Infects looked up too, caught in some dim memory.

A momentary distraction from the need to gorge and purge and gorge again.

The lighter began to burn Nero's fingers, the metal housing glowing orange.

"Run," he said, gritting his teeth. Sad Girl and Estrada did, weaving through the flame-addled Z toward the cliff edge. Petal put her arms around Nero's neck.

"Go!"

"I'm not going anywhere."

The smell of burnt skin filled the air, excruciating as it cauterized the gash in his palm. It was beyond hurt. It was beyond pain. It was pure Zen.

Five seconds more. Give them a chance.

Four.

Three.

Two.

One.

Nero cursed, gripped his wrist, and dropped the lighter. Melted fat from his palm spilled into the snow with a hiss, oily steam rising.

The Infects roared and grabbed them.

"Bye," Petal said.

"Bye," Nero said, pressing his lips against hers.

All around them mouths opened, teeth clicked, jaws distended.

And then one by one, they began to fall.

Gunshots recoiled across the clearing.

Three Z dropped. Six. Nine. Rows fell over like they'd been shoved by an invisible hand.

Or a bullet to the brain stem.

Between collapsing Infects, Nero could see Sno-Cats pull up at the edge of the trail, soldiers in white camo pouring out of bay doors. Sad Girl and Estrada were on their stomachs, hands over their heads, being cuffed. There were roars, screams, the unmistakable sounds of hand-to-hand combat. The soldiers wore face masks and held machine guns that seemed to fire darts instead of bullets.

They set up a skirmish line, some on one knee while others stood behind, shooting with precision.

Almost as if they were trained for it.

An officer in full military garb, and with no protective gear, swung a riding crop while yelling and giving orders. Soldiers began tagging and bagging downed Infects, securing their arms with steel cuffs, slipping leather harnesses with red gag balls over their heads and into their mouths, clamping padlocks into the loops. Others dragged the captured Infects back to the Sno-Cats for loading.

A few Infects managed to rush through the line and pull away soldiers, who screamed as they were feasted on. Other soldiers, wearing all red, responded quickly, firing real bullets. Infect heads exploded. Another wave of men in black attended to the bitten soldiers, jabbing hypodermics into their necks and fitting them with head harnesses.

Men in white coats picked through the bodies. A cleanup

crew sprayed something from a huge hose. Doctors wearing biohazard suits took samples. Search dogs howled in volleys.

And then a team of firefighters set fire to the lodge.

Swann turned and charged. The remaining Infects followed. There was a crack of rifle reports.

Swann took the first dart.

And kept coming.

She took six darts.

And kept coming.

She took nine darts.

And kept coming.

The tenth planted itself deep into her forehead.

And she finally collapsed.

Nero and Petal put their hands up as soldiers reached them. One, a major, stepped forward. Nero could see through her protective shielding. It was a woman.

"That was smart. Signaling with the lighter," she said.

He looked down at the raw rectangular brand, the outline of lips and a tongue seared into the center of his palm, and nodded.

The woman raised her rifle.

"We're not Infects," Petal said. "We're survivors."

"We know what you are," the woman said, sighting Nero with a red laser. It focused on his heart.

"All right, so we're convicts. What are you going to do? Shoot us?"

"Yes," she said.

And then fired.

Tuesday, October 3

7:00 a.m.	Wake-up bell, meds distribution
7:15	Coffee and crumb cake in Terranaut Lounge
7:45	Blood draw, ankle tap
8:00	Full breakfast in caf, morning affirmations with Counselor Cobbler
9:00	Hatha yoga in meditation room, figure drawing in studio, Lift 'n' Spin in gymnasium with Counselor Yates
11–11:45	Choice time
noon	Full lunch in caf, afternoon affirmations with Counselor Tse
1:00 p.m.	Blood draw, tox screen
1:45–3:00	Plastic surgery open house, volleyball
3:30	Community Voice meeting, ceramics workshop
5:00	Full dinner in caf, evening affirmations with Counselor Ricketts
7:15	Blood draw, atrial tap
7:45	Tonight's movie: *Oh, No, You Didn't!*, starring Charlie Murphy, Carrot Top, and Juliette Lewis
9:45	Juice and cookies in Recovery Room
10:15 p.m.	Lights-out

The End Is Just the Beginning

THE FACILITY WAS LARGE AND IMMACULATELY clean. Every room was full, all three wings, teeming with kids and adults in orange or pink hospital gowns and slippers.

Nu-Clients.

Children were kept in one section, teens in another. Adults stayed in a group living unit.

The walls were gray and solid. There were long rectangular windows made of thick glass, close to the ceiling. All doors required a key card, which the counselors kept at the end of chains attached to their belts.

Nero sat on a comfortable white chair in an open rec room. Boblegum and Kim Fowley were talking quietly on the couch across from him. Bruce Leroy and Tripper were calmly playing cards by the faux fireplace. Tripper's fourth round of tattoo removal had just finished, his skin pink and glossy and raw. The two children from the porta potty were jumping rope in the hallway. Lush and Exene gossiped on the floor over diet colas. Almost everyone was disfigured in some way. Mostly from bites. But also from skin tearing, deep fingernail gouges, flesh gobbling, organ rending, and other invasions. Some injuries were too gruesome, too far gone to repair despite the fact that the plastic surgery clinic ran twenty-four hours a day and skin grafts were as common as wiped noses. Almost everyone was in some stage of repair, from full reconstruction to minor spackling, like houses slapped together by a drunken carpenter.

Or chiseled apart by a genius sculptor.

Not all the Nu-Clients were capable of interacting. Some sat in corners, staring off into the middle distance. Others spoke only to themselves. A few had gone mute entirely. Mr. Bator refused to wear his prosthetic. Velma, seemingly unaware of her surroundings, drooled on herself in the corner. And not all of them had made it. Heavy D died of grievous injuries, Swann having eaten most of his vitals. Jack Oh was found with a steak knife in his orbital bone. Yeltsin's head was never found. A larger group had been shot by soldiers.

But those who had been rescued were eligible for Nu-Client housing and reeducation after being given an antidote.

Made from Petal's blood.

It killed what the counselors called "the avian plague."

More than killed it.

Her blood tracked down infected cells and took them apart, prying out junk DNA like delicate marrow from a spicy Szechuan sauce.

And then ate it.

It took a while for the balance of infection to turn, over an aggressive course of injections, but when it did, humanity tended to reassert itself. After weeks of sedation and round-the-clock transfusions, most Nu-Clients were lucid, if still badly scarred from their experiences.

Or as the sign said, *We are all Terranauts in Transition.*

For some, memory was mostly a random haze, but for others it was harrowingly clear.

Grisly images. Dark thoughts in strobe. Bottomless guilt. PTSD.

They all found their own way to cope.

To heal.

To begin to heal.

They saw psychoanalysts, listened to classical music, did primal-scream therapy, learned to meditate. Every night, there was a Getting Over Cannibalism group and a Violence Was roundtable. Nu-Clients in general seemed both relieved and ashamed by the idea that their having "gone Z" was simply a matter of infection and not the result of a dirty bomb or biblical injunction.

A disease like any other.

Diabetes or alcoholism.

From which one could be cured.

Even absolved from intent.

At the Friday-night "Go Tell It on the Mountain" Community Meeting, Nu-Clients got up and apologized tearfully to those they'd hurt, to those they'd bitten, to those whose flesh they'd eaten.

They confessed.

And began to analyze their guilt.

Lush (Annie Hsu) often spoke. So did Cupcake (Pam Nardo) and Tripper (Darby C. Rash). But Bruce Leroy (Marcellus Lee) was the most frequent speaker, endlessly taking the podium, racked with sobs, reliving his wrongs. He tore metaphorically at his brutalized chest, questioned his humanity, his essential goodness, until he was surrounded and given group hugs in front of the plaques memorializing Counselor Jack Oh (Jackson Ort) and Heavy D (Sammy Swester).

Later, in hallways and corners, Nu-Clients discussed their dreams.

What it meant to be an Infect.

Whether the word *zombie* in itself was offensive.

How desperately they missed being part of a hive mind.

And then there were the theories.

Mostly of the conspiracy variety.

Corporate malfeasance.

Government experiments.

Military industrial.

Fluoride in the water.

Dick Cheney.

General stupidity.

And whether it was wrong to admit they sometimes wished they could have part of Z back.

An identity. A purpose. A community.

Being Z at least meant being something.

Unreservedly.

Without fear or analysis.

ZOMBRULE #24: *You have to have a brain to understand consequences. And you have to have a personality to believe in them. In either case, undead or in bed, rules are stupid. Break them.*

Nero tried hard to assimilate with the rehabbers. He followed instructions, kept up appearances, gave out hugs or advice when needed.

While Petal was locked in the IT basement.

To stay sharp, he palmed his sedatives and coagulants and cell boosters and gave them to Mr. Bator, who gobbled them like cashews and then lay on the front carpet, watching TV in a fetal clench.

While Petal sat in a cage.

Just like she'd been doing in the lodge.

While people above her healed.

While people above her confessed and repented.

Nero was not going to let it happen this time.

Not again.

Petal wasn't staying down there.

Even one second longer than she had to.

Nero was never going back to Nick. And he didn't think any-one else should revert either, although most of the others reclaimed their real names.

Sad Girl (Candy Hayes) worked as an orderly, handing out medication and cigarettes and magazines, her finger-nails painted black, wearing rings and jewelry and tight green dresses. War Pig (Reggie Cole) spent most of his time in the smoking room, lighting a new Camel no-filter before his last one was even done, biting his thumbnails, and looking around nervously. He refused to speak to Raekwon (Trishelle Huggins). She couldn't understand why, often crying and ask-ing others to intervene, but War Pig would get up without a word and walk out of any room she entered.

Then there was Idle (Patterson Nordstrom Jr.) and Billy (Stanton Auchischloss), who weren't actually brothers — let alone related at all. They were heavily sedated and kept under lockdown in a special wing, too far gone even for the therapists to deal with. They screamed and clawed at their ankle braces, yelled for their mommies in voices that echoed throughout the halls, pulling hair out in twisted chunks. Both of them were gaunt and pale, tans long gone, braces yanked out by the root in bloody protest. They looked like a pair of darkling ferrets, covered in scratches, covered in feces, now almost entirely bald.

Nero remained calm, went to all the meetings, ate the Jell-O, offered up his thoughts and feelings. At least the ones he thought the counselors wanted to hear. But filling a bite wound with silicone or lasering a scar changed nothing. He didn't mention Joanjet, although she wasn't in the facility and didn't have a plaque on the wall. He didn't ask questions, demand answers, or insist on being let out, as some others had — others who were escorted soon afterward to the Heavy Sedation Wing, a place no one had actually seen, and from which nobody had yet returned.

Nero had been the model patient.

But he wasn't a model, and he wasn't a patient.

You still need to be patient though, he told himself.

Just like the Rock would have.

Except the Rock was gone.

Nero had woken up the first morning in the facility feeling dull and slow, an IV of antidote and sedatives in his arm, and it was like his attic had been cleaned. Disinfected. Emptied by a moving crew. All dusty floors and bare joists and cloister-quiet.

The Rock had simply split.

And Nero hated to admit it, but he sort of missed him (it?).

Especially during the long hours after lights-out.

Rhinoplasty Home Kit

LIKE EVERY OTHER DAY SINCE HE'D AWOKEN in the facility, Nero skipped nuCalisthenics and took a walk around the hallways instead. As head trustee, he was the only one allowed to do so.

In the interior, there were no counselors.

There were heavily armed soldiers in black Kevlar.

A number of them watching the surgical recovery bay.

Where there was only one person still recovering.

Swann.

She lay in a coma on a stainless-steel pallet. Hooked up to dozens of tubes and monitors. Nero stood outside the mesh-lined window, watching her breathe. Without the crazy hair and dried blood, she looked almost normal again.

Almost beautiful.

He wondered what she was thinking about beneath those closed lids. What she might be dreaming of.

If she remembered.

The night she came to him in the lodge.

Or maybe it was he who had come to her.

Right before they came together.

Nero stared at his badly scarred hand, a thick and ugly rectangle of dead tissue crossed by enormous stitches, like a flag struck by lightning, the faint image of the Stones' cartoon lips burned beneath.

Mick's tongue had finally closed the wound.

After Swann's tongue had opened it.

In any case, she was as (un)popular as ever, the subject of most Nu-Client discussions and meetings and therapy sessions.

And dreams.

They called her the Blondmare.

They called her the Bride of Chunkenstein.

They called her Pure Fucking Evil.

No one wanted Swann to wake up.

In fact, if she weren't behind wire-reinforced glass, one of them probably would have made sure she didn't.

Soon a guard would come and escort Nero into the rear of the facility, past labs and locked offices and a heavily rein-forced flight of stairs.

To see Petal.

They were allowed to spend an hour together every day.

She was housed in the sublevel, in a tiny concrete room, behind a thick glass viewing window. She had a bed and a side table, some books and magazines, a small treadmill in the corner, and a steel toilet that extended from the wall. She wore thin, gauzy nightgowns, with her hair up in barrettes. Her bare arms were bruised and pocked and raw from where they drew blood through a metal collection slot. They'd installed permanent insertion points around her neck, over the main arteries, which remained red and wet like a necklace of tiny roses.

It made Nero so angry, he wanted to fly into a rage.

Every time.

Rush the guard. Crack skulls.

But that would be stupid. He wouldn't make it ten feet.

And then they'd both be locked up.

A pulse monitor went off in Swann's room. She didn't seem to move, but a light pinged and blipped, finally tripping an electronic alarm.

No one came.

No doctors were summoned over loudspeakers.

There were no calls for anything *stat*.

As Nero leaned closer to the glass, wondering if he should do something, an enormous guard grabbed his shoulder and pulled him away.

"Is it time already?"

"Yeah, but not for your little girlfriend."

"Then what are you pawing me for?"

The guard smiled. His breath was terrible, like raw meat.

"The Man wants to see you."

Sanctum Sanctorum

THEY WALKED PAST MOTHBALLED HOLDING
tanks and surgery bays, down a long hallway and through a
series of thick steel security gates that ended in a vestibule
lined with leather and gold trim.

The guard knocked twice on a dark mahogany door.

"Enter," said a voice.

The guard motioned with his metal baton, and Nero
stepped in.

The room was hot and steamy. Dark. In the rear was a
cone of yellow light.

In the center of that light sat Win Fuld.

In a leather chair.

His feet up on a heavy oak desk.

"Nicky boy!"

Win Fuld grinned his lipless grin, now completely white, eyebrows gone, his forehead one long sheet of pale, veiny skin. An oxygen tank rested behind his leg. He centered the mask and breathed from it deeply, then spoke through the rubber cone.

"How's my favorite Nu-Client?"

Nero said nothing.

"Slow on the uptake? Must be the sedatives. They have a fogging effect. But hey, sometimes a little fog feels *good*, huh?"

The oxygen tank hissed.

A heart monitor pounded.

Win Fuld rose unsteadily and motioned Nero over. "I imagine you'll want to see this."

On the far wall of the office were framed pictures, front pages of the *San Francisco Daily Beacon.*

The first headline read "GI's Chow Super-Chicken on Way to Guadalcanal!"

"We started experimenting in 1941. Rebozzo's was given a large government grant to increase poultry production for the war effort."

The next paper said "Worker Riot at Rebozzo Plant, Federal Agents Kill 36 'Bezerkers.'"

"Some of the early trials didn't go so well."

The next said "Atrocities Alleged in Vietnamese Hamlet. 'Gruesome' Site Razed in Air Strike."

"An unfortunate necessity."

The next said "Entire Religious Cult in Waco, Texas, Dies

in 'Accidental' Conflagration. Branch Davidians Involved in Bizarre Rites."

"Still not clear on that one."

The final headline, from 1999, said "Ecstasy-Fueled Rave Goes Horribly Wrong; Dozens Bitten and Trampled in Bloody Nightclub Panic."

"Kids and their dope, huh?"

At the end of the row was a framed pamphlet, hand-printed like a religious tract or conspiracy fanzine, with huge fonts and excessive exclamation points. It was riddled with typos. The masthead said "Corporate Meat Is Corporate Murder." Underneath that was the anacronym CORMICOM. Beneath were articles with titles like: "Rebozzo Aviraculture's Secret Labs. Govornment Invulved in Genetic Experimenta-tion on Poultry!" "Food Chain Unsafe! Fast-Frood Franchises Found to be Responsible for Mysterious Illness Outbreaks!" "Deadly Chicken Virus Alleged to Have Escaped From Lab!" "Q: What's Worse Than Mad Cow Disease? A: Even Angrier Nuggets."

Win Fuld chuckled. A patch of skin curled down over his eyebrow like a strip of old wallpaper. He fished a safety pin from a bowl on his desk and tacked the flesh back in place. Nero noticed another pin just above the line of his collar. And one on the back of his wrist. "In a speech ten years ago, our dipshit president actually labeled CORMICOM a terrorist group. Terror? Mostly they break into farms and free cows from their pens in the middle of the night. Then, of course, the animals starve to death or get hit by cars. Another victory for the people."

Nero recognized the pamphlet. He'd seen protesters outside Rebozzo's gates trying to hand them to workers, yelling things like "Murderers!" and "Solidarity!" He'd never paid them much attention.

Fuld went on: "You're a hero to them, you know. After your . . . liberation of the Rebozzo Fryers? You were very briefly the Che Guevara of chicken."

"The who?"

Win Fuld laughed. "My point precisely."

Nero looked at the newspapers again. "You're telling me there's been zombies since, like, before Hitler?"

Win Fuld wheeled his oxygen tank back to the desk.

"The walking dead? Rising from the grave, that sort of thing? Ridiculous. No, we are just a people of insatiable appetites. A hungry mob is an angry mob. Sometimes that hunger metastasizes. You can call it a plague, you can call it the End-Time, or you can call it Tuesday. Mostly it's just lazy R & D."

An egg timer went off. Win Fuld's gums began to bleed. He slid a leather case from his top drawer. Inside was a hypodermic needle. He carefully filled it with a black liquid and then plunged it into his arm.

Blood into blood.

Blood into Fuld.

Petal's blood into Fuld.

Nero wanted to vomit.

Instead he watched, mesmerized.

Win Fuld's eyes closed.

His entire body shivered.

He growled for a second, drooled, slapped himself in the face, and then continued.

"It's impossible, in any case, to control the virus. Are birds meant to be penned and caged at all, let alone on an industrial scale? No. But the demand for their crunchy goodness is too great to be denied. Production outpaces reproduction. And so, modifications are necessary."

"Prototypes."

"Exactly. I myself ate hundreds of them. You, your father, your sister. The other men on our R & D team. Including Anton Gazes."

"Petal's father worked with you?"

"Until his breakdown. Not unlike your own father's. Ingestion affected us all differently. You seem to have developed a limited resistance. I, on the other hand, must continually reinject the cure. Young Petal, as far as we can tell, is fully immune."

Nero looked down at his hand. The cut. Swann's tongue. He never turned, but he should have.

"I want to talk to Bobo Rebozzo."

Win Fuld laughed. "Highly unlikely."

"What, he's not here?"

The reoxygenation system clicked. A mist of vitamin A fell from the ceiling.

"There is no Bobo Rebozzo."

Nero rubbed his temples.

"At least there hasn't been since he died in the outbreak of '53. Rebozzo's a marketing prop. A clown in a yellow suit. I own all this."

"But Swann is his daughter."

"Swann is my daughter."

Nero tried to imagine someone actually having sex with Win Fuld.

"You sent your own child to Inward Trek?"

Win Fuld wiped his gums with a silk handkerchief. "I had no doubt she would . . . survive, even prosper, in adverse conditions."

"You know what she did out there, right? If she wakes up, she's never going to be the same. No matter how many surgeries she gets or classes she takes. No one could be."

Win Fuld inhaled from the oxygen mask. His gums seeped darkly. He didn't blink, didn't twitch, barely registered a pulse as he spoke in a funny helium voice. "That's okay. She was sort of an entitled brat before, don't you think?"

The heating vents dripped sweat. The walls beaded with it.

"So why did you call me here?"

Win Fuld spread his hands, palms up. "I want to offer you a job."

"That's funny. Really."

"Miss Gazes, as you should have figured out by now, is filled with something extremely valuable. It literally pulses through her. But lately she's been less than cooperative. Not eating properly. Refusing the needle."

"You don't need her permission. You can just take what you want. Which is exactly what you're doing already."

"Ah, but that's not so. Nothing sedates her. Nothing knocks her out. The techs are afraid to enter the room. Putting her arm through the collection slot of her own volition just makes everything so much easier on everyone."

Nero said nothing.

Win Fuld tried to smile. A needle holding the corner of his lip together slipped out and tumbled to the floor. "We can break the cycle of the virus. We are close to synthesizing the antidote. Isn't that worth a few months of your girlfriend being locked up?"

"While I just forget everything that happened?"

Win Fuld shrugged. "Until it all happens again."

"And you keep making money selling poison."

"But people love poison. They *crave* it. If we didn't sell it to them, one fried nugget at a time, then there'd really be a revolution."

Nero stood. It was almost like Fuld had wanted the outbreak to happen. Was having a building full of Nu-Clients the point all along? There were other things besides an antidote you could develop. But you'd need infected subjects to experiment on first. Maybe the clients themselves were where the real money was. You couldn't do human research — even in Cambodia — anymore.

"No deal."

"Of course, you could stay here with us. Rehabbing. Getting in touch with yourself. Living a comfortable life. Eating at the cafeteria . . . forever."

Nero flexed his hand, watched scar tissue strain against healthy skin. "None of the Nu-Clients are ever getting out, are they?"

"Are you interested in the job or not, Mr. Sole?"

"What's it pay?"

Win Fuld smiled. "Your real life. Some of it, in any case. You can go home. Back to school if you wish. Another successful IT rehabilitation. All you need to do is report here daily. Visit Miss Gazes. Keep her happy and productive."

Nero hated himself for being so easily manipulated, while at the same time unable to hide his excitement at the chance to get out of the facility. To go home. See Amanda. Breathe real air. Laze around the house like a regular tool, even for a day.

Even for an hour.

"Deal."

"Hard bargaining, but I think you made the right choice."

Nero ignored the disgusting yellow thing that Win Fuld called a hand.

"Your father will be informed that you have completed your IT sentence on time and are coming home soon, fully rehabilitated. I will instruct the nurses to ease off on your medication. In the meantime, Miss Gazes's cooperation must improve a hundred percent."

Nero shook his head. "She'll never forgive me for this. And I don't blame her."

"For what, exactly?"

"I got her arrested. I got her sent to IT in the first place. If I hadn't let that first load of fryers get to packaging —"

Win Fuld waved for the guard. "She didn't get arrested because of you."

Nero closed his mouth. It took every bit of strength he had to open it again. "What did you say?"

"Miss Gazes got arrested for trying to set the Blue Room on fire."

Win Fuld opened a drawer and pulled out a stack of half-burned CORMICOM pamphlets.

"And she tried to light it with these."

The guard opened the door, grabbed Nero's shoulder, and escorted him through.

The World, and Still and Still and Still and Still, the World

NICK SAT IN THE BACK OF THE CLASSROOM AS
Miss Smollet *mwa-mwa-mwa'd* her way through a biology
lesson. He'd missed three months and was given triple homework every night in order to catch up. It was either that or
stay back a year and repeat the grade.

He didn't have a year to spare.

Next to him sat Jett Ballou, who'd had to hustle to get the
seat, since pretty much everyone was dying to sit next to Nick.

A girl across the room, Katie Wells, kept texting him her
phone number.

He was mobbed at his locker, mobbed at the caf, mobbed
while not playing dodgeball in the middle of games of
dodgeball.

"What happened in prison?"

"Dude, did you shiv anyone?"

"Were you tier boss?"

"How about the rape? Was there rape?"

"Did you get a homemade tat?"

"Did you meet Charles Manson?"

Nick tried to explain that it was just a lame juvie camp, that it wasn't like in the movies, wasn't at all what they thought. But the more he talked, the more they winked and nodded as if in on some unspoken secret, like, the first rule of doing time is that you never did time.

"Oh, yeah, okay. Sure, man. I get it."

"I'm serious, it was no big deal."

"Uh-huh, uh-huh. Cool."

Nick went to his next class shaking his head, surrounded by kids walking in packs, all wearing the same hoodies, listening to the same music, reading the same books, using the same slang. He felt ten years older, like he'd been fired from a couple of jobs and gone through a few divorces, but instead of that otherness making him seem even less palatable than before, now it was all about the rock star.

At lunch he chose a small table in the corner. There was a rush to take the other seats, two girls in orange sweaters briefly pulling each other's hair. Nick looked at the faces around the table — pink, straining, wanting so badly to impress.

And felt nothing. No kinship, friendship, interest.

Even worse, no one seemed to remember Petal, or even care. There'd been a small funeral. Jett Ballou said some people from Rebozzo's had gone. Three days later, everything was back to normal.

Whatever normal meant anymore.

It all seemed so fake. And meaningless.

Was this what he'd fought so hard to get back to?

Instead of fifth-period math there was an assembly. A policeman from town had died in the Shasta County fire. So had some sophomore's brother, who'd been in the army. Rumor had it that Nick's IT group had been near those woods, so he was given a special seat in the front row and treated with deference by students and teachers alike. First there was a moment of silence. Then a fire chief talked about how fires could be prevented in the future. The mayor talked about studying hard and not doing graffiti. A forest ranger asked for volunteers to spend the weekend replanting trees.

Someone laughed. "The weekend?"

There was a huge cheer as the lights dimmed and music boomed out of the sound system. It was Tawnii Täme's new album, the one produced by Dirk Rock and Spumaland, where she tried her hand at a little light rapping.

Then a dozen men and women in polyester uniforms sprinted down the aisles.

Each carrying a huge warmer bag.

Or a cooler.

While an announcement thanked Fresh Bukket for generously donating lunch.

As the food was set up at folding tables on the stage and people jostled to get in line to fill their plates, a guy in a chicken costume did backflips down the center aisle. He leaped onstage, swung around his yellow wings, and poked teachers with his beak. It got huge laughs. The chicken tossed SMOKE MY NUGGETS shirts into the crowd, then tossed rights and lefts and uppercuts with his comically huge boxing gloves.

The kids went crazy.

And then they went for seconds.

After school, Nick got three offers for rides home.

He stood out by the entrance and thumbed instead.

Which only cranked his rep another notch.

The Dude was in the kitchen, watching TV.

Except he wasn't dressed like a dude anymore.

He wore slacks and a button-down shirt. His beard was shaved off except for a neat soul patch. The sandals were gone. The fingerless gloves were gone. The fanny pack was gone.

The tan stayed.

Nick played it deadpan, pretending to make dinner even though there was nothing in the fridge. He rearranged slices of bread on a plate while the Dude jabbed at the remote. It landed on a reality show called *Minuscule vs. Majuscule*, where a midget and a former basketball player competed for prizes in challenges that almost always involved one of them getting kicked in the balls.

"I need a favor, Nicky," the Dude finally said.

"Yeah. To be honest? I'm actually kind of busy."

"That pile of bread can't wait?"

Nick stopped massaging the loaf.

"Fine. What is it?"

The Dude went to the bathroom and came back with a towel around his shoulders, the ends tucked into his shirt. He held up a pair of scissors.

"You're kidding."

"Nope, they got to go."

"All of it?"

"All of it."

"You're saying you want me to cut your hair."

"I'm saying I want you to cut my hair."

Nick cringed at the thought of touching his father's dreads. But the Dude's face was so oddly sincere he couldn't say no.

Nick closed his eyes and grabbed a handful of Dadlock.

"Ouch."

Then sank the metal in.

"Take it easy there."

As it turned out, it was sorta fun to chop them off.

"Now, that's more like it."

The Dude whistled while Nick worked, scissors snipping away. Hair tumbled down in waves, forming mounds across the floor, a feast of snakes.

"So what's this all about?" Nick asked when he'd finally hacked through a square acre.

"I got a job."

"Say that again."

"I got a job."

"One more time."

"I got a job."

"You got a *job*?"

"I did indeed."

"You're *employed*?"

"Gainfully."

"You're kidding me."

The Dude grinned. "Kind of amazed myself, but the call came yesterday morning. I start Monday. Put the old chemistry degree back to work, draw a regular paycheck. They know I've been a little out of the loop but love my potential."

"Wow. Is it a new company? Some start-up?"

"Nope. It's Rebozzo's."

Nick slipped, almost taking off his father's ear.

"Yeah, Captain Fuld called. Did quite a bit of apologizing, actually. But he insists they need fresh thinking on the R & D team. An experienced hand who's seen the ropes. Win wants to make things right, get me back in the fold."

"And you already said yes?"

"Sure did. Went to the store and put a new suit on the old Visa. 'Course, it got denied."

"So you stole it?"

"Nope, pawned my wedding ring and put the rest on layaway."

Nick cut deeply through the last bundle of greasy cable.

All that was left was a tight, even buzz.

The Dude looked fifty pounds lighter.

He got up and checked himself in the mirror, smiling like he'd just been paroled, given a bus ticket, and told to keep going until he crossed the state line. "Super job. Even with your record, you're a lock for barber school."

Nick swept up hair while the Dude jabbed at the remote.

Friday-night wrestling came on. A cage match.

Slaughterfist was going for a cruiserweight belt against the Masticator.

"You like wrestling now?"

The Dude shrugged. "Well, I've always sort of dug Sir Ziggurat. And Massive James Sasser has some slick moves. I guess you're usually pulling the night shift while it's on."

Nick dropped the dustpan. Tufts of hair wafted across the floor.

There was no way.

None.

It was impossible.

Wasn't it?

The Masticator got Slaughterfist in an elbow grip and then tossed him out of the ring. Slaughterfist's manager came up from behind and clobbered the Masticator with a folding metal chair.

"Who are you rooting for?"

"Oh, I don't care. My real favorite isn't on tonight."

"Why not?"

"Well, he doesn't really wrestle anymore. Sort of went Hollywood and got too big for his Speedo."

Nick swallowed. Twice.

"What's his name?"

"The Rock."

Nick closed his eyes and sat down, almost missing the chair. Something in his brain began to itch. He unflexed a muscle in his cortex, a slit that had opened a long time ago.

"It was you?"

"What was me?"

"The voice. Our . . . connection."

The Dude flicked the remote. "Sorry, kid, you're speaking Chinese."

Nick leaned over, speaking softly. "You were practically holding my hand all the way up to the lodge."

"What lodge? You mean Rebozzo's?"

"But how did you know which way to turn? How did you know where to go?"

The Dude frowned, making the *whoa* sign. "Well, if you

mean have I been there before, the answer is yes. Plenty of times. Corporate retreats. Team building. Trust exercises. I know that trail like the back of my hand."

Nick looked down at the burn in the center of his palm.

"But what about all the rest? The jokes."

"There were jokes?"

"And the wise-assing. You gave me advice."

"I did?"

"You know you did." Nick said. "You totally know."

The Dude looked uncomfortable. He tried to grin it away. "Hey, I guess that's what fathers are for."

Nick stared at the shorn man in front of him, a grizzled whippet in a cheap suit. He wasn't ever going to work at Rebozzo's. They'd never even let him in the gates. Win Fuld was screwing with both of them.

Proving a point.

"Dad, do you remember the summer I was twelve?"

"Ah, not really, no."

"I kept thinking I heard music. Totally loud and random. In my head."

"That's weird."

"Was it you?"

"Me?"

"Yeah, you sending it."

"I don't understand."

"Try harder."

The Dude thought for a minute. "Well, your mother used to say she heard Mozart in her sleep. Or sometimes would ask if I could turn down the radio when it was already off."

"Mom? Really?"

"This may be difficult to accept, Nick, but I think you're old enough to know the truth."

"What truth?"

"A slight instability runs in our family."

"You're kidding."

"Nope."

"Strange, I hadn't noticed."

"Well, I didn't want to say anything until you were old enough to handle it."

"Thanks."

"Hey, you bet."

Nick tossed a steak dinner in the microwave. When it was done, he put it in front of his father, along with a glass of water and a napkin. The Dude leaned over and turned down the volume.

"Nick?"

"Yeah?"

"Did you know the Rock's real name is Dwayne?"

"No. I didn't know that."

"Point is, a guy called the Rock gets to tell the world to eat it in a way that your average Dwayne never could. Which is cool. But in the end, it's not your name that defines you; it's your actions."

Nick stared at Nero's reflection in the microwave door.

"Would one of those defining actions include me getting you some Jell-O?"

The Dude laughed. "Absolutely."

When it was jouncing in the center of the table, and the Dude had a death grip on his favorite wooden spoon, Nick turned to go upstairs.

But stopped in the doorway.

"Mom told me once that you guys met at a concert."

"It's true. In California. God, that seems like a lifetime ago."

"Who did you see?"

"The Rolling Stones."

"At Altamont?"

The Dude slurped a cherry cube. "That's right. Altamont Raceway. Nineteen sixty-nine. How did you know?"

Nick reached in his pocket, about to slam the lighter on the table, until he remembered for the millionth time that Win Fuld had confiscated it.

"How does anyone know anything anymore?"

"Amen," the Dude said, turning up the volume.

Hey, Little Sister, Shotgun

NICK WENT UP TO AMANDA'S ROOM, LIKE HE did every night since he'd gotten home. She didn't sit under the table in the kitchen anymore. Nick had always thought she'd done so out of sheer weirdness or obstinacy. Now he realized that she did it for the Dude's sake. To be near him without crowding him. To comfort him.

But the Dude was on a roll, excited about his new job. He didn't need her there anymore. Or at least not right there.

It was scary how much Amanda had grown in ninety days, almost a preteen. Sassier. Present. On her computer all the time. Even if she was mostly slashing her way through the Battle of Actium or ruling post-apocalypse Vegas at the point of a Luger.

He knocked on the door. She was at her laptop, pounding keys. He sat on the floor, next to her chair.

Amanda laughed. *"Trading Places?"*

"I never knew how cool it was down here."

"I knew there was? Something different? About you the moment you? Came home?"

"You have no idea."

She continued to tap away, IM'ing with a bunch of friends.

Making jokes about bands.

And game characters.

LOL'ing in a welter of girl-power nerd-dom.

Amanda.

Having a conversation.

With other people.

Amazing.

"You want to know where I was?" Nick finally asked. "The last three months?"

Amanda closed her message screen and brought up two different games in progress. She did three button combinations, released rockets, released throwing stars, enacted a force field, eviscerated a wizard and some rogue elves. She landed a ship on the frozen slope of Proxima Prime, extracted a hold full of Kraytonium from the planet's crust, sold it on the Rigelian black market, made a killing, bought a wormhole pass and a tactical nuke, sieged Leningrad, overhauled her pulse drive, and then defeated the last remaining knight of the Order of Crowley.

"In prison? It's okay? I won't judge? You?"

"No, there was more to it than that."

Amanda executed a flying knee that took out a trio of killer clowns. "Tell me?"

Nick sighed. "Okay, first of all, there was this guy named Bruce Leroy."

"You mean like? African? American? Bruce Lee?"

"Exactly."

"I want him? On my team?"

"Me too," Nick said.

And then he told her.

Everything.

From the minute he stepped onto the IT van to the conversation with Petal he'd had the day before.

It took over two hours.

Amanda finally pushed away her keyboard and turned to him. Her hair was parted even more severely than usual.

Nick was positive she was going to laugh. Or get angry. Or, the most frightening possibility, not react at all.

Instead she said, "I guess I always sort of knew? That zombies? Were real?"

"So you, uh, believe me?"

"Of course?"

He let out a long gust of air. "Um, okay. That's sort of amazing."

Amanda shrugged. "Not really? Your story? Has too much? Detail to be made up?"

He nodded. "True."

"Also? I've been monitoring some sites? You're not the only one? Saying this shit?"

"Amanda!" Nick said. "You just swore!"

"So? Fucking? What?"

He laughed, looking at his tiny, dark, dead-serious sister. And then hugged her. Hard. Amanda hated to be hugged. But she let him. When he pulled back, she snapped her fingers.

"Okay, three things? One, do I have to? Call you Nero?"

"You can call me anything you want."

"Okay, Nick? Second thing?"

"Shoot."

"Thank you for? Sticking up for? Mr. Bator?"

"You're welcome."

"Third, you need to get? Petal out of there? Sounds like? She's dying?"

It was bizarre. Amanda had accepted it all, without blinking. Nick thought his own friends were jaded, but Amanda was something else entirely. Her capacity to be amazed had already skipped a generation. By the time she was in high school, it'd be a worldwide collective yawn when aliens landed a pie pan on the White House lawn and then vaporized the president.

"I know, A-dog. Believe me."

"Unless she's? Already dead?"

Nick stiffened. "Yeah, unless."

"So we need? Tanks? A SEAL unit? Maybe even? Two?"

"True, but not very realistic."

Amanda frowned, nodded. "But then? What?"

"The only weapon that's free."

"Decommissioned? Cold War ordinance?"

"No, information."

Amanda spun back to her computer, and with a few taps brought up links to Fresh Bukket. Marketing, customer complaints, fan sites. Dead rat found in mashed potatoes. Conspiracy stuff, sales numbers, the Sole Fryer recall. The Rebozzo Fryer launch. She pulled up the CORMICOM site. Rants, accusations, dime-store Assanges. Even stuff about the Dude, pictures of him with young Win Fuld and Anton Gazes.

Prototypes.

Side effects.

Strange viruses in Bombay and Cairo.

Hazmat troops, Quantico, zombie black sites, Zach holding pens.

Who really shot John Lennon.

Then there were calls to action. Protests, sit-ins, boycotts that no one cared about or would ever join. Boilerplate about how we're all already zombies. Walking through our lives, doing nothing but consuming, the usual self-righteous bumper-sticker whining about individuality, a noncleverness that was void of actual solutions. One headline said "Embrace Your New Space on the Food Chain!" Another said "We Are All Zombie Nuggets. Some of Us Are Just Extra Crispy!"

"Thanks, but I know all that stuff already."

"Hold? On?"

Amanda bore down through layer after layer of rumor, a bullshit tiramisu. One in particular came up repeatedly.

"People say there's? Colonies of them? Up in the hills?"

Nick read it all. Much of the stuff was clearly nonsense, dudes talking smack, saying they were CIA. Saying they were in the Fire. Saying they were infected, right there at the computer. Saying it made your junk bigger. Saying they wanted to meet other infected girls and party.

Then came a pair of articles that were different.

One was posted by a soldier who had doubts about his mission. He was angry. Disgusted by his orders. Haunted by the carnage he'd witnessed. And had backup info. Satellite photos. Camps. CDC maps of contagion spread. Reticulate patterns. Recombination theory. Classified documents detailing the order to burn fifteen thousand square miles of forest.

The other was posted by hikers claiming they'd spotted Infect militias deep in the woods of Montana and Idaho. That they'd crept close and seen them training, organizing, not acting like zombies at all. They were calling them the Evolved. Of course, none had pictures, just excuses. Camera battery dead, cell phone shorted out, video not available.

The next link went to a Chinese chat room, the text of the site in Mandarin.

"It says click here and beware?" Amanda translated.

"How do you know that?"

She just shrugged.

The link bounced them into an ongoing chat that was coded. Amanda clicked around, ran it through some encryption software, and then a translator.

"What are you, some sort of hacker genius?"

"No?" she said, voice even more whispery than usual. "Anyone can do that? It's just to? Keep out the noobs?"

Soldier34532: But they'd changed. They didn't attack, didn't bite. The Evolved have an agenda, I'm telling you.

PreachPeach9: That's what I heard too. Zombies with the ability to reason. To problem solve. It's, like, Kafka or some shit. Or was that Kant?

TheNutcutter: Whatever. You guys are morons.

HeadSnapp: Hi! Who wants to talk about mixed martial arts?

Soldier34532: They've moved on from their basest needs. It was bound to happen. Even the stupidest animals adapt, gain skills, improve their chances for survival. Either that or they die out. But the Evolved haven't died out. They're flourishing. It's natural selection.

BillyGrammerer: Or unnatural selection.

H.M.S.Beegle: Check the fossil record. They found

zombie teeth from before Christ in some cave in the Negev.

TheNutcutter: Oh, yeah? How exactly can you tell zombie teeth from any other teeth? Did they find Judas's fanny pack, too?

ColonCleanse: The government says this entire Z routine is all a bunch of crap. So does my friend Tim.

OrksDrink40s: Ah, yes. The government. The same people who brought you Lee Harvey Oswald and Iran-Contra. The same people who sold you tax cuts for the rich.

Prelapsarian1: What are you, socialist?

OrksDrink40s: No, I'm just not stupid.

Cronenberg: Do you even know what socialist means, Ork?

OrksDrink40s: Yeah, it means the government is better equipped to handle certain social services, like your lobotomy, or delivering the mail, than Goldman Sachs is.

Prelapsarian1: Eff U, Socialombie!

FunionInParadise66: Can we get back to, like, the Zomb-A-Pocalypse, please? While we still have time?

TheNutcutter: So tell me one thing, where did this "virus" come from?

Nick leaned over and typed.

Soul2Sole: It came from Fresh Bukket.

GBeckG: Ha! At least it tastes oh so good on the way down.

Soldier34532: I was there on the ridge when they broke through our lines. Attacked the Sno-Cats. Total animals. Berzerkers. Now they're like . . . next-gen zombies. They've learned to control themselves. They're living in tents. Rumor is that when you have the virus long enough, you begin to evolve.

GBeckG: Soldier's a fag.

PreachPeach9: Training themselves for what, Soldier? And how do they control the virus?

Soldier34532: I dunno. Maybe the reason people act like zombies is because they haven't learned to *let* the virus control them yet. Maybe the biting comes from the human part of them not letting go. Once it's in there long enough, maybe the two parts, human and zombie, finally make peace.

PreachPeach9: Peace with what?

Soldier34532: The inevitable.

OrksDrink4os: If zombiedom is a reversion to the essential self, it's entirely possible that Z is the next stop in human development.

TheNutcutter: Which means the fat, the rich, the cynical, the entitled, the liars, and the bored all have something coming.

OrksDrink40s: A date to meet their own monster.

TheNutcutter: Not coincide with it. Not buy it off. Become it.

OrksDrink40s: Turns out revolution isn't all bombs and tear gas and braless hippies shouting slogans after all.

TheNutcutter: Holy shit, it's a coup on the microscopic level! The revolution will not only not be televised; it will be unable to be seen by the naked human eye!

OrksDrink40s: All they need is a Z leader. Some guy with good hair and a cleft chin.

BaruchThePoet: Actually, there's a woman, not a zombie. Who they say is in charge. She's like Golda Meir. Total Badass. Lara Croft.

Soldier34532: J. Own Jhet.

TiffTame8: What's that?

Soldier34532: Her name, I guess?

TiffTame8: Sounds Russian.

Soldier34532: Well, that's what she calls herself. I've never seen her. They say she's still human. Whatever that means anymore.

GBeckG: Oh, my God, do you people need to get a —

The screen went blank. Then blue text filled it from top to bottom: FORBIDDEN SITE — CLOSED INDEFINITELY.

"Darn it? That was good?"

They found a lot more sites, mostly the same thing but more digressive, even less convincing. A few others were closed down while they read. Some went quiet just out of boredom.

Amanda clicked over to a new game. It was called *Discovery 1492*. She was an explorer leading a motley crew of conquistadors into the heart of Mayan civilization. And wiping it out with Daisy Cutters and TEC-9s.

"I say we? Blow it all up and? Start over?"

"What do you mean?"

"America? Humanity? The world's a? Thinly veiled apocalypse? Already?"

"I know, but —"

"Pixilated violence? Is just another sign of? Cultural collapse?"

"It is?"

"Yes?"

"But it's all you ever do."

Amanda lit up a row of teepees with a napalm cannon. Her voice got extremely low.

"Why fight it? It's time that something major shifted? Before it's too late? People are always terrified? When the change comes? You think they didn't cower? At the edge of the Renaissance?"

"Yeah, I guess."

"A Caravaggio probably? Seemed to them? Just like a zombie does? To us?"

Nick laughed. "Wow. Not only is that amazingly perceptive, but you realize that's the most consecutive words you've strung together since you were born?"

"It's the first? Time I ever? Needed to?"

Nick watched Amanda's explorer take off his helmet and armor, then turn and start firing on his fellow conquistadors. She double-clicked and a line of claymores exploded under the mercenaries. Little text bubbles started popping up, like *Hey!* and *WTF?* and *Stop it!* and *Traitor!* Amanda took out a team of artillery gunners and then laid down suppressing fire as the regrouped Indians whooped, stormed over the hill, and mopped up invaders with knives and rocks and wooden clubs.

She threw down the controller and turned to Nick. "I want to? Evolve? Just like them?"

"You don't need to. You're perfect."

Amanda made a vomit face. "Don't patronize? I know what? I am?"

"Which is?"

"Totally ready for everything? To be? Very different?"

"It's not just you, though, is it?"

"All of us want to? Aren't you paying attention? The world is? Terminally bored?"

Nick rubbed his temples, suddenly knowing exactly what he had to do. And how to do it.

"But even if the whole world is a hole of suck, maybe it's still better than what's coming."

Amanda's voice was barely audible.

"It's not?"

"You're sure?"

"I am?"

He nodded, kissing her forehead.

"Thanks, A-dog."

"Of course?"

"And don't tell the Du . . . don't tell Dad, okay?"

Amanda rolled her eyes and loaded a new game. Within seconds she was driving a tank made of human bone into South Central L.A.

"Nick?"

"Yeah?"

"Close the door?"

"Sure."

"But next time you? Open it?"

"Yeah?"

"You better be coming for me?"

Amanda racked the .50-cal, loaded a sleeve of uranium-tipped shells, and started piling up serious bonus points.

Conjugal Visit

AFTER SCHOOL, NERO DROVE THE CELICA TO the IT facility and parked in the gated lot, behind three circles of electrified fence. After he was escorted in, he said hello to Bruce Leroy and Exene, who were playing chess, and then sat in the TV lounge with Mr. Bator, who refused to speak but seemed to enjoy having company while watching TV. A rerun of *Too Much Love for One Abode.* was on. It was a sit-com about a middle-class couple, the Abodes, who'd adopted nine Albanian children. The children took turns comically butchering idioms and being amazed by the largesse of the American supermarket: "Campbell must be very powerful man, no? They name for him so many kinds of soup!"

Mr. Bator laughed, sort of, a wet slurp that came from the tear that used to be his face.

"You ready?"

A guard escorted Nero along the usual route. He sat down on the other side of the thick glass. Petal was lying in bed, looking gaunt and drawn in cutoff jumpsuit bottoms and a T-shirt that said GANG OF FOUR in black Magic Marker. There was an IV in the crook of her arm, a blood bag slowly filling up on the floor. Her white hair was whiter than ever, cut in a severe angle across her face.

Nero waved.

Petal put down her copy of *The Prince*, sat across from him, and pressed the button that let them talk through a speaker in the metal housing.

"Brains," she said.

"Must. Have. Brains," he said back.

It was a private joke that wasn't very private. The guard yawned, but they knew he was listening.

"Fuld offered me a job."

Petal raised an eyebrow. "You should take it. I bet there's a great health plan."

"I already did. It's one of the reasons I'm here."

"To talk me into being a good kitty? Meow on command?"

"Exactly. In exchange, when this is all over, he's going to let you out. Everyone else too."

"Did you get that promise on paper?"

"Signed on the dotted line."

She leaned back, provocatively crossing her bare legs on the table.

Her slightly gray and bruised and punctured legs.

Legs that he could not allow to be abused.

For even a minute longer.

"Well, it's settled then."

"Fuld also told me you tried to burn down the Blue Room."

She frowned. "Not really. I was just having a bad day."

"Argument with your other boyfriend?"

"Total PMS."

"Why didn't you tell me before?"

Petal leaned into the speaker and spoke quietly. "Because it was a stupid gesture that didn't change anything, and because deep down I know if I had the chance, I'd do it again."

"You would?"

"Yes."

"Right now?"

"Yes."

A buzzer went off.

Petal's blood bag was full. She pulled out the IV roughly. A nurse who looked like the bass player from ZZ Top came into the vestibule in scrubs and blew a whistle.

"Clavicle tap."

Petal handed the bag through the collection slot. The nurse whisked it away with two gloved fingers, holding her breath. Petal grabbed a fresh bag from the table, then racked the needle into her neck, like plugging in a pair of headphones, while giving the finger to the nurse's back.

Nero could not believe how much she'd changed.

Shy and quiet? Sorry, that girl was long gone.

Trusting? No, sir.

Prepared to do as she was told? Not hardly.

A reformed arsonist? Yeah, except for the reformed part.

Over the months in the facility, the infection had remained static, but Petal had blossomed.

Fuld thought he had her locked down, in control. Tap the main line, turn on the faucet.

But Petal was the only immune.

The carrier of a pure strain of Z.

It was like being pregnant, but without all the belly.

"So let's deliver it," Nero finally said. "Cut the cord. We're our only way in, and our only way out."

"Are you serious?"

"Yes."

"Right now?"

"Yes."

"Are you scared?"

"No. Yes. A little."

"Good," she said. "You should be."

Nero looked over, made sure the guard wasn't watching, and slid his hand through the collection slot. It didn't really fit, but he shoved it beneath the metal lip, scraping off a layer of skin.

It didn't matter. He wouldn't need it in a few minutes.

Petal took his hand and stroked it, turning her head so she could rest his palm against her cheek.

She kissed his fingertips, kissed his thumb.

"Is this insane?" he asked.

"No more insane than what was done to us."

"What will people do?"

"They'll adapt."

"What if they don't?"

"Then they won't."

Nero thought about it. "You're right."

"Hey, no one asked penicillin's permission to exist. No one asked the Internet to wait around on some hard drive until everyone was ready."

"Then stop talking and do it," he whispered.

Petal opened her mouth.

Lips drawn back from two rows of perfect white teeth.

And bit through Nick, deep into Nero.

Lovingly.

At least at first.

And then hungrily.

A fine mist of blood sprayed across the wall.

"Stop."

She bit deeper, began to drink.

"Stop!"

Petal looked up, eyes glazed, breathing heavily.

He pulled his hand away and hid it under his shirt.

"What did it taste like?"

Her teeth were red. "Good. Gross. Both."

"Everything is both. Have you ever noticed that?"

"Yes," she said, looking at him with such love and appreciation he considered the possibility that he might actually deserve it.

"So what do we do now?"

"Wait."

"For what?"

"For your skin to begin to twitch."

"My skin is already twitching."

"For a buzz to rise in your ears."

"A buzz has totally risen."

Petal smiled. Her eyes were a blue million miles. She leaned up against the glass and whispered.

"Then, honey, we're here."

As if on cue, the guard turned, yawned, said time was up. "Kissy hour's over."

Nero stood, feeling ridiculously strong. "I'll be back."

"How long?"

He looked at the watch he wasn't wearing. Only one person had the key card to open her door. "Not long at all."

"C'mon, Romeo," the guard said.

Petal laughed, wiping her mouth. "How appropriate. Star-crossed lovers. Houses divided. Juliet gives him poison, and then the whole world changes."

Nero followed the guard into the hall, hypnotized by the pulse in his neck, his unsullied flesh, his irresistible new-car smell.

He could have stood there, breathing it in, forever.

"Can we hurry it up, chief?"

"No," Nero said. It was getting hard to talk. His mouth was swollen and sore. "You must. Be patient."

"Right."

The guard slid foil off a piece of Juicy Fruit and slipped it between his teeth. He was big, with a neatly trimmed goatee and tattoos poking from a tight shirt, all pecs and delts and combat training.

All of it useless.

Or at least it would be soon.

He opened the security door and extended his hand sarcastically. "After you, Fruit Loop."

Nero grabbed the guard and bit deeply into the flesh of his upper arm, then pushed him to the ground. The guard, in shock, started to flail for the antibiotics they all carried in a flap on their belt.

"Don't bother. Doesn't work. Just there to make you. Feel better."

The guard gulped the pills anyway, at least the ones that didn't scatter across the floor, and scrambled back against the wall. Nero cuffed him to a chair.

"Why?" he asked, eyes animal with fear. "Why on purpose?"

It was a fair question.

A toughie.

Hard to answer.

Maybe the virus was inevitable.

Maybe it was even God.

Someone bit into an apple, and then everything changed.

Someone bit into a security guard, and then everything changed again.

Nick was Nick was Nick was Nick.

Then he was Nero.

And, ultimately, Nero was not going to allow his girlfriend to rot in a cell one minute longer.

Was it worth sacrificing the whole world for?

Maybe.

But how did you explain all that to a security guard who was asking questions as a cheap distraction while trying to fish a Taser from of his back pocket?

Nero blinked, slapped his own face, forced himself to maintain.

Because his head buzzed.

It screamed and ached.

He was Adam, naked.

Petal was Eve, naked.

They were Zadam and Zeve.

The apple and the serpent and the hands and the teeth.

All he had to do was go forth and multiply.

Nero walked into the cafeteria. War Pig was sitting by himself, eating oatmeal. His red curls had been shaved off. There were purple rings under his eyes.

"Hey," he said glumly. "You look like you could use a cup of coffee."

Nero leaned over and bit him on the shoulder.

"What the fuck, man!"

Nero wanted to respond but couldn't.

War Pig jumped up. "That is *so* not funny."

Nero kept going, walking into the TV lounge where Sad Girl and Estrada were lying on the couch.

"Oh, no," Sad Girl said.

"You kicked it off again, eh?" Estrada asked, looking into Nero's eyes.

"I knew it," Sad Girl said, throwing her magazine on the floor. "Cupcake's plan. Cut a hole in the door and let it happen, right? Join the other team and you are the other team?"

"Yes."

"But I like it here. When we got our release dates, I was even gonna ask if we could stay for extra rehab."

Nero looked at Estrada. "You too?"

"If she wants, yeah. We got good food, free rent, our own room. Man, people here care what happens to us. They get it. No one out there cares, do they?"

"No," Nero said.

"That's right. Never did. What do I got waiting for me on the streets? Empty time until I get arrested again."

"No more arrests. Time starts. Now."

"No." Sad Girl said.

"Babe?" Estrada said.

"Babe *what*?"

"Be cool."

"Cool? Are you *shitting* me?"

Estrada held out his hand.

Nero bit it.

Sad Girl closed her eyes and raised her arm. Nero leaned over. At the last second she pulled back and ran into the bathroom.

"She'll come around," Estrada said, admiring the wound Nero had left. "Women, huh?"

"Yeah," Nero was barely able to say. "Wu-man."

They bumped knuckles.

"I believe in you, Fiddler. And now the city is most definitely burning."

"Burn-ing," Nero said.

Estrada laughed and then walked toward the art studio.

A counselor tried to stop him and got molars for his trouble.

Hollow-point rounds ricocheted down the hall.

Screams rained down from above.

Nero felt a clanging in his head, the madness, coming on like the first rush of unheard music or some unnameable drug. But it was fine and high and tight. It was static, a ball of energy, stomach hollow, face stolen. New parts of him were opening, like a stack of tiny presents, ribbons being pulled off one at a time, as other parts closed.

Voices rumbled, low and insect-like.

The first inklings of communication.

Communion.

War Pig shuffled by, a smile on his face. Tripper followed, slick head gleaming. Cupcake held her arms out, beatific. Mr. Bator, a look of release in his eyes, sank himself into the cafeteria lady.

Nero figured it would take about an hour until the facility and everyone in it had turned. Some would be out of control, but eventually he would lead them. As Swann had. Like Joanjet was doing. In the mountains.

He would teach them that it wasn't a virus; it was a blessing.

That they weren't a mindless horde; they were an army.

With no agenda and nothing to lose.

Except a culture that had been lost a long time ago.

The future in the rearview.

Darwin with a twist.

There was commotion around the front offices. Men shouting instructions, yelling over handheld radios. Gunfire. A guard ran by, armed with a shotgun. She stopped, staring at Nero. It was the female soldier. The major who'd shot him in the clearing by the lodge. There was a bite on her chin, a chunk of flesh hanging free. Blood dripped slowly to the floor.

"Are you turned?" she asked.

Nero shrugged. "Is there. A difference. Anymore?"

Static squalled through her shoulder radio. She cursed, racked more shells, and ran down the hall.

Nero went in the other direction, took the long way, avoiding the commotion.

The next wing was empty.

By the time he came to the end, there was no one guarding it at all.

He knocked on the pane of safety glass.

Nothing.

He did it again. Louder.

Nothing.

He closed his eyes and thought, *Wake up!*

Swann's eyes flickered open.

She yawned and stretched.

Then turned her head.

And winked.

An alarm went off, and then another.

Klaxons reverberated across tile floors.

The sprinklers engaged.

There was yelling.

Crying.

Chaos.

Nero stood there, getting wet.

Getting wetter.

Getting clean.

Swann ran a hand through her hair, tore IVs from her arm, pulled magnetic leads from her chest, leather restraints from her neck, and the red plastic gag ball from her mouth.

Then charged the plate glass and slammed against it.

"Hi," Nero said, although it may have sounded like "Ngurrgh."

Swann raised her hand to smash at the glass, then stopped and raised an eyebrow instead.

"I'll be back," he said, walking slowly down the corridor.

Trying not to shamble.

And succeeding.

As soon as they got out of the facility, Nero and Sad Girl and Petal and Estrada were going to load into the Celica. Maybe put Swann in the trunk. Roll down all their windows, crank up the radio, and go for a ride.

So were a lot of other people.

The IT vans were hitting the highway again, in formation.

Slogan intact: *We're All in This Together.*

See if Bruce Leroy was down.

Find Joanjet.

Make a few pit stops, expand the team.

Except it wasn't going to be the Infects this round.

They were going by a new name.

The Evolved.

But before they could do anything, he had to find Win Fuld.

And have a little talk.

Nero took Nick by the hand and led him straight on down the hall.

CASE NUMBER   08-1134-09898

INCIDENT DATE   11-18-2010

INCIDENT TIME   13:27-14:13 hours

COPIES TO   Juvenile court

ARRESTING OFFICER   Sgt. Mark Mothersbaugh

SUSPECT(s)   Sammy Swester

Age	18	Race	Caucasian
Height	5'7"	Hair	Yellow, curly
Weight	312	Eyes	Brown

Distinguishing Characteristics:

Hasn't missed a whole lot of meals, wearing
XENA: WARRIOR PRINCESS T-shirt and 70s
Kareem-style sweatbands. Thick glasses.
No ankles to speak of. Sweaty and breathing
heavily.

Narrative:

On the above date and time, I was assigned
to Car #92, patrolling solo. I was
dispatched to 500 Memorial Drive #246 on
a report of an identity theft. This is
a Hayward Tech dorm building. While en
route, I was updated by ECC that the
suspect was a male student, overweight,
described as wearing multiple sweatbands,

who had hacked into a fellow student's
account and stolen compromising photos
and other data. ECC provided me with her
name, Anna Tang, an Asian female with
many visible tattoos and green lipstick,
wearing a long black coat and thigh-high
leather boots. Upon arrival, Victim Tang
immediately took me to her dorm room and
turned on her computer. Every file on her
desktop had somehow been corrupted. All
the files, hundreds of them, had been
replaced with photos of suspect Swester,
lying naked on his bed, wearing only the
aforementioned sweatbands, as well as what
some might describe as a smile. Suspect
Swester without his clothes is not an
enticing sight either to this officer or to
Victim Tang, which she expressed repeatedly
and in multiple languages, one I believe
to be Taiwanese. Victim Tang burst into
tears, giving me Suspect Swester's room
number and urging me to utilize my weapon
"so it hurts." When I said could not do
so, she repeatedly commented, "Then can
you at least tase him, bro?" I assured
her that tasing did not seem necessary
as yet but was an option that remained

on the table. Upon knocking on his door,
Swester said "Entrez, Anna, <u>mon amour</u>" in
a French accent, obviously false. When I
entered, identifying myself, the suspect
was lying naked on the bed, in almost an
exact approximation of the photograph,
except for several bags of snack chips
and pastry boxes arrayed around him.
While not seeming entirely unsurprised to
see me, he refused to answer questions,
instead employing television-grade legal
jargon, most of it centering on his
Miranda rights, as well as First Amendment
freedoms, including "expressions of the
flesh." At that point, I took Mr. Swester
into custody.

---

* **DO NOT WRITE BELOW THIS LINE** *
INWARD TREK HANDLER NOTES:

Sentenced   Inward Trek boot camp, 3 months

Camp Nickname   Heavy D

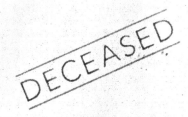

CASE NUMBER _____ 02-6389-028732

INCIDENT DATE _____ 12-02-2010

INCIDENT TIME _____ 08:27-10:13 hours

COPIES TO _____ Juvenile court

ARRESTING OFFICER _____ Ofc. John Graham Mellor

SUSPECT(s) _____ Daniel Bevelaqua

Age	15	Race	Caucasian
Height	5'4"	Hair	Brown
Weight	121	Eyes	Blue

Distinguishing Characteristics:

Thin, timid, extremely large nose, walks
bent forward as if suffering from a spinal
problem. In general gives the impression
that a strong wind may pick him up and
sweep him beyond the breakers. Really,
the kid has a truly massive nose that you
probably could not trace on this piece of
paper.

Narrative:

On the above date and time, I was assigned
to Car #33 along with Officer Caulfield.
We were dispatched to 1090 Kearney Street,
where suspect was found sitting on the
floor of a very large and well-appointed

apartment, weeping. Next to him was a
very attractive young lady, shot in the
chest. The apartment's owner, one Alberto
"Alley Rat" Tintoretto, made the call
after hearing glass break downstairs. He
secured his gun, a legal S&W .38 of which
he is the registered owner. Upon seeing the
young lady, who at the time was wearing a
black ski mask, leafing through his desk
drawers, Tintoretto fired once, a direct
hit. It wasn't until he pulled the mask off
that Mr. Tintoretto realized he'd shot a
teenage girl. There was a knock. Thinking
it was the police, Tintoretto opened the
door, allowing the suspect entrance. Upon
seeing the young girl, he rushed to her
side, breaking into tears. Tintoretto
waited for us to arrive, listening to the
boy weep and mourn. At the station, I
discovered he was none other than Danny
"Kid Nose" Bevelaqua, who has many priors
for B&E and receiving stolen goods and
is known as a local tough, despite his
appearance. However, he was not party to
the crime and no charges were pressed
against him. The woman was later ID'd as
Lucy Furillo, his longtime girlfriend. The

Nose was searched before release and found
to have a small amount of cocaine on him,
for which he was sentenced as a separate
matter. Before being led away, Bevelaqua
repeatedly and tearfully swore to this
officer that he was "done with the life"
and "would never hurt anyone again."

- -
* DO NOT WRITE BELOW THIS LINE *
INWARD TREK HANDLER NOTES:
- -

Sentenced   Inward Trek boot camp, 3 months

Camp Nickname   Mr. Bator

CASE NUMBER   02-8836-110283

INCIDENT DATE   10-27-2010

INCIDENT TIME   01:27-03:39 hours

COPIES TO   Juvenile court

ARRESTING OFFICER   Ofc. Angelo Gianni

SUSPECT(s)   Darby C. Rash

Age   17   Race   Caucasian

Height   5'3"   Hair   Shaved head

Weight   140   Eyes   Green

Distinguishing Characteristics:

Numerous neck, chest, arm, and leg tattoos.
Suspect claims they are "band tats."
Has shaved head and Aryan sympathizer
appearance. Did not sit still entire time
in custody.

Narrative:

On the above date and time, I was assigned
to Car #3 along with Officer P. Smear.
We were dispatched to 106 Potrero Street
#3177 on a 62-20, Taking Candy from a Baby.
My first one ever. I double-checked with
dispatch, thinking this must be a joke
of some sort, a prank being played by the
other guys, since it's my first month on the

force. Dispatch insisted it was no joke.
When we arrived at location, a woman, the
young boy's mother, had suspect pinned to
the ground, holding him until we arrived.
Suspect, wearing leather jacket, wallet
chain, and Doc Martens, was crying and
asking to be released. The mother, in
sweatpants and blond ponytail, who I would
estimate weighing 110 pounds wet, refused,
grinding her knee into suspect's back. When
questioned, suspect admitted to attempting
to "just take a few bites" of the young
boy's supersize Butter Fingered bar while
the mother was distracted with her cell
phone. When the boy refused, suspect
grabbed bar and shoved it into his mouth.
The boy began to cry. Suspect searched
the boy's pockets for more candy. When
the mother confronted him, suspect used
foul language, threatening to "beat her
skank ass down." Mother, who informed this
officer that she is a brown belt in Tae Bo
and regular devotee of Pilates, quickly
forced suspect to the ground with a series
of neck punches and crotch kicks. At this
point, suspect begged us to arrest him if
we would just get the woman off his back.

The Butter Fingered wrapper was found
in his pocket. Samples of chocolate from
around his mouth were swabbed and taken
into evidence. I then put suspect in the
back of the cruiser, whereupon he cried the
entire way to the station. Numerous calls
to his foster parents went unanswered.

- -
*   **DO NOT WRITE BELOW THIS LINE**   *
        INWARD TREK HANDLER NOTES:
- -

Sentenced   Inward Trek boot camp, 3 months

Camp Nickname   Tripper

CASE NUMBER _____ 09-6627-919199

INCIDENT DATE _____ 09-27-2010

INCIDENT TIME _____ 14:27-16:59 hours

COPIES TO _____ Juvenile court

ARRESTING OFFICER ___ Ofc. Vincent Stigma

SUSPECT(s) _____ Danny Trujillo

Age	17	Race	Hispanic/Latino
Height	5'9"	Hair	Dark black, slicked back
Weight	166	Eyes	Brown

Distinguishing Characteristics:

Sour countenance, heavy-lidded stare,
"tear" tattoo below left eye.

Narrative:

On the above date and time, I was assigned
to Car #3 along with Officer Preslar.
We were dispatched to 2297 Broadway on
a report of "domestic dispute." When
arriving at location, we found suspect
sitting calmly on couch watching TV. On
the floor was his uncle Eugenio. Suspect
readily admitted beating his uncle with
his fists "for a very long time" and said
"because I couldn't take it anymore." When
asked what "it" was, suspect lifted up his

shirt and showed grotesque amounts of scar
tissue that he claimed had come from belt-
whipping from his uncle as punishments
while growing up. The sizes and layering
of the scars seemed to support this claim.
An ambulance was called for the uncle,
and child protective services for the
suspect. We subsequently learned there had
been many complaints about the uncle by
neighbors. A judge ruled the beating to be
self-defense, but due to the suspect's gang
affiliations, it was determined that he
serve an indeterminate period in juvenile
detention regardless.

----

* DO NOT WRITE BELOW THIS LINE *
INWARD TREK HANDLER NOTES:

Sentenced   **Inward Trek boot camp, 3 months**

Camp Nickname   **Estrada**

CASE NUMBER _____ 02-9238-836728

INCIDENT DATE _____ 11-22-2010

INCIDENT TIME _____ 18:27-19:13 hours

COPIES TO _____ Juvenile court

ARRESTING OFFICER ____ Det. William Michael Albert Broad

SUSPECT(s) _____ Patterson Nordstrom Jr. and

Stanton Auchischloss

Age(s)   16, 17   Race(s) Caucasian, Caucasian

Height(s) 5'6", 5'6"Hair(s) Bottle blond, bottle blond

Weight(s) 121, 122 Eyes   Blue, blue

Distinguishing Characteristics:

Short, peroxided, Maverick from Top Gun—
style hair, insistence that they are twins
when there are documented age differences,
let alone different last names. Possible
brain damage, tendency to finish each
other's sentences, to speak in a slang that
is difficult to process, possibly for its
objective level of stupidity. Dyed hair
stands straight up, preppy collar stands
straight up, arrogant smirks, elaborate
chrome braces.

Narrative:

On the above date and time, I was assigned
to Car #3 along with Officer B. Traven.

We were dispatched to 1212 Haight Street
on a report of Blocking the Sidewalk
and "possible terroristic activity." Upon
arrival, we noticed a group of perhaps
forty people, mostly young, mostly smelling
strongly of marijuana and patchouli. They
were holding Occupy Wall Street posters
and various signs with slogans disparaging
the president, Congress, foreclosures,
mortgages, default swaps, etc. Several
people were playing acoustic guitars and
singing. Others were juggling or playing
hacky sack. This "protest" was taking
place between a Lehman Brothers office and
a Gap clothing store. Two large banners
were unfurled, reading SWEATSHOP WORKERS
ARE SLAVE WORKERS! and THERE'S A REASON
YOUR CLOTHES ARE SO CHEAP! When asked
to disperse, most of the protesters did,
except for a very tall boy with white-blond
dyed hair that stood straight up in what
can only be described as late Billy Idol.
This officer realizes he is dating himself
with that reference. Young Billy Idol
in a large black trench coat refused to
listen or move and continued to read from
a piece of paper, what he later referred

to as "mad poetry, yo." A younger officer
at the station identified the "poetry"
as the lyrics of a band named Slayer. At
that time we noticed that the Gap window
behind him had recently been spray-painted
with the words CORPORATE WHORES. Next
to the lettering was what appeared to be
a drawing of a vagina. It's possible that
it was actually a bagel. Orange paint
matching the paint on the window was found
on suspect's fingers. A can of spray paint
of the same color was found in suspect's
pocket. When the suspect was asked why he'd
vandalized the property, he replied, "Have
you ever read a newspaper?" In any case,
the boy in the trench coat was asked for
a third and final time to disperse. When
he did not, I attempted to place him in
cuffs. This was difficult because when
I grabbed his arm, he fell apart. The
reason for this is that it was not one
boy, but two boys. Suspect Nordstrom was on
suspect Auchischloss's shoulders, making
them look like one person beneath the long
coat. We finally cuffed both suspects, to
the displeasure of the jeering and only
semidispersed crowd, who began to toss

objects at us, like croissants, muffins,
Allen Ginsberg retrospectives, and tofrutti
containers. Suspects were noticed by this
officer in the rearview mirror kissing on
way to precinct. When told to stop, they
refused. When asked why, they said, "We
having a white wedding in Vermont, yo, and
you ain't invited."

They were booked and released to the
custody of their (different) mothers.

- -
DO NOT WRITE BELOW THIS LINE
INWARD TREK HANDLER NOTES:
- -

Sentenced   Inward Trek boot camp, 3 months

Camp Nickname   Idle and Billy

DECEASED/
RECLAMATION
STILL PENDING

ZOMBIEFACTS QUESTION TIME

with Dr. Henry E. Kyburg, head of necrotic studies at the Herschel Gordon Lewis Department of the University of Western Upstate

Q: Why don't zombies eat every part of a body before they move on to the next one?

A: Do you eat all the toppings on your pizza, or do you pick some off? Do you always wipe your plate clean, or do you get tired of the pheasant compote in balsamic reduction after a few bites? Zombies are an amalgam of teeth, hands, gristle, and vague memories. Sometimes the memory of a bad anchovy takes precedence over the logic of calorie intake.

Q: Do zombies freeze?

A: Yes. The small amount of liquids and oils remaining in most zombies will freeze at zero degrees Celsius and below. Antarctica is a perfectly safe plague-free zone — until global warming takes complete effect. When thawed, Z are capable of resuming full activity. Theoretically, the freezing and thawing should destroy every cell wall in their bodies, but it doesn't. We have yet to determine why not.

Q: I just read this book in which the United States fights off a zombie outbreak and eventually cleans the entire country of the things, winning the battle and restoring order. Is this even possible?

A: Well, most necrologists and other zombology professionals generally agree on the Bauer Breakdown, otherwise known as the "6-3-1 model." Essentially it postulates a numerical likelihood for every ten given people during the initial wave of infection. Namely, six will turn Z, three will die outright (suicide, heart attack, car accident, etc.) without turning, and one will "survive," or remain human. If we extrapolate these numbers, given a U.S. population of roughly 300 million, that means 180 million will be zombies, 90 million will die immediately, and 30 million will survive. If those 30 million were somehow able to establish a provisional government and a fighting force, they would need to kill 180 million zombies — almost all of them by individual head shot. This, of course, would be almost, if not entirely, impossible. Just to eradicate 10 percent of the beasts — using a (very generous) 50 percent accuracy rate — would require 36 million bullets alone. That's more than 1 million bullets per survivor. It also presumes that each of those survivors is healthy, fighting capable, and sane. No, the fantasy of organized ballistics-based eradication is just that: a fantasy.

Q: Are zombies really just bulimics with bad skin and an unfair reputation?

A: Who let this person in?

Q: What is the one thing that the movies always get wrong about zombies?

A: Children. It's a grim but true fact that a vast percentage of children will not survive the initial outbreak — some death estimates are as high as 94 percent for children up to age twelve within the first month. Preteen children are slower, weaker, and lack adequate reasoning or problem-solving skills. They are easy targets for zombies. Most movies that show hordes walking down streets or through malls rarely reflect the likely age composition of any given zombie group when younger casualty rates are factored in. In fact, parents who try to protect their children have a 96 percent higher mortality rate than single or individual survivors. Protecting or comforting a child in the open, trying to explain random horrific violence or the nature of evil, seeing to a child's needs, scavenging for two, and counting on the child's not drawing zombies to your location or hideout with assorted whining, crying, and the like are all nearly impossible. Should humanity survive a zombie attack and regain the upper hand, it may very well perish anyway, as repopulation of an entire age group would prove extremely difficult. Any true post-zombie scenario would be less about getting the lights back on and more about unrestrained procreation.

Q: Do zombies ever have to take a shit after eating all that fatty meat?

A: Zombie excretion is unheard of. Bowel activity ceases with the onset of the virus. A highly active zombie should theoretically be more weighed down or even incapacitated by the sheer flesh poundage it ingests, as opposed to a zombie yet to feed. Even so, we have not noticed a diminishment of motor function in the field due to being "overserved."

Q: How can they exist if they don't breathe?

A: The zombie brain is much like a D-cell battery with the barest remnant of a charge. It requires no internal oxygen replenishment. There is some speculation that zombies absorb oxygen through the skin in a crude method akin to reverse transpiration. While this theory has its adherents, I don't put much stock in it. Zombie lungs might as well be a pair of old rubber boots. And, of course, their blood does not require cleaning. Oxygen, therefore, is largely superfluous.

Q: If they are decomposing, that means their muscles are decomposing too, which means they would be totally weak, if not crippled, right? So how come zombies are so dang strong?

A: Zombie locomotion is entirely without precedent in the natural world and would seem to defy logic — even demented logic. Not to mention basic anatomy, biology, and chemistry.

You are correct that they should not be able move once the muscle, tendons, and fasciae degrade. Even shambling should be beyond them. And yet it is not.

Q: What are the most important items to acquire during a zombie siege?

A: A head-mounted flashlight. Batteries. Matches. A pistol fitted with a silencer (opening up on a horde with an AK-47 may momentarily clear your lawn, but will almost certainly draw every other zombie within a three-mile radius to your location). Ammunition. Freeze-dried food. Iodine tablets. Basic medicines. Cooking oil. Needle and thread. Light, warm clothes. Water-resistant outerwear. A hammock for sleeping in trees. A blizzard-rated sleeping bag. A cudgel or other heavy bludgeoning weapon with a short handle (baseball bats and fire axes sound good on paper but are often useless, as they have zero leverage and swing radius in tight quarters — a five-pound roofer's hammer is nearly the perfect weapon). A small, sturdy backpack. Good boots. A hunting knife. A screwdriver and pliers. A crowbar. A propane stove and canisters. Binoculars. The ability to develop and nurture a survival-level degree of sanity in the face of systematic madness.

Q: Can they bite through thick leather? What about Kevlar? If you had a motorcycle helmet, boots, and full Kevlar gear on, could you just walk through a crowd of them?

A: Zombie dentistry is a small but burgeoning subscience upon which I am not entirely qualified to comment, but it is interesting how strong zombie teeth tend to be. What *can't* a zombie bite through? There are undoubtedly various cutting-edge fibers and protective coverings that will repel the incisor or molar in question. The problem is that they'll keep trying, no matter what. And the flesh beneath the protective covering will begin to suffer damage regardless. Large-scale edema, abrasion, and even organ malfunction may follow. Finally, though, any protective covering is only as good as its ability to withstand a horde of zombies and their pernicious hands and teeth from removing it. Unless a motorcycle helmet is welded to your skull, at some point it is likely to be flung aside and access granted to the more delicate prizes within.

Q: What's the worst thing you can do should the Zomb-A-Pocalypse occur?

A: Barricade yourself in somewhere. Of course, it's a natural impulse to lock doors, push bureaus and other heavy items in front of attic entrances, and the like. But most people forget that their temporary safety will soon become a slow, torturous death trap. If you've locked yourself in the basement of a house filled with zombies, those zombies are unlikely to leave. And sooner or later you are going to run out of food and water — or at least fresh air from having to remain in proximity to your own excrement. Freedom of movement is essential to survival. Out in an open field dodging slow shamblers is vastly preferable to a week's safety that becomes a self-inflicted hellhole. The one steadfast rule of all plague scenarios: supplies always run out.

Q: Why do they want to eat flesh? Why not tofu? Or Wheat Thins?

A: For the very same reason you prefer a hamburger to a cucumber. Fat, salt, protein, flavor. There is some possibility that, much like the innate human need to procreate, zombies have a preconscious desire to "turn" all those who do not resemble them. If everyone's ugly, then no one is ugly. If everyone exists in a welter of putrefaction, then hygiene ceases to be a concern. The problem there, from a zombie survival viewpoint, is what do they do with themselves when the last human has been fed upon?

Q: Why don't they just want to eat brains? I thought all they wanted was brains. Must. Have. Brains.

A: The dictates of B-movie zombie lore have no bearing on reality or scientific fact.

Q: Why don't they bleed?

A: Zombies do bleed when freshly turned. After that, they tend to seep a thick, coagulated gel until, with time, they become more or less fully desiccated.

Q: If a zombie falls and rots in the forest but there's no one there to hear it, does it make a sound?

A: This is a foolish question that I have no interest in answering. So I'll ask you something instead: if a moron wants to know nothing, and is only interested in making cheap jokes, are chunks of said moron vastly more likely to soon be residing in a zombie esophagus than someone who takes his survival seriously? Clearly, yes.

Q: Thank you for your time.

A: You are more certainly welcome. Particularly since time is the one thing we have very little left of.

THE OFFICIAL® ALL-INCLUSIVE USDZA-SANCTIONED ZOMBIE HANDLE/NICKNAME LIST

Swarm

Z Dogs

Lurkers

Necrosapiens

Zoil

Meat Junkies

Zulch

Dead Headz

Zed Heads

Revenants

Revs

Shamblers

Nico Clauxs

Citizen Zane

Coprophages

The Undead

Slackjaws

Zach

Sid and Nancy

Braindrain

The Awakened

Them Thangs

The Plague

Rumsfelds

The Infects

Target Practice

Zee

Kannibale

Ghouls

The Medusans

BerZerkers

Rots

Baked Ziti and Flesh Sauce

Zen Chunks

Red Zeppelins

The Hoard

Boogiemenz

Skels

The Unclean

Necromorphs

Thus Spoke Zombathustra

Stale Skin

Zoftig Fleshpigs

Shin Bags

ZBilly ZJoel

Moaners

Zanucks

Zonks

Uncle Zeddie

Chompers

Stank Zappa and the
   Muthaz of Invention

The Living Impaired

Zombicapped

Bubba

The Reavers

Zax

Skin Jobs

Night Soilers

Dick Nixons

Zebulons

Rage Cage

Wraiths

Zmaggots

Zeligs

Shamburglers

Zabagliones

Stalkers

Babe Didrikson Zahariases

Zero Population Growth

Barry Zito's ERA

Zygodactals

Brain Bagels

Chopper

Face-Tearing Zwitterions

The Clergy of Zymurgy

SpamArchy

The Misfits

Anthropophagites

Flesh Tribe

Caribes

The Devolved

The Evolved

Acknowledgments

THE AUTHOR WOULD LIKE TO THANK YOU
for not thinking too unkindly of him for having
the gall to refer to himself as "the author." A
huge thank you to Christian "Zomb-Power"
Bauer for his many insights and readings of
various iterations. He is a prince among men.
Also a very heartfelt thanks to Jordan Brown,
Steven Malk, Ty King, Matt Heller, Jarrett and
Aaron at Dark Coast Press, Henry Kyburg,
Daryl Miller-Salomons, Larry Benner, Nathan
Pyritz, James Weinberg, Matt Roeser, Hannah
Mahoney, Kristine Serio, Brad Listi, Greg Olear,
Joe Daly, Tracy Miracle, Carter Hasegawa, Liz
Bicknell, everyone over at Candlewick Press,
Shawn Harris, and George A. Romero.